LETHAL HARVEST

A JAKE CASHEN CRIME THRILLER

DECLAN JAMES

Lethal Harvest

A Detective Jake Cashen Novel

By
Declan James

ONE

S he stared at him. Always judging. Always looking down at him. Her frozen gaze, wide-eyed, accusatory. Her mouth stuck open in her final scream. He held her face in front of him, ready to call him another name. But she would never get the chance to berate him again.

He lifted her head higher, coiling his fingers through her thick, gray hair.

"Say it!" he shouted. "Call me a liar one more time. Call me a thief!"

He heard her shriek. It echoed through his bones and made the blood roar in his ears. Her jaw went slack. He took a step back. Her face. Her stupid, judgmental look.

"Say it," he dared her once more. "Come on!"

He jerked her forward. Something shifted. Broke free. He held on to her, pulling her head upward. This time, her body fell away below it, crumpling to the floor of the barn. Rivers of blood soaked the wooden floor and ran through the uneven oak slats.

Now it was his turn to scream. He couldn't let go of her. It was as if his fingers were glued to her hair. She was a nightmare now. A ghoul. He was nose to nose with her, gripping her severed head.

"No. No. No!"

He took a staggering step forward. Think. Move. Do something! What had he tried to do?

Her blood was everywhere. Why hadn't he thought she would bleed?

It was then he realized he was still holding the machete in his right hand. Blood dripped from the blade. There was far too much of it to clean up. He became aware of the pain shooting up his right arm. She had been harder to cut through than he anticipated.

God. He hadn't been thinking at all.

Adrenaline coursing through him now, the walls of the barn closed in on him. Heat smothered him. He couldn't breathe. Stumbling out into the yard, he shook his arm, trying to free the gruesome souvenir of his night's work from his fingers.

It was like she wouldn't let go. Even now. Her hateful expression forever locked in place. He did the only thing he could think to do. He drew his arm back, arced it over his head, and threw her into the cornfield.

The crows would make quick work of her, he hoped. But there was so much blood. He'd made a mess.

Sticky blood caked his gloves. Thank God for those. He couldn't even remember putting them on. They were hers. Gardening gloves. They'd been sitting on the kitchen counter of all places.

Trembling, he stepped over her body. There was nothing to be done about it now. Wild thoughts raced through his mind. He should take something. He owed it to her, after all. If it weren't for her, he could have made something of himself. He *was* making something of himself. Little by little, climbing back out of the hole. But then she stripped everything away. It only took one word from her. And she knew it. She knew exactly what she was doing the whole time.

"You're nothing but a thief!" she'd said. "You think I don't see you for what you are? A loser. A grifter. How dare you come into *my* home! You don't belong here!"

Don't belong here. Don't belong here. Don't belong here.

Rage bubbled to the surface, stealing the breath from his lungs.

She made him do it. Gave him no choice. She had everyone fooled. Such a nice lady. A pillar of the town. But she was the worst of it.

"That's what you get!" he shouted into the night sky. Rage gave way to laughter. He doubled over from it. She hadn't been afraid. Not until that last second, when she must have seen the real danger in his eyes. He would live on that forever. It had finally dawned on her he was not someone she should have messed with. She should have respected him. Appreciated him. Treated him like a human being, not something she needed to scrape off her shoe.

As he thought it, he wiped his own shoe on the grass. Blood and bits of something rubbed off and his laughter rose once more.

Was there time to bury her? Is that what's done? He thought about going back into the house. He'd left a mess there. No. Not him. She had done it. She had given him no choice.

No choice. There had never been any choice. There had only been what she wanted. Ruby Ingall. She played God with people's lives.

No more. Never again. He had reclaimed his own destiny and shut her up for good.

Sweat beaded his brow. It ran into his eyes, making it difficult to see. The barn loomed in front of him, casting long shadows over the lawn. He heard a crash. Something fell from a cupboard inside. He startled, crouched down. Her vile cat darted out the pet door off the kitchen. It had something in its teeth.

He had half a mind to chase it down and chop it to bits like he'd done to her. She treated the thing better than she did people. But the cat was too quick.

"You're on your own now," he muttered, his voice sounding far away and foreign to his ears.

It was time to go. If he stayed longer, he would only make things worse. He wiped his brow with his forearm, smearing blood on his face. She'd cut him. The bitch.

He went to the pump on the side of the barn. Lifting it, the cool water began to flow. He rinsed the blade of the machete. It gleamed in the moonlight. Satisfied he'd washed it cleaner than when he picked it up, he took it back into the barn, careful to leave her body where it lay.

His throat burned. Had she scratched him there? He couldn't remember. He went back to the pump. He stuck his head under the stream and drank. It tasted good. Ice cold water. It felt like a baptism of sorts. And it was.

Because after tonight, he was a new man.

He was free.

Two

"It's a bad idea."

Jake's rear end hadn't even touched the booth seat before his grandfather started in.

"Okay," Jake said with a sigh. He could tell by the look on the old man's face, whatever this was about, Max Cashen was winding up for a full-on rant. Max pointed a gnarled finger at Jake's face.

"It's a bad idea. I told her nothing good was gonna come of it. I want no part of it. You should have no part of it. But she's gonna work on you like she always does and you're gonna cave and then we're all gonna suffer."

"Gramps," Jake said. "It's been kind of a long day. Whatever this is, you think it can wait until the weekend?"

Cashen's Irish Pub, or "Sips" as the locals had started to call it, was fast filling up. Jake wasn't the only person in town looking to leave his troubles behind for an hour before heading on home. Though Jake's troubles tended to follow him wherever he went. The lone crimes-against-person detective in Worthington County. He didn't exactly have a job he could clock out of and forget.

His sister Gemma owned the bar, one of about a dozen professional ventures she'd taken over the last two decades. Most of those had turned into disastrous misadventures. But after six months, Jake had to admit, the place was booming. She kept a back booth just for Jake. His grandfather usually liked to hold court at the copper top table in the center of the dining room. Tonight, though, he was loaded for bear and sitting directly across from Jake.

"If you don't talk some sense into her, she's gonna do more than screw up her own life this time. I'm telling you."

Jake looked across the dining room. Gemma stood behind the bar, giving orders to one of the female servers. She'd hired a couple of new ones. Now that summer had officially ended, she'd lost a few of the college-aged wait staff who had helped her open the bar. Gemma caught Jake's eye. Her face fell as she too could read Grandpa's body language. Gemma put a hand on the girl's shoulder and gave her an encouraging smile. Her smile morphed into a mask he knew she wore sometimes when trying to deal with Grandpa Max. She made her way over to Jake's booth.

"Scoot," she ordered Grandpa. "And don't listen to whatever he's been telling you. You're not minding your own business again, I take it."

Grandpa shook his head. He slapped his palms on the table and heaved himself to his feet. "I've warned you. Both of you. I wash my hands of it now." With that, he slid out of the booth and made his way over to his copper top. Gemma sat down in his place.

"Do I even want to ask?" Jake said.

"I didn't want to talk to you about this right now. I was going to give you a chance to have a beer. Or five."

"It's Thursday," he said. "I still work in the morning. I didn't come here to get plastered."

"You're right. This can wait. I'll talk to you this weekend." Something caught her eye. She gestured to someone over Jake's shoulder. He turned, but couldn't see who she was signaling to. But now she wore that fake smile for Jake. He knew it wasn't a good omen.

"Just tell me what's up," he said. "You're clearly itching to. And the old man certainly has opinions. What do you need?"

Gemma's shoulders dropped. "I don't need anything. Don't act like I can't clean up my own messes."

Jake raised a hand in surrender. She was prickly today. The only person who had a worse temper than Grandpa Max was his sister. By the heat coloring her cheeks, he knew he was in land mine territory.

"What is it?" he said.

Gemma folded her hands. "I know what you're going to say. I know what you're going to think. Believe me, I've weighed all the pros and cons. I'm aware of the pitfalls. And I know how this is probably going to end, but ..."

"Gemma, for God's sake. What?"

"Dickie," she blurted.

"Dickie."

"Dickie." She nodded.

Jake felt tension harden his shoulders. His own rage bubbled to the surface. Dickie. She could only mean Dickie Gerald, her most recent ex-husband and father to their nine-year-old son, Aidan. Dickie had a lousy track record with his sister and had gotten physical with her in the years Jake lived out of town.

"What's he done?"

"Nothing. Or ... nothing recently. Except ... he's gotten sober."

Jake went still, bracing himself for whatever else Gemma had to tell him. His grandfather's warning echoed. Whatever this was, was a bad idea. One Grandpa Max had tried to warn her away from when he caught wind of it. If it involved Dickie Gerald, Jake knew the old man was likely right.

"I'm not an idiot," she said. "I know people rarely change long term. I know what Dickie's capable of."

"Gemma, for the love of God, do not tell me you're taking that creep back."

"I'm not telling you that. Of course not. What I'm telling you ... I'm giving you a heads-up. That's all. I was ... I'm ... I've allowed Dickie some limited, supervised visitation with Aidan."

Jake took a sip of his beer. Maybe having five would be a good idea after all.

"How'd that go?" he asked. "And when. Where was I? Please tell me you're not the one supervising this visitation alone."

She didn't answer. A new pit formed in Jake's stomach. The look on her face told him he'd guessed the situation correctly.

"Gemma, I don't want you alone with Dickie. Ever."

She put a hand up. "I'm not here to discuss that. That's not why I'm bringing it up. But since I have. Aidan's been asking. He wants to know his dad. They've been communicating."

"How? Aidan doesn't have a phone."

"He asked me to call him. Dickie reached out to me a few months ago."

"A few months ago? I'm only hearing about this now?"

"Jake, listen. Please. Part of me hates all of this, too. Most of me. But the fact remains that Dickie is Aidan's dad. I know full well how this is probably going to turn out. Dickie's going to show up for a little while. But he's Dickie. He'll revert to form. He'll disappoint Aidan. I hate it. I want to protect him from it. It's just ... Aidan's not a baby anymore. Before we know it, he's going to be a teenager. He's going to hit that age where I won't be able to tell him anything. So better he learns who Dickie is now before he gets old enough to run off and do something stupid like try to go live with him."

Her logic was dizzying. Though part of it made sense. Let Aidan learn for himself the kind of man Dickie was.

"Well," he said. "I guess I'm glad you told me. I'd rather hear it from you than run into that ass ... er ... Dickie. But I meant what I said. I don't want you alone with him. The next time he visits Aidan, I want to be there."

"When Dickie's sober, he's harmless. He's a mouse who can barely squeak. Believe me, I know the signs. I can sense it on him a mile away. One look at him and I know if Dickie's been drinking or not. You have to trust me on that."

Jake wasn't satisfied, but he knew his sister well enough to know it wasn't worth arguing about. Not now. She kept her posture rigid, her lips pursed. He knew there was something else she wasn't telling him.

"What?" he said, feeling that pit reform in his stomach.

"He's asked me for a favor."

"A favor? Letting him see his kid isn't favor enough?"

"He could have taken me to court on that one. I told you. Aidan's getting older. The next time we wind up in court, the judge is probably going to want to hear from Aidan. I don't want to put him through that. To his credit, neither does Dickie. So far, he's behaving. I'm not naïve enough to believe this time's going to stick. I'm clear-headed on that. But ..."

"But what?"

"But ... well ... Dickie's as together as I've ever known him to be. He's actually going to meetings. Seeing a therapist. Don't roll your eyes at me, but this time seems different."

"Oh, Gemma."

"I told you. I know the odds of it lasting are slim. I mean it. I have my eyes fully open here. Dickie asked me ... er ... actually you ... to do something for him."

"Me? He wants me to do something for him? How about I refrain from bashing his nose in for beating on my sister? Consider that the favor he gets from me."

"Jake, that's not helpful. And he's not asking for much. I promise. He's asking for five minutes. He just wants to talk to you. Five minutes. That's it."

"Why?"

She sat back. "Honestly? I'm not sure. He just said he has to give you something. And he has to do it in person."

"I'm not interested in anything Dickie Gerald has to give me."

"Jake, please. I'm not doing any of this for Dickie. I'm doing it for Aidan. Whether you like it or not, he *is* Aidan's dad. If there is even the slightest chance that man can keep his shit together and be a halfway decent human being, Aidan deserves it. I don't want to rock the boat."

"How long has this been going on?" Jake asked.

"What do you mean?"

"You know what I mean. How long ago did you let Dickie back into your life and not tell me about it?"

Gemma dropped her chin. He knew that look, too. Christ.

"How long have you been lying to me?"

"I never lied," she snapped. "I just didn't tell you."

"Gemma ..."

"Four months," she said.

"What?"

"Since last May. Just before school let out."

"All summer. You're telling me Aidan's been spending time with Dickie all summer?"

"Once a week," she said. "And it's been minimal. We met at the park to start. Then Aidan's favorite fast food place. They got lunch. A couple of weeks ago, Dickie took Aidan to the zoo. I went too with some friends."

"Why are you even telling me anything? You're going to do whatever you want anyway."

"It's my life!" she shouted, then immediately dropped to a whisper. "It's my business. I told you. I've been careful. But this is as long as I've ever seen Dickie sober. I'm hopeful. But not stupid. It's been little by little. So far, Dickie's lived up to every condition I set for him. And Aidan's happy. It's been good for him. For now, at least. Dickie might break his heart, but for now ... he's getting to know his dad."

"What do you want from me, then?"

"Five minutes. That's all. Dickie asked. Hear what he has to say. Whatever it is. If you want to tell him to go piss up a rope, that's your business. If you want to threaten him within an inch of his life if he screws this thing up, well, he's earned that and more. But he's asked to talk to you for five minutes. He knows full well how you feel."

"When?" Jake muttered.

Gemma bit her lip. She looked over Jake's shoulder again. He felt the cold fingers of dread snaking up his spine. He'd been had. No wonder Grandpa was so riled up before Jake even sat down.

"He's here?"

"We thought this would be a good, neutral place," Gemma said.

"You mean you know I'm not likely to break his damn nose in the middle of your bar? Don't be too sure. If that weasel tries something ..."

"He won't," she said. Gemma raised her hand and waved two fingers. Jake went stiff, refusing to turn his head. A moment later, Dickie Gerald stood at the end of the booth. He was clean-shaven, smiling nervously, and crushing a baseball cap in his hands.

J ake didn't want to admit it. Didn't even really want to look at the guy. But as Gemma found an excuse to disappear and Dickie Gerald slid into the booth opposite him, Jake had to admit the man looked better than he'd ever seen him. Usually scrawny and unkempt, Dickie's face had filled out. His generally sallow complexion was replaced with a tan, healthy glow.

He wore a clean shirt and his eyes were clear. Jake was used to seeing them bloodshot from the overindulgence of cheap whiskey.

"Thank you," Dickie started. "I know I'm not your favorite person."

Jake resisted the urge to tell him exactly what kind of person he thought Dickie was. Five minutes. That's what he'd agreed to give him. For Aidan.

"What's this about?" Jake asked, checking his smartwatch. He set a timer and tilted the screen so Dickie could see it. "Five minutes. Clock's running, Dickie."

"Thank you. I mean it, man. I know what you think of me."

"It's not what I think that's your problem. It's what I know."

"I'm not proud of my past. I've done a lot of things I regret. I messed everything up with Gemma. That's gotta be my biggest regret. She's the best thing that ever happened to me and I screwed it all up. I know that."

"No," Jake said. "She's not the best thing that ever happened to you. Aidan is. So what I want to know. Are you using that boy to get to her? Is that your play? Because you've never shown any interest in being a dad to that kid in the ten years since you found out he was coming."

"He's my son," Dickie said, emphasizing the word "my."

"No," Jake said. "See, that would imply that you've acted like a father to him. My sister may have a soft heart when it comes to him. It can cloud her judgment. Make no mistake, I don't suffer from the same problem."

"Well, what happens between me and Aidan and me and Gemma and Aidan is our business."

"Until you hurt them," Jake said. "That's when it becomes my business. Do you understand what I'm telling you? I don't care what step you're on, Dickie. If this is you making some kind of amends, I'm not interested."

"Jake, I get it. I do. You said your piece. You're welcome to it. I deserve it. I know that. But I'm really not here to talk about Aidan or Gemma. That's not what this is about. This is about ... someone else."

Jake sat back. There were only about three minutes left on his timer.

"I'm here about my cousin. On his behalf. Believe me, I knew how this was going to go with you. I don't wanna talk to you. I don't even wanna be in the same room with you, either."

Jake started to rise. "Good. So let's not be."

Dickie reached out and grabbed Jake's wrist. Jake felt coiled, like a rattlesnake ready to strike. Dickie must have seen something in his face and pulled his hand back.

"Please," he said. "Just let me say what I came to say and give you what I promised to give you. Then we can go our separate ways. As far as Gemma and Aidan, like I said. As much as you hate me, you can't change the fact that Aidan's my boy. I'm in his life and I'm gonna stay in his life. But this isn't about that."

"Your five minutes are up."

"My cousin," Dickie said. He reached into the back pocket of his jeans and pulled out a crumpled but sealed envelope. "This is for you. He asked me to give it to you."

Something in Jake told him he should just keep going. Turn his back on Dickie. Not take whatever bait he was dangling. Life in Blackhand Hills might have turned out vastly different if he had.

But before he could really form a solid thought, Dickie slapped that battered envelope into his hand.

Jake didn't look at it. He sat back down.

"My cousin," Dickie continued. "He's a dead man anyway, okay? He knows that. Only ... he doesn't deserve to be."

"What the hell are you talking about?"

"My cousin is Wesley Hall," Dickie said.

The name held no meaning to Jake. Not then. Dickie dropped it like it should have.

"He's at Chillicothe. In about six weeks, they're gonna stick a needle in his arm and that'll be the end of it."

"Christ," Jake muttered. "You've got a cousin on death row? That's what this is about? You expect me to do something about it?"

"No. No, man. I don't. I just promised to give you that letter. That's all. Except, I know Wes. He didn't hurt nobody. I know it."

"Great," Jake said. "A ringing endorsement. Why don't you call the governor?"

"Man, I get it. I know how this sounds. You hate my guts. You know what? I hate yours. Yeah. Twelve steps. I'm working the program. I am. And I'm sorry for what I did to Gemma. Only I never did anything to you, so ..."

Jake crushed the letter in his fist. He had half a mind to throw the thing at Dickie. "See, that's the thing. If you hurt my sister, I end you."

"Wes is innocent. That's the thing. He didn't kill that old lady and they're gonna juice him just the same. That ain't right. Even you know that. He said he's been trying to get somebody to read one of his letters for years. All his appeals got turned down. He's out of time."

As if on cue, Jake's watch timer started beeping. He pressed the side button and silenced it. Dickie smiled.

"Read the letter. That's all I ask."

"All you asked was for five minutes. Then all you asked was for me to take this damn thing. Now you want me to read it."

"Do whatever you gotta do. My conscience is clear now. I can tell Wes I tried. It won't be on my head anymore. I'll tell his ma. I'm doing this for her as much as anybody else. She's always been good to me, my Aunt Laurie. You should talk to her."

Dickie got up. "Finish your beer," he said. "We got nothing left to talk about. I've done my part."

Mercifully, Dickie turned on his heel and walked straight out the front door. Jake felt some of the tension leave his shoulders. Gemma reappeared almost immediately.

"Thank you," she said. "I appreciate it. And I told you. He looks different."

"Looks aren't everything," Jake said. Gemma held a pitcher in her hand. She refilled Jake's beer mug. He practically inhaled the second one.

"What is that, anyway?" Gemma said. "The letter. Dickie said he just wanted to make sure he put it in your hand. I see he did that much."

Jake set his mug down. Half intending to rip the thing in half, he turned it over and read the return address.

Wesley Wayne Hall. When Dickie said it at first, it didn't ring any bells. But now, seeing it in writing, all three names spelled out, it sent a stab of recognition through Jake. He quickly pulled up the browser on his phone and typed the name in.

The first headline that popped up made his stomach churn.

"Christ," he whispered. "You gotta be kidding me."

Gemma leaned in and read the name on the envelope. Unlike Jake, she recognized it immediately. Her jaw dropped. She looked back at the door Dickie had just exited.

"That son of a bitch," she said.

THREE

"People want to forget that fall. I can never forget. We didn't feel safe. For weeks, months, we lived in terror. But Ed Zender didn't give up. Now a monster is locked up where he can't hurt any of us ever again."

Jake pressed pause. The salt-and-pepper-haired woman stared straight at the camera after she'd delivered her last line. She seemed vaguely familiar. He'd probably seen her at the grocery store a time or two. She looked like everyone's grandmother in her red-and-white-checkered house dress. She stood on her own porch with vast cornfields ready to be harvested in the distance.

Jake pressed play. The image of an empty jail cell filled the screen. In one corner, a mugshot appeared featuring a white male, brown shaggy hair, a dirty face with deep lines around his mouth. His eyes were wild, bloodshot, his cheek bruised.

"The most dangerous criminal in Worthington County history," the voice over actor declared. The voice was familiar. Jake could have sworn he'd heard it announcing Hollywood movie trailers. "On death row because of one man and his tireless pursuit for justice. This November, cast your vote to put that same man, Ed Zender, in charge of *your* safety. Determined. Principled. Experienced. Place your trust in Ed Zender for sheriff. The only choice for real safety."

The graphic faded and dissolved to a shot of Ed Zender in front of the Public Safety building wearing a suit and tie, an American flag pin on his lapel.

"I'm Ed Zender and I approve this message."

Jake rewound the commercial, freezing it at the image of the empty jail cell and mugshot.

"That ad is on every five minutes, I swear."

Deputy Erica "Birdie" Wayne walked into Jake's office holding her mug of coffee. Jake had already downed three cups of his own. He had a fresh pot brewing in the corner.

"I hear it in my sleep," Birdie said.

"Do you think people still care?" Jake asked.

Birdie stood next to Jake as he leaned against the table in the far corner of the office. The video played on a flat screen television mounted to the wall. It was a new addition to the office, courtesy of the existing sheriff, and the boss Jake hoped to keep, Meg Landry.

"About him?" Birdie asked, gesturing with her mug toward the image on the screen. "Wesley Wayne Hall? Honestly, if this were any other year, maybe they wouldn't. I hadn't heard that name in years. How convenient for Ed that Hall's last appeal tanked. I heard a rumor that he's trying to get permission to be one of the witnesses when they execute him in November."

"I wasn't here when that all went down," Jake said.

Birdie set her mug down on the table and sat in one of the chairs. "It was my senior year in high school. I think Ruby Ingall's grandson was a freshman. He's the one who found her. Awful stuff. We heard she was decapitated. It wasn't too long before Halloween if I remember right. There were all sorts of rumors floating around about what happened out on her farm. People were scared. That part's true."

Jake rewound the video and paused it at the beginning, showing the older woman talking about how she credited Ed for being the town's savior that fall.

"That's Corrine Forbush. She lives ... or lived ... on one of the the neighboring farms. I'm actually surprised she was willing to put her face on that ad," Birdie said.

"You think Ed paid her?"

"I hope not. I mean ... Ed *did* clear the Ruby Ingall murder. That's pretty much his one claim to fame as a detective from what everyone's saying."

"Who's everyone?" Jake asked. "People have been pretty tight-lipped around me."

Birdie nodded. "They know how much you like Landry."

There was something in her expression. She was holding something back. Jake had known Birdie since she was practically in diapers. Her older brother Ben had been one of his very best friends growing up. His murder is what had brought Birdie back to town and eventually working for the Sheriff's Department.

"What else are they saying about me?"

She chewed her lip. "Nothing. Not around me anyway."

Jake hit the power button on the remote, sending the screen to black.

"Why are you studying that?" Birdie asked.

Jake walked over to his desk and picked up the crumpled envelope Dickie Gerald had thrust upon him last night. He handed it to Birdie.

Picking up her mug with one hand, she took the letter in the other. As she took a long sip, she read the outside of the envelope.

"Where did you get this?" she asked.

"You wouldn't believe me if I told you."

"There's no postmark on it. Seriously, where did you get this?"

"Dickie Gerald," he said. "He's managed to work himself back into Gemma's good graces. She made me talk to him for five minutes last night."

"I think good graces is a bit of an exaggeration," Birdie said. Then her face fell as she realized her error.

"You knew?"

"Jake ..."

"You knew Gemma's been seeing Dickie?"

"She's not seeing him. Don't make it sound like that. She's doing it for Aidan. She's giving him a chance to see who his dad is. It was bound to happen sooner or later."

"She talked to you about it?" Jake fumed.

"She asked my opinion, yes."

"Which was?"

"I told her to be careful. I told her Dickie Gerald isn't someone I'd trust. And I told her to tell you before you found out about it from somebody else. I'm glad she did."

Jake grumbled. He didn't like the idea of Birdie and Gemma discussing either Dickie Gerald or him behind his back.

"He's his dad, Jake," Birdie said. "Like I said, this was bound to happen sooner or later."

"Later is soon enough," he said.

"What about this?" Birdie asked, deftly changing the subject and drawing Jake's focus back to the letter.

"What about it?"

"Are you going to open it? And how the hell did Dickie Gerald come into possession of a letter from Wesley Wayne Hall?"

"Apparently they're cousins."

Birdie snorted a laugh. "Those Gerald boys are cousins with everybody. Something tells me Hall isn't that close to him if he thought Dickie was his best avenue to you."

"Dickie's apparently close with Hall's mother or something. I don't know."

Birdie set her cup down. She reached across the table and grabbed a letter opener off Jake's desk. Before he could tell her not to, she sliced one end of the letter open and slid the contents out.

She spread the letter on the table and began to read it. From Jake's vantage point, he just saw scrawling, shaky handwriting written with a black marker that smudged the page.

"Throw it away," Jake said. "Shred it."

Birdie got to the end of it. She turned the page over but there was no more writing on the other side.

"Well, he could use an editor. But you should read it."

"Birdie, I get dozens of those things every month. You probably do too. Let me guess. He got screwed over by the system. He's innocent. He wants me to hunt down the real killer. You said it yourself. Hall's last appeal tanked. He's about to get a needle in his arm. He saw his mugshot on that commercial so now he's trying to capitalize on it."

She smoothed the paper flat on the table.

"Did you know the Ingall family?" she asked.

"Not really. I mean, I knew of them. My grandpa was acquainted with Ruby Ingall's husband back in the day. I think he knew him from the lodge. I remember him talking about helping Ruby out on their family farm after her husband died. The son took it over or something?"

"The grandson," Birdie said. "Sam."

"The one who found her body?" Jake asked.

"Right. That farm has been in Sam Ingall's family for a hundred and fifty years or some such."

"Well, good for the kid," Jake said. "I find it interesting it's not *his* face on that commercial. I don't imagine the Ingall family appreciates this all being dredged up for political points."

"No. I don't imagine they do. But Jake, you should read this."

She handed him the letter. He had half a mind to do exactly what he suggested Birdie should do with it. He eyed the shredder in the corner. Instead, he sat at the table opposite Birdie and indulged her.

Dear Detective Jake Cashen,
    I am already dead. I know that. I know everyone wants me to be. I know what they think

of me. I know what you probably think of me. But you don't know me. Let me be clear.

I didn't kill Ruby Ingall. And I know what that sounds like. I know you probably get letters like this all the time. Everyone in here says they're not guilty. Why should I be any different?

I also know I probably didn't win myself any points by sending this letter through a man you probably hate. I know who my cousin is. I know you probably think Dickie Gerald is a con man, a liar, and a thief. He is all of that. And worse. But he's family and he's trying to turn his life around. If he put this letter in your hand ... if you're taking the time to read it ... then I am grateful.

I am asking for your time. I know that's a big ask. But time is the only thing I have left and I don't have much. In just a few weeks, I'll be dead anyway if you can't help me. When I'm dead, then there will be no way to undo what was done. There will be no way for people to know the truth.

I didn't kill Ruby Ingall. I DID NOT KILL RUBY INGALL. I swear this on my life. Though I know you may think that isn't worth much. But the thing you DO need to know. It has taken me years to understand what happened. To accept the fact that I was used. I was a convenience. I was nothing. I have seen what they're saying about my case on the news. They're saying Detective Zender is some kind of savior. That I am the monster he locked away.

I am not a monster. I am an innocent man. And I can prove it. If you give me just a small amount of your time, I can explain what I know. I cannot put it in a letter. I need to see you in person. Please. I am humbling myself before you. I believe you are a good man. I believe you want to seek the truth. I can give you that. I can prove what I'm saying. For fifteen years, I have been locked away for a crime I did not commit. A crime that Ed Zender knows I did not commit. How can a man like that be elected sheriff? People need to know. Please. Just give me a few minutes of your time. I've given your name to the prison as an approved visitor. If you don't like what I have to say, if you don't believe me, then you can walk away and never look back.

There's nobody else I can ask. I'm begging you. Do it for the King of the Hilltop.

A tremor ran through him. The King of the Hilltop. Jake slid the note back toward Birdie. "It's garbage," he said. "I told you. We get hundreds of letters like that."

Birdie picked it up. "Jake ... does he mean what I think he means? The King of the Hilltop?"

"He's rambling. It's nothing."

"You sure about that? Because to me it seems pretty clear, he's talking about Rex ..."

"No!" Jake cut her off. He didn't want her to say Rex Bardo's name out loud. He was known as King Rex to the wider world of Blackhand Hills and law enforcement. The kingpin of the region's organized crime syndicate known as the Hilltop Boys. Rex was in federal prison. Jake had formed a relationship of sorts with him. How in the hell could someone like Wesley Wayne Hall know that? And why would Bardo get involved in a local murder if Hall was telling the truth?

"I should burn the damn thing," Jake muttered.

"You're right. Only, what would be the harm in having a conversation with the guy?"

"What?"

"He went to a whole lot of trouble to get this letter in your hand. You specifically. Why?"

"Who knows? Maybe he read my name in the paper. Saw me at a press conference. I'm in Zender's old job now."

"He doesn't sound dumb," Birdie said. "He called Dickie out pretty accurately."

"Like that's hard? Dickie's low-hanging fruit on the idiot tree, Birdie."

"True. But Ed's gotten a lot of traction off that ad. Doesn't it stick in your craw that he's using Ruby Ingall's murder investigation to score political points?"

"It makes me angry for her family," he said. "Voters will see through that."

"I hope so. It's just ... if this were the other way around. If Landry were the one claiming credit for putting Wesley Wayne Hall behind bars, don't you think her opponent would go pay him a visit at his prompting? Just to see what he has to say?"

"He's got nothing to say. He's going to proclaim his innocence like every other guy in there."

"Sure. Sure. Of course. It's just ... he's specific, Jake. He's calling Ed Zender out by name. You've been bristling every time that commercial comes on. We both know what kind of detective Ed really was. Right? And that phrase, King of the Hilltop. You know it's not random. I mean ... if he who you don't want me to name is going around telling people he's got some in with you. That's no good either, right?"

"What's your point, Birdie?"

"Just go talk to the guy. There's no harm in it. He's right about one thing. In a couple of weeks, none of this will matter. Hall will be dead and Ed will ... well ..."

"He'll what?"

"He might be sheriff."

A chill went through Jake as she said it. Ed Zender. Sheriff. There was no telling what that would do to the department.

"You're off tomorrow," Birdie said. "What's to stop you from taking a drive out to Chillicothe?"

"Birdie ..."

She folded the letter and put it back in its envelope. She rose and walked over to Jake. Smiling, she slid the letter into his lapel pocket and patted his chest.

"Go," she said. "Talk to the guy. At the very least, you'll get to come back here and tell me I told you so. Then I'll owe you lunch. I'll take you to Papa's Diner. Spiros is putting moussaka back on the menu next week."

Jake's mouth watered just thinking of it. Birdie knew what buttons to push.

"A conversation," he said. "That's all."

Birdie stepped back and smiled. Between Gemma, Birdie, and even damn Dickie Gerald, Jake had the sneaking sensation that he'd been outmaneuvered. At the same time, that blasted commercial kept replaying in his mind.

Ed Zender. Savior of the county.

Over Jake's dead body.

Four

It was easy to feel claustrophobic in a place like Chillicothe Prison. Jake sat in a dark, dank, windowless room with concrete walls. At the other end of the hall, the most forsaken of men sat in 74 square foot cells awaiting the day they'd be driven forty miles away to the death chamber of the Lucasville Southern Ohio Correctional Facility. There, in a cold, sterile examination room, they would be strapped to a table and a lethal dose of midazolam of hydromorphone would be poured into their veins, those drugs having recently been declared *safe* again for such purposes.

Six weeks from now, Wesley Wayne Hall would make that final journey. Today, though, he shuffled into the interview room in prison tans and pounds of chains shackling his wrists and ankles.

Jake came with no expectations. The only image he had of Hall was his mugshot taken a few weeks after Ruby Ingall's decapitated head was found in a cornfield. It would have taken a fair bit of strength to make the cut. Slicing through muscle, sinew, then bone. Jake knew the coroner determined seventy-five-year-old

Ruby had mercifully already been dead before those cuts were made. No. Strangled to death before her killer desecrated her body in her family's one-hundred-and fifty-year-old barn, the oldest one still standing in Worthington County.

Hall had no emotion on his face as he made his way to the metal chair opposite Jake. A long table separated them. The prison guard pressed down on Hall's left shoulder, forcing him into the chair. A moment later, he threaded Hall's wrist chains through a metal loop on the table, then hooked his leg irons to the table, bolted to the floor.

"I'll just be outside," the guard said. A big guy. Muscular. Gruff. He made good on his statement and left Jake and Hall alone, pulling the steel door shut with an echoing clang.

"I didn't think you'd come," Hall said. His voice was gravelly, likely from long periods of nonuse. The man hadn't had a visitor in over two years, Jake learned. The guards would later tell Jake that Hall rarely spoke to any of them. A model prisoner, though. He did what he was told. Caused no trouble.

Jake reached into his suit coat pocket and pulled out the crumpled letter Dickie Gerald had shoved into his hand that fateful night at Gemma's bar.

"You got my attention," Jake said. "You wanna get the big thing out of the way first?"

Hall's eyes narrowed. He was ten years older than Jake, not quite fifty. But he looked north of seventy. Deeply creased, dark brown eyes. A heavily jowled mouth. At six foot one, he'd weighed a fit, one hundred and eighty pounds the day of his arrest. He'd gained at least a hundred pounds since then.

"The big thing," Hall repeated, though it wasn't a question.

"What do you know about the King of the Hilltop?" Jake said, almost spitting it.

"I've just heard things," Hall answered.

"Heard things. You want to know what I've heard? You don't talk to anybody. For the past few months, they've had you in solitary confinement."

"I didn't say I've talked to anybody. That's the best way to hear things, Detective. It's no secret that you go see Rex Bardo. It's a small world. Prison is even smaller. People talk. I listen."

"You think Rex Bardo cares what happens to you?"

"Do you?"

Jake rubbed his jaw. "Honestly? No."

"But you came."

"I came because of this," Jake said, jabbing a finger on the letter. "You've made some assumptions. You've traded on a tenuous family connection. And you've thrown my name around in circles it doesn't belong. So yeah. I'm curious."

"I'm sorry about my cousin. Dickie and I aren't close. But my mother has tried hard with him. She was probably more of a mother figure to him than his own mother was. She was a junkie. The funny thing is, if you'd have asked me when we were growing up which one of us would end up in a place like this, I would have bet on Dickie. So would everybody else. I don't belong here, Mr. Cashen. And I'm out of options. So yes. I made an assumption. I gambled that you might be curious enough to come out and have a conversation with me if somebody like Rex Bardo took an interest in it."

"What do you have to do with Rex Bardo?" Jake asked.

Hall shifted in his chair, making his irons rattle. "Nothing," he said. "I'll make you a promise, Detective. Everything I tell you is gonna be the truth. That King of the Hilltop crap is the last fib you'll hear from me. I told you. I've just heard things. I don't know Bardo. I never had anything to do with the Hilltop Boys. As a matter of fact, when we were kids, it was Dickie who had the ambition to run with that crowd. I was the one who told him it would lead to nothing good. But they wouldn't have him. People like Dickie aren't cut out for that kind of life. Bardo's too smart to associate himself with somebody like my cousin. And he's too smart to associate with somebody like me."

"A gamble," Jake said. "A pretty stupid one."

"Yeah? What? You think if it gets back to Rex Bardo that I used his name, he's gonna have somebody get to me? Kill me? You read the news? I'm a dead man anyway. You're looking at somebody who has nothing to lose."

Jake sat back. "This was a waste of my time." He regretted not following every instinct he had back at the office. What the hell was he even doing here? The mere mention of Rex Bardo had been enough to make him throw away his better judgment. He started to rise.

"Please," Hall said. "That's the one time you're gonna hear me beg, Detective. Please. Just give me a few minutes of your time. That's all I'm asking. It's not a waste of your time if Ed Zender is really about to be elected sheriff. That would make him your boss, right?"

Jake tried to read Wesley Wayne Hall. The man's eyes seemed cold, not desperate. Resigned. And yet, he'd lured Jake out here.

"He's using my name," Hall said. "He's putting all my business out there to score political points. I'm going to die. And he's trying to dance on my grave on his way to that sheriff's job. That's not right. You're a good man, aren't you? An honest cop? That's why you came out here. You didn't like the fact somebody might be talking about your association with Rex Bardo. You wanted to see what was real. Well, I'm telling you. Yeah. People are talking. It's been noticed that you've paid old Rex so many visits in prison. But nobody knows shit about anything. It's just talk. That's because there's nothing to know. Isn't that right? You're not like Zender at all. I told you, I made a gamble. That's the biggest one of all."

"What do you mean I'm not like Zender?"

"I mean Ed Zender has no business wearing a badge, let alone the big one. He's the reason I'm sitting here. He's going to have my blood on his hands in a few weeks. And he's figured out a way to make that the reason people want to elect him."

"You're out of options," Jake said. "Out of time. In my experience, desperate men make desperate choices."

"I didn't kill Ruby Ingall. I'm telling you Ed Zender knows it."

"So that's it? You just want me to believe you're an innocent man?"

"No," Hall said, surprising Jake. "I'm not innocent. I said I didn't kill old lady Ruby. Those are two different things."

Jake sat back down. "Fine. I'm here. I'll give you five minutes."

"I worked for Ruby. Odd jobs around the farm. She needed a handyman. None of her kids knew how to do anything useful. They were soft. So she hired me. It went pretty good for a while. A long while. Then she turned on me. She said I stole from her. The thing is, from her point of view, that's probably exactly what it looked like. I was low on gas so I took some from her barn and poured it into my truck. I was gonna replace it. She didn't give me the chance to explain any of that. She just made an assumption that I was some dirtbag thief. Then she went around and told all the other farmers in the area not to have anything to do with me. They listened. Whatever Ruby said, went. They ran me off. I hated her after that. Okay? I'm telling you that right upfront. She did me wrong. We had words. I told her how I felt. I told a few other people how I felt. But I didn't kill her. I was just an easy mark. Ed Zender took that and ran with it."

"You think Zender framed you?"

"Have you looked into my case? All the evidence?"

"No."

"Maybe you should. I wasn't there the night Ruby Ingall got herself killed. And I don't know who did it. I wish I did. If she treated me that bad, she probably did it to somebody else too. She must have just pissed off the wrong person and it finally caught up to her. But it wasn't me. I wasn't there. I can prove it."

"If you can prove it," Jake said. "Why didn't you?"

"Because I'm telling you, Ed Zender made up his mind to pin this thing on me and that was it."

"What is it that you want from me?" Jake said. "You had a trial. You had a lawyer. You were convicted, Hall."

"I was railroaded. I'm telling you, man. You asked me what I wanted from you. How about you do the job Ed Zender wouldn't? I gave him names. I told him who I was with that night. Scotty Moore. We worked jobs together around some of the local farms. You can ask around. Somebody might know him. That night we were scrapping. Scotty can verify it. Zender never even talked to him. And Allison? Allison Sobecki. She and I were going together at the time. You know this whole thing? She almost killed herself over it."

"What are you talking about?"

"Allison lied. She got on the stand and told a bunch of lies about how she saw me coming home that night covered in blood. It wasn't true. It never happened. She'll tell you. Ed Zender got to her. Bullied her. Threatened to throw her in jail for the rest of her life, too. So she said what she had to say to get clear of it."

Jake shook his head. "You expect me to believe Ed Zender engaged in witness tampering? Why?"

"You'd have to ask him that. I'm just telling you. Talk to Allison. You got a piece of paper? I'll tell you how to get a hold of her. If you find Scotty Moore, he'll tell you, too."

"Why didn't he just tell someone fifteen years ago?"

"We had a falling-out back then. Petty stuff. But I'm telling you, Zender never even bothered talking to Scotty. I don't know why. But I've talked to him. I wrote him a letter maybe eight years ago. I found out through the grapevine where he was staying. And he wrote back. He was willing to come forward then. But then he stopped returning my letters. I don't know. Maybe he's dead. I haven't heard that he was. But you should be able to figure that out quick enough. I can give you some names. People I know he was working for long after I ended up in here. Maybe they know how to find him. But he told me he tried to talk to Zender. Told the truth. We were together the night Ruby Ingall got hers. But nobody told the jury that."

"Why is that?" Jake asked. "You had an attorney."

"I would have been better off without one. The guy was a drunk. Some piece of crap public defender. I heard he got disbarred a few years after my trial. You can look that up too. Barry Wymer. He smelled like cheap bourbon throughout the whole trial. The prosecutor steamrolled him. The evidence they had on me? It was garbage. That blood they found on the workbench? That could have been from way before all this. I cut myself sharpening a mower blade."

Hall held up his thumb and pointed to a crescent-shaped scar along the base of it. To Jake, it seemed like nothing more than a convenient visual aid.

"I told Wymer all of this. He never brought it up at trial. I'm not lying. These are all things you can verify. I'm telling you."

It was a tantalizing story, if true. But could Ed Zender have really been that stupid or careless back in the day? Not tracking down an alibi witness was one thing. There could have been a hundred reasons for that. But threatening a witness? It didn't sound like the Zender Jake knew. It sounded a lot more like the desperate ramblings of a marked man.

"I know what you're thinking," Hall said. "I know you want to walk out of here and forget you ever met me."

"Trust me. You have no idea what I'm thinking."

"I'm not asking you for much."

"Really? Seems to me you're asking me for an awful lot. I don't know you. Don't even really know anything about your case. You got my attention by telling a lie."

"I didn't lie. Tell me how I lied. I didn't say I knew Rex Bardo. Didn't say he vouched for me. You came here because of whatever you've got on your own conscience about that man. You're right when you said I'm desperate. That it was a desperate trick. Sure. It was. But it was a good one. It got you here. The rest of it? You can check. Wymer got exposed for the crap lawyer he was. Allison will tell you what Zender did to her to get her to lie. She'll tell the truth now. She'll sign whatever you want her to sign. She's right with God now. She's just scared. But I think she can trust you. I think you're nothing like Ed Zender. Are you?"

Jake didn't answer. He wouldn't give Wesley Wayne Hall that much. It was enough he was sitting across the table from him.

"Talk to Allison. Just a conversation. You got that paper?"

Jake reached into his jacket pocket and pulled out a small notebook and pen. He slid it across the table. Hall took the pen and scrawled out a name, phone number and address. He wrote a second name and slid the notebook and pen back to Jake.

Jake read the first name. Allison Sobecki. The address was in Worthington County, just a few miles from his own home.

"She's a good girl," Hall said. "Too good for me if I'm telling the truth. Her life took a few bad turns because of me. I'm sorry for that. But I'm not sorry for this. I didn't kill old Ruby. I'm not a violent man. I've done things I regret. But I'm not a liar. And I'm not a murderer. I know that's what everybody says in here. I know you have no reason to believe a word I'm saying. But you're here. And I gotta figure that's because it's like I said. You're not like Ed Zender. If there's even a slight chance that I'm innocent and you can help prove it, you'd want to, wouldn't you? If it means that a dirty cop is about to become your new boss?"

"That's a hell of a leap, Hall."

"Is it? Cuz what I hear is Zender's gonna win. I hear a big reason is because people think he saved them. From me."

Hall wasn't wrong. Ever since Zender's campaign started running those ads featuring Ruby Ingall's murder, he'd been up in the polls.

"They're gonna kill me," Hall said. "I'm out of appeals. Nobody will listen to me."

"What makes you think I will?" Jake said, though he already knew the answer. As Hall lifted his chin, Jake had the strongest sense that Hall knew it, too.

"Because if you don't, never mind the needle in my arm ... who's going to save those same people from Ed Zender?"

FIVE

The Tuesday Breakfast Club had become a fixture in the back room of Papa's Diner in downtown Stanley, the Worthington County seat. Its participants called themselves the Wise Men though the diner's proprietress, Tessa Papatonis, preferred calling them the Wise Asses and the name had kind of stuck. Its three core members had all retired from the Sheriff's Department years ago. Virgil Adamski had worked in the property room. Bill Nutter had served as the crimes-to-property detective before Gary Majewski took over. Chuck Thompson had spent a couple of years in Jake's job two decades ago before moving over to a command position.

The three of them were deep in conversation as Jake walked into the diner. Tessa saw him and scooted around the counter to pull Jake into a hug and kiss him on the cheek.

"You stay away too long," she said. "Where have you been keeping yourself?" Tessa's husband, Spiros, sang something in Greek while he worked the griddle in the back. He turned slightly, gave Jake a wave over his shoulder, then went back to expertly flipping pancakes.

"Around," Jake said. "It's been a little crazy at work."

Tessa waved him off. "All the more reason for you to stop and see me. You're getting too skinny." She poked Jake's rib and swatted him on the rear with the towel she had over her shoulder, deploying it with the speed of a rattlesnake.

"Jake!" Chuck Thompson shouted out.

"Go on," Tessa said. "They're ornery today."

"They're ornery every day," Jake said. Tessa nodded. Spiros yelled something out at his wife.

"Keep your pants on!" she yelled back, then gave Jake a good-natured shove in the direction of the Wise Men. He knew she'd have his breakfast in front of him, including an obscene amount of pancakes, within two minutes. Right now, coffee was the urgency. Jake took a seat at the table, joining the Tuesday Breakfast Club.

He overturned a coffee mug and reached for the carafe at the center of the table. Tessa had just filled it. The aroma hit Jake first, like a jolt to the veins.

"We've missed you," Nutter said. "How's it going in Landry's office?"

Jake took a sip of steaming black coffee, not caring if it scalded him on the way down. It was good. Strong. Necessary.

"You mean the election or the job?" he asked.

"We're worried," Chuck said. "Word is the county commissioners are gonna endorse Zender next week."

"That's not a surprise," Jake said. "They've been gunning for Meg since she took office. It's just noise."

Virgil put his own mug down. "Come off it. This is us. She's in trouble, Jake. Everybody knows it. Tim Brouchard's hired some slick PR team from New York of all places. That commercial he's got running about Wesley Wayne Hall is making an impact. It's a stroke of genius."

"Funny you should mention that," Jake said.

Chuck and Virgil exchanged a look that told him Virgil's immediate pivot to the Hall case hadn't just been a coincidence.

Jake's shoulders dropped. "You already know I took a little field trip, don't you? Christ. How?"

"Calm down," Chuck said. "Nobody's spying on you. I've just still got friends out at Chillicothe. And Wesley Hall doesn't get many visitors."

"Who else knows?" Jake asked, then realized it was a pointless question. If word had reached these three, it was probably all over the county by now.

"Don't sweat it," Chuck insisted. "This wasn't gossip. Not the kind you're thinking of."

"Still," Bill said. "If we already know you paid Hall a visit, how long do you think it's gonna take before Zender or his people find out?"

"I had my reasons," Jake said. "And I was going to run it by the three of you. That's actually why I'm here."

Virgil's smile widened. "Aw. Now you're gonna hurt all three of Chuck's feelings. He thought you just missed him."

Jake smirked. "I did."

"So, what did you want to talk to us about?" Bill asked.

Jake pulled out the letter Hall wrote to him by way of Dickie Gerald. There was no point keeping any of it to himself at this point. Not with these three. He tossed it to the other side of the table. Chuck and Bill put their readers on. It took about a minute before all three men had finished reading it.

"I probably got a thousand of those things during my career," Chuck said. "We all have."

"I know," Jake said.

"You went to see that bastard just off this?" Bill asked.

"More or less," Jake answered. "And it went about how you'd expect. I just ... there's a couple of things Hall said that seemed like something to follow up on. You guys were there during that era. It had to have been the biggest thing going at the time."

"Sure," Chuck said. "Ruby Ingall was good people. Everybody wanted to make sure she and her family got justice."

"But Ed?" Jake said. "Look, we all know what he's like. By the time he finally retired from being a detective, he was barely going through the motions. I didn't know him back in the day. But none of you have ever given me the impression he was a very good cop. I'm not looking to smear him. But Hall said some things. I was hoping to get a feel from you guys as to what might be true."

"What's he saying?" Bill asked, taking off his readers.

Jake looked around. The diner wasn't very full. Just two tables up toward the front, well out of earshot.

"Hall had a girlfriend," Jake started.

"Yeah," Chuck said. "She testified against him. Jury ate it up. She said she remembered Hall coming home and running to the basement to wash blood off his hands and his clothes. It was something like eleven at night and he started a load of laundry. She said he never did laundry."

"Good memory," Bill said. "I forgot about that."

"Yeah," Jake said. "Only now Hall's insisting the girlfriend's willing to recant all that. He says she's now claiming Ed got aggressive with her. Coached her."

Virgil whistled. "You talk to her?"

"Not yet," Jake said. "I just ... I don't know. Ed's ... Ed. You think he was capable of doing something like that?"

The men were silent for a moment, perhaps choosing their next words carefully. It was Chuck who finally spoke up.

"I just remember at the time thinking it was bad luck Ed drew that case. Borowski would have been better suited for it."

The mention of Frank Borowski made Jake bristle. Frank had been his mentor, his coach, a father figure. He was the reason Jake decided to pursue a career in law enforcement. The man had been a legend. Now ... he was a fugitive.

"Why wasn't he?" Jake asked. "O'Neal was still sheriff back then. He could have put whoever he wanted to on that case."

"He was gone," Bill said. "In those days, Frank would sometimes pool his vacation. Take it all at once. He'd head out to Montana to elk hunt. Or Florida for some fishing trip. Be gone for six weeks at a time. Not even Ruby Ingall losing her head would have been enough to bring him back. The man was a master at compartmentalization."

Until he wasn't, Jake thought. But he pushed those thoughts away. Frank Borowski was a lost cause, a wild goose he knew better than to chase.

"But Ed," he said. "This story about him roughing up Wesley Hall's girlfriend. Could there be any truth to it?"

Nutter shrugged. "Maybe." The other two men shot him fast scowls.

"It's just us," Nutter protested. "Yeah. If it turned out to be true, what Hall's saying, and that's a big if. I can't say it would entirely surprise me. And shouldn't surprise either of you guys."

"No," Chuck reluctantly admitted. "Over the years, Ed and Frank had less and less to do with each other outside of sharing an office. Frank didn't like how Ed operated. A big part of that was exactly this kind of hot dog shit."

"Frank was worried Ed could skirt the line when it came to some more ... aggressive ... tactics," Virgil said.

"Is there a record of any of it?" Jake asked. "Was he ever disciplined?"

"Nothing that ever stuck," Chuck said. "But it got heated between Frank and Ed. I know that. Ed was scared of Frank and Frank knew it. So, after a while, that worked to Frank's advantage. Ed calmed down. But as far as the Ruby Ingall case, Ed was working solo. Frank had nothing to do with it."

That didn't exactly ease Jake's concerns. It meant Ed Zender, at his very worst, would have been able to run that investigation however he wanted.

"You believe this guy?" Bill asked. "Hall?"

"He has every reason to lie," Jake said. "He gave me two names though. This girlfriend. She's still local. He also named an alibi witness that as far as I know, was never called to testify. You know anything about that?"

Bill shook his head. He would have worked out of the same office space as Frank Borowski and Ed Zender back in the day. "I don't remember any of that. Hall didn't have an alibi. He had a lawyer though."

"A lousy one," Chuck chimed in. "You remember Barry Wymer?"

"Oh yeah," Bill said.

"And not fondly, I take it," Jake said.

Bill shrugged. "I think he's dead now. But he got into some trouble with the bar. Drinking or substance abuse or something. Can't say he was much of a favorite down at the courthouse."

"Do you believe this guy?" Bill asked again.

Jake ran a finger over the rim of his coffee mug. "I don't know. Probably not. It's just ..."

"It's Ed," Virgil finished for him. "You know. Frank was mystified by how Ed cleared that case so fast. I do remember that. It was all wrapped up before Frank got back into town. But we sat at this very table talking about it. Frank said Ed might have benefited from the Blind Squirrel Theory."

"As in, even they find a nut every once in a while?" Jake asked.

"You got it," Virgil said. "I don't know. Maybe you go talk to the girlfriend if she's local. On the down-low if you can. I'd say it's worth that much."

"Can of worms," Chuck cautioned. "Jake, if anybody finds out you're getting into this, you know it could cause problems for Landry."

"I didn't make this a political issue," Jake said. "Zender did. He's the one using it as his badge of honor in his campaign."

"And Hall knows it," Virgil said. "You don't think that could be the reason he reached out?"

"Of course it is," Jake said. "But the man is set to get a needle in his arm in about six weeks. Right before the election. The timing couldn't have been more perfect for Ed. Somebody should at least take a second look."

"It's just gonna be sticky if it ends up being you," Chuck said.

"But who else will?" Jake asked. "I'm talking about one conversation. For my own peace of mind. I talk to this girlfriend. Odds are, she won't be credible. Or the second she realizes she could get in trouble for perjuring herself, she'll change her story back."

"You should do it," Bill said. Virgil and Chuck didn't look so sure. "I mean it. If that bastard's lying about how that investigation went down, I'd want to know. And let's not pretend Ed Zender as sheriff is gonna be good for anybody."

"No," Virgil said. "Just be careful, Jake. Have you considered the possibility somebody else put Wesley Wayne Hall up to this? I mean, him dragging you into it? You specifically? It just ... it feels like a spider web. A trap."

"If you do this," Chuck said, "I need you to make me a promise. Right here, Jake."

He seemed angry. Chuck's knuckles went white as he clenched his fists on either side of his breakfast plate.

"What, Chuck?" Jake asked.

"Ruby. I knew her. Your grandpa knew her. She could be a real battle-axe. But ... she was one of a kind. That's a good family out there. You should talk to them. If this thing turns into a ... thing. They shouldn't hear about it on the internet or somewhere. They should hear it from you. It wasn't just Ruby's murder. That was bad enough. But that family has suffered. Got ripped apart from all of this."

"I understand," Jake said. "And you know me. I wouldn't take any of this lightly. And it's just a conversation."

The moment he uttered the words though, he realized he'd said them before. Going to see Wesley Wayne Hall was just supposed to be a conversation. But as he looked at the expressions on Bill Nutter, Chuck Thompson, and Virgil Adamski's faces, he knew they were thinking along the same lines.

Ed Zender had probably arrested the right man. Wesley Wayne Hall was probably guilty as sin. Probably.

But Jake knew an election and a man's life could depend on the truth. He couldn't afford to be wrong.

Six

Allison Sobecki lived in the southwest corner of Worthington County, all the way over in Durris Township. If you threw a rock from her front porch, it could land in Vinton County. The home was a two-story Craftsman situated on an eight-acre lot that used to be a soybean field. As Jake pulled up, an older man with long, wiry gray hair and well-worn blue overalls leaned over the hood of a 1967 Dodge Charger, his ear to the engine.

The man barely looked up as Jake approached. He had to weave between two mountain bikes, four angry chickens, and a calico cat that darted out from under the porch.

"Hello," Jake said. "I'm looking for ..."

"She's inside," the man shouted, not pulling his head out from under the hood. "Ally!"

The screen door on the porch flung open. A woman came out. She was pretty. Probably right around Jake's age. She had bleached blonde hair that came to the middle of her back. She wore frayed, cut-off jean shorts that displayed intricate tattoos on her muscled thighs and red cowboy boots that hugged her calves.

"You, Jake?" she called out.

"Jake Cashen," he said. He gave a curt wave to the older man and joined the woman on the porch. She shook his hand and opened the screen door wider, allowing Jake to step inside.

"Sorry about the mess," she said. "I just got off work. The boys have been off school the last couple of days. Some kind of teacher in-service. They're not so good about picking up after themselves when I'm not home."

The front living room was littered with various toys, building blocks, empty potato chip bags, and at least five half-empty bottles of water. Allison picked those up and tossed them in a kitchen garbage can just off the living room.

"We can talk in here," she said. "The boys are plugged into their screens upstairs."

"The boys?" Jake asked.

"Leo and Damian," she said. "They're twins. They're ten. Cody's seventeen. He's at work today. He's got a job at the gas station on Lexington. I don't really like him working there. It's so close to the interstate. But my pops says it's good for him."

"That your pops?" Jake asked, gesturing toward the pole barn and the Dodge Charger.

"Yeah," she said. "Sorry. He's a lot friendlier than he seems. He just gets a one-track mind when he's working on something. He's retired from GM. A mechanic. He's been doing side jobs under the table for a couple of years since he moved in with me. You need anything worked on? He's one of the best and his prices are reasonable. It started out as just something to keep him busy every once in a while. He's booked solid now into next month."

"I'm not surprised," Jake said. "A good mechanic is worth his weight in gold."

"That's what I told him," she said. "You want something to drink? I've got water in the fridge. Some iced tea? Or maybe a beer? You're off duty, right? It's Saturday."

"I'm off duty. But thanks. I'm fine."

Allison gestured toward the two overstuffed chairs in the corner of the living room. She also had a sectional couch in front of a flat-screen TV on the wall. Jake took a seat at the end of the couch. Allison sat in one of the chairs.

"I appreciate you coming out," she said just as Jake was about to thank her for letting him.

"You know why I'm here," he said.

Allison shifted, closing her hands together. She slid them between her knees. A protective posture. As if she were closing into herself.

"You've been in communication with Wesley Hall?" Jake asked.

"Some," she said. "We've written some letters. It's been a little while. A couple of months. I went out there to see him a few years ago. And ... he called. Two days ago."

"I saw him too," Jake said. "Last week. You know why?"

She nodded. "I know why. That's what the call was about. He was hoping you'd get in touch with me. I gotta be honest. I'm surprised you did."

"If I'm being honest. So am I. Allison, Wes has some pretty interesting things to say about what's happened to him. I agreed to at least have a conversation with you. But again ... if we're being honest ..."

"You think he killed Ruby Ingall?" she finished his sentence. "Everybody thinks he killed Ruby Ingall."

"Do you?"

She bit her lip. "I don't know. I only know my part in this. Which is bad enough. But I can't give Wes an alibi. I'm done lying, Detective Cashen. And that's what I have to tell you."

Jake sat back. She didn't seem nervous. She wasn't sweating. She kept her gaze locked with his. She displayed none of the typical body language of someone who was lying to him. Of course, it could also mean she was a practiced liar.

"Your testimony in Wesley's trial was pretty damning. You understand that it's one of the reasons he was convicted."

She shuddered. "I know. I'm sorry for that. I truly am. It's something I've had to figure out how to live with. It took me down. Way down."

"What do you mean?"

She tilted her head slightly, regarding him. "Why does Wes trust you?"

"I'm sorry?"

"He must. You came all this way. He knows exactly what cops can do to him. What they've already done to him."

"He says Ed Zender had it out for him. He says his lawyer had it out for him. I'm not gonna sit here and pretend I haven't heard that kind of thing a million times from people like him. Wes knows he's got nothing left to lose. He has every reason to lie to me."

"I don't. I could just stay how I've been. Faded back into the woodwork. I told you. It took me a long time to put my past behind me. What I did. What I said."

"He says you admitted to lying on the stand. He says you made everything up. That you didn't see Wesley come home the night of Ruby Ingall's murder covered in blood. You understand the consequences of that?"

"I understand it's one of the reasons Wesley's about to get executed. Yes."

"That's not what I mean. I mean the consequences to you. If Wesley's story is right. That you lied under oath. Never mind Wesley Wayne Hall. That's perjury. Obstruction of justice. That's a prosecutable crime, Ms. Sobecki."

"Allison," she said.

"Okay. Allison. I just want you to be very careful. Yeah. I'm off duty. But I'm a cop. You get that. I'm not out here as some favor to Wesley Hall."

"You're out here because you don't want Ed Zender to win that election."

"No," Jake said sharply. "I'm out here because I have questions I think are important enough to ask. So I won't take up a lot of your time. This thing has already taken up enough of mine. Do you have something you want to tell me?"

"I think I will have a glass of water," she said. "You sure you don't want one?" She rose and walked into the kitchen. Jake waved her off. A moment later, she came back with a water bottle. She unscrewed the cap and put it on the coffee table in front of the couch. She sat down and took a long swig. Her hands shook.

"You need to understand how things were," she said. "I got involved with Wes at a low point in my life. I was twenty years old and had a kid already. That's my Cody. He was only two at the time. His dad, my ex. He was a friend of my dad's. A lot younger. But they worked together. I thought he was solid. He was. He thought I had Cody to trap him. I didn't. I swear I didn't. My pops and me ... we weren't really on speaking terms at the time. I was a bit of a rebel. Never finished high school. I ran away when I was fifteen. A few years after that, I met Michael, Cody's dad. I thought he was going to be my answer to everything. That he was gonna take care of me. Of us. I know my part in all of it. I was smoking a lot of weed back then. It progressed. I got hooked on some bad stuff. I'm not proud of any of that."

Jake had taken the time to pull up Allison Sobecki's rap sheet before coming out. She'd been arrested for possession a few times. Did a ninety-day stint in the county jail. At the time of Ruby Ingall's murder, she was on probation.

"Allison," Jake said. "I'm not here to judge you for your past."

"No," she said. "I didn't think that you were. But you have to understand what was going on. I lost my son. Michael took Cody away from me. I was going to rehab. I was working on myself. I just needed Michael to help me out a little. But he wouldn't give Cody back. He wouldn't even let me see him. Then he got the courts involved. I lost my visitation. I was a mess. Out of my mind. I told you. I'm not proud of the choices I made. But I was trying to turn everything around. I've been clean and sober for thirteen years."

Thirteen years. Jake kept his face neutral. So she was using during the time of Ruby's murder. During her statement to the police. Her testimony.

"I'm glad for you," he said and he meant it.

"I don't make the greatest choices when it comes to men. Wes wasn't good for me either. I mean, he was nice to me. Never hit me or anything. But he was rudderless. That's what my pops called him. Going from job to job. Didn't have benefits. Then he got into all that trouble with Ruby. I mean, before her getting killed. She accused him of stealing from her. I was so angry with him when he came home and told me that. Because I believed it. I loved Wes at the time. Or I thought I did. But why didn't he just ask that old woman if he could borrow some gas? If he'd have just done that, maybe this whole thing would have turned out different. Wes has a temper. I'll admit that. He's not violent though. Or he wasn't back then. But he's stubborn and can be mean. So I have no doubt he shot his mouth off to her and about her. I know he did. Only ... I don't think he killed her."

"What happened that night, Allison? What do you remember?"

"Nothing. Just ... nothing. Wes wasn't home. He told me he'd gone scrapping. Which he did, I think. I went to bed. When I woke up, he was sleeping in the bed beside me. Same as always. It was just a normal night. A normal day. Then everything got shot all to hell."

"What about what you told Zender? About getting up in the middle of the night and seeing him come in covered in blood? The laundry?"

She shook her head. Her eyes filled with tears. "That didn't happen."

"You lied? Again, do you understand the ramifications of that?"

"I know. But I didn't just make it up. The reason I told you about Michael and Cody. During that time, I was trying desperately to get Cody back. Or even just to get my visitation restored. But Michael had a fancy lawyer. He had money. I was on probation. I was clean then. That I swear. I relapsed later, after everything went down. But not then. Not when Ruby got killed. Not when I talked to Ed Zender and he made me ..."

Jake went stone cold. She gasped as she said the last bit. Her unfinished sentence just hung there.

"What do you mean?" Jake finally said. "Ed Zender made you what?"

"He knew, okay? He told me he knew about the threats Wes made around town. And he was really angry with her. He *did* say those things people came forward about. But you gotta understand. She ruined him. He was making good money on the farms around town. He was in demand. Things were finally starting to happen for him. For us. And Ruby Ingall just took it all away. But the rest of it? It wasn't true. God. I'm so sorry. I know it was my fault."

"What was your fault?"

"He kept coming back. Over and over. Kept hounding me. Telling me he knew I knew what really happened."

"Ed. You're saying Ed kept hounding you?"

"Yes. Detective Zender. He said ... he knew about Cody. He told me if I wanted to get my son back that I'd better cooperate and say what I knew. But I did. I told him everything."

Jake ran a hand over his jaw. He had a day's worth of stubble, it being the weekend.

"Allison, I'm going to need you to be very specific. Did you or did you not see Wesley Wayne Hall covered in blood the night Ruby Ingall was killed?"

The front screen door opened. Allison's father walked in, wiping his hands on a shop towel. He gave Jake a menacing stare, but moved off into the kitchen.

"It's okay, Pops," Allison said. "I need to get this out."

"We haven't met," her father said. "I'm George Cummings, Allison's father."

"Good to meet you," Jake said, though George didn't offer his hand.

"Everything okay in here?" George asked.

"It's fine," Allison said. "I'm okay. I told you."

"You want me to stay?" George asked his daughter.

"No," she said. "He's not like ... he's not like the other one."

"He's a cop," George said. He stared at Jake for a moment, then moved off down the hall and out of sight.

"He's just worried about me," she said.

"He's being a dad."

Allison's tears spilled out. "We weren't on good terms all those years ago. It's only been recently. Pops, he's ... he's working the program too. He's been sober thirty years. He was the first to recognize the signs when I started getting into trouble. He kicked me out. I was so angry with him for so long. But now ... if it were one of my boys. I just hope I'd have the strength to do the same. He saved me. I know that now."

"He's a good man, then."

"Are you?" Her eyes bored into him.

"What do you think?"

"People say you are. You don't think I just do what Wes tells me to do, do you? I've asked around."

"Allison, what are you trying to tell me?"

"Ed Zender knew what to do to get me to say what he wanted me to say."

"What he wanted you to say? Are you trying to tell me Zender coached you?"

"I was clean. I swear to God. I told him that too. But he said it wouldn't matter. He said one call to my probation officer, telling him I wasn't cooperating with his investigation. Or that he'd seen paraphernalia in my house. He'd violate my probation. Make it so I'd lose in court if I tried to get my visitation back."

Jake stayed motionless. He kept his expression neutral. "The laundry story. The blood ..."

"He didn't tell me to say that. Not specifically. I just ... I knew what he wanted. He told me I knew something more than I was telling. I swear I didn't though. It was just like I told you. I woke up and Wes was sleeping beside me. I didn't hear when he came in. But Zender ... he kept on at me and on at me. He said I had to have seen something. I had to know something. That I was covering it up. That there had to have been blood. That Wes couldn't have just come home and me not seeing him covered in blood and what did he do with it? He had me up against the wall. His hands on me. I couldn't breathe. I couldn't get away."

"You're telling me Ed Zender laid his hands on you?" Jake asked. His voice had gotten so low it didn't even sound familiar to his own ears.

"Yes," she said. "He didn't hit me. He was just ... I couldn't leave. He was gonna hold me there until he was good and ready to let me go. Intimidating me. He asked me what my probation officer, what Cody's father would think if they found me with a needle sticking out of my arm the next day. I was scared to death. I believed he could do it. Shoot me up against my will. And I knew Wes hated Ruby Ingall. Zender kept saying it over and over. That he knew

Wes was guilty. That he had the truth. So I better just say what I knew or I'd be in jail right alongside of him. That I'd never see Cody again and he'd know what kind of trash his mama really was."

She was full-on crying now. Jake could hear George Cummings moving in another part of the house.

"He broke me. Okay? Ed Zender broke me. I told him what he wanted to hear. That yes. I saw blood all over Wes when he came home. That he went down to the basement and did a load of laundry and took a shower before he came to bed. And once I did it ... it just all got away from me. You have to understand. I believed Wes was guilty at that point. He had to be. Zender swore it. He said they had all the evidence. I couldn't go back. I believed he could make trouble for me. I was thinking of Cody and what I had to do to get him back."

"Did it work?" Jake asked, his voice still sounding cold to him. He didn't mean it to be. He just didn't know if he could believe this woman's story.

"What do you mean?"

"Wes was convicted. But did you get to see your son?"

She squeezed her eyes shut. "No. Not for years. I was ... I was a zombie back then. Just trying to survive. And I relapsed. I did all the things Zender threatened to do to me. Only I did it to myself. I brought it on myself. That's nobody's fault but mine. But Wes? What I said? It's a lie. I'm telling you the truth now. I swear it. I swear it on my life. I swear it on my sons' heads. I never saw Wes with blood on him that night. I never saw him washing his clothes. I just woke up the next morning and he was sleeping next to me. That's all. The rest of it? I said it because I was scared. Terrified. And I didn't think it would matter. Now I know I was wrong. If Wes dies, that'll be partly my fault, too."

"You perjured yourself," Jake said.

"I think it's time for you to get going, Detective." George Cummings seemed to materialize from the shadows. He formed a menacing presence in the hallway.

"We aren't finished," Jake said, rising.

"You are for today," George said. "The next time you wanna talk to Ally, she'll want to have her lawyer present."

"Pop," she said.

"Enough," George boomed. "You got what you came for. Now go."

What he came for. Jake didn't even remember if he said goodbye as he let himself out of the house. He barely remembered getting behind the wheel and driving off.

Ed Zender. Jake had known him to be lazy and incompetent in his later years as a detective. But was he truly capable of witness tampering? If Allison Sobecki's story was true, Ed himself had committed a crime, let alone the impact on Wesley Wayne Hall.

It couldn't be true? Could it? The deeper he got into this, the worse things seemed to be. Each layer of the onion revealed more rot underneath. And the stench kept leading him right to Ed Zender's door.

SEVEN

Monday morning before roll call, Jake took Birdie aside and asked her to quietly gather what she could from the evidence room on Ruby Ingall's murder. As he left her, he stood outside Meg Landry's office door, debating whether he should tell her anything yet. Right now, he had little more than suspicions. Maybe later, after he looked at the murder file, he might feel differently. He turned on his heel, ready to walk quietly back to his office. Meg's door swung open.

"Jake?" she said. "Good. I meant to come find you. Get in here, will you?"

Jake walked in. Meg closed the door behind them.

"Give me some good news," she said. "I could use it."

"Things aren't that bad," he said.

Landry picked up a newspaper off her desk and tossed it to him. She had it folded to the local news section. The headline was bracing. Meg was down almost ten points in the latest polling.

"These don't mean anything," Jake said. "How many times have you actually answered some pollster? Most people hang up the phone. Zealots and whackadoos, that's who answers this stuff." He tossed the paper right into her trash can.

"I just thought you and I should have a conversation. In the event I'm out of a job next year. You need to be prepared. I'm putting some things in place. But I want you to reconsider my suggestion for you to take the sergeant's test. You'll be better protected if you're in command, Jake."

"I like the job I have just fine."

"And you can still do it. This can just be a formality. But Ed will have far fewer avenues to screw with you."

"I'm not afraid of Ed."

"Yeah? Well, I am. In fact, I'm terrified of what he might do. I'm hearing things. Scary things. He's vindictive, Jake. Everyone knows he's no fan of yours."

"Meg, I can take care of myself. But why are you so fatalistic this morning? Giving up the fight already?"

"Oh hell no, are you kidding me? Not a chance. There's still the town hall later this week. Plenty of time for Ed to show himself for the fool he really is."

"You'll wipe the floor with him."

"You better be there. Front row. It'll be nice to see a friendly face in the audience."

Meg knew how much Jake hated those kinds of events. He tried to stay as far away from politics as possible. "Okay," he said. "But I'm serious."

"What am I gonna do if I lose? I don't know, Jake. Paige has two years of high school left. I don't want to think about the possibility of pulling her to move somewhere else. I don't know. Maybe I'll become a housewife. Take up knitting. Do bake sales."

"That actually sounds like heaven."

"Doesn't it?" Meg said. "I don't know. But I'll figure it out."

"I have no doubt."

"So ... good news. Give me some."

Once again, Jake debated telling her what he knew about the Ingall case. But it was dangerous. Better Meg stayed far away from it. He didn't want it looking like Meg was directing the whole thing. Using her office to find dirt on Ed Zender.

"I'm working on it," Jake said. Meg gave him a curious expression. They'd known each other long enough that she could read his tone.

"Okaaay," she said. "Something you wanna fill me in on?"

"Not just yet. Give me a few days."

Meg's desk phone rang. Jake took it as an exit strategy. Meg held a finger up, gesturing for him to wait. Jake pretended not to see it. He made a clean getaway. He just hoped he did indeed have good news for her. Soon.

By the end of the shift, Birdie proved to him once again why she belonged in the detective bureau and not in field ops. Maybe, he thought. If Meg Landry wins this damn election, she can start putting people where they need to be. Right now, the county commissioners kept breathing down everyone's neck, threatening more budget cuts.

"In here," Birdie said. She had Jake follow her down to one of the empty basement storage rooms. It was dank, dusty, full of cobwebs, but Birdie had been busy.

"I figured we're better off down here than up in your office," she said. "You didn't say as much, but I got the impression the fewer people poke their noses into what you're doing, the better."

"I'm not sure what I'm doing. Not yet."

Birdie flicked the light switch. She'd commandeered two long tables and a couple of folding chairs. Several boxes sat on the floor, but two of the tables were in the beginning stages of organization.

"I laid out what was collected at the scene," she said. "I called in a favor at the courthouse. That table over there is cross-checked with everything that was actually entered into evidence at Wesley Wayne Hall's trial."

"Birdie, this is really great. You made quick work of it."

And she had. Jake walked over to the trial table. Birdie appeared to have everything arranged in the order it was introduced at trial. Crime scene photos. The machete used to cut off poor Ruby Ingall's head. She had also printed cards with every witness called along with which pieces of evidence the prosecutor had introduced during their testimony.

The second table, containing the rest of the evidence collected but not necessarily introduced at trial, was far less organized. This didn't surprise Jake. When investigating any crime, never mind a murder, it was often hard to know what might later end up important. You did the best you could to preserve as much as you could.

Jake saw dozens of bags of evidence. Household items. A set of kitchen knives. A hair brush. A set of muddy work boots. Farm implements. A few aging corn cobs that had disintegrated to little more than dust. There were also several bags filled with broken glass. One clearly used to be a saucer. It had broken into three large pieces. Another bag contained tiny pieces of blue, iridescent glass. He held it up in the dim light. The pieces changed colors, like a prism. There was no telling what they used to be.

"What a mess," he said, putting the bag of blue glass down.

"That's putting it mildly. With the exception of what I pulled from the courthouse, everything else was basically just tossed in four big boxes with no rhyme or reason. I'm still trying to make sense of it all."

"You've done an amazing job so far from what I can tell."

"Let's just say this isn't my first rodeo."

He knew it wasn't. Before coming to work for Worthington County, Birdie had worked in Army intelligence, investigating anything from espionage, drugs, murder, or counterintelligence. It wasn't something she talked about much, which Jake could understand. She'd once told him she'd worked a few cases that ended up on the front page of the *New York Times*. He never pried beyond that.

"You have a read on anything yet?" he asked.

Birdie blew a hair away from her forehead. She stood with her hands on her hips. "Well, like I said. It was all a damn mess. The kind of thing that flat out gives me hives."

"That's Ed," Jake said. "We didn't work together long. But he was cutting corners that gave me hives a couple of years ago."

"I'm not surprised. Also, it doesn't look like he got BCI involved to process the crime scene."

Jake's stomach churned a bit. This didn't surprise him, either. Jake wouldn't think of running a murder investigation without turning the crime scene over to Ohio's Bureau of Criminal Investigation. Agent Mark Ramirez had delivered solid work that had helped Jake put several cold-blooded killers behind bars for good.

"The first day I met Ramirez," Jake said, "he told me to watch out for Ed. That was his chief complaint. That he was handling too much on his own. He warned me someday it was gonna come back to bite us."

"All right," Birdie said. "I've seen enough to have a pretty bad feeling about what went down on this one. And I know you well enough to know you wouldn't crawl into this particular can of worms without a damn good reason. You gonna tell me what you found out from Hall and his girlfriend?"

Jake turned one of the folding chairs and sat down. Birdie took his lead and sat in the other one.

"The girlfriend," he started. "Did you read through her statement?"

"Yeah. Tim Brouchard put her on the stand. She was a material witness. Claimed Hall came home covered in blood in the middle of the night and immediately went to the basement washing machine, stripped off all his clothes, and did a load of laundry."

Birdie reached for a stack of papers on the table with Ed's stuff. She handed it to Jake. He thumbed through Allison Sobecki's statement.

"I don't have the trial transcript yet," Birdie said. "I can order it, but wanted to wait until you gave me the go-ahead. I managed to get all of this stuff on the QT. If I start ordering transcripts, that's gonna draw more attention."

"Good thinking," he said. "Though from what I understand, the girl's story stayed consistent on the stand."

"So, what did she have to say when you met her?"

Jake took a breath. He gave Birdie the highlights from his visit to Allison Sobecki's house.

He hadn't known Birdie to be shocked by much, but by the time he finished, she sat with her jaw slack.

"Jake," she said. "You realize that's a crime. If Ed did even half of what the Sobecki girl is claiming, he could be prosecuted."

"If it could be proven," Jake said. "So far, it would be her word against his."

"Do you believe her?"

He scratched his chin. "I don't know. Maybe. I just don't see what motivation she could have to lie. Ed wouldn't be the only one potentially guilty of a crime. She admitted to perjury. Defensible, maybe, if Ed truly did threaten her like that. But the safer thing for her to do now would be just to keep her mouth shut. She's had a complicated history with law enforcement even before tangling with Ed. And that's the other thing that makes her problematic. Admittedly, she's a former junkie. She's got a record. She'd have credibility issues in any criminal prosecution against Ed."

"Then what's all this for?" Birdie asked, spreading her arms and gesturing to the piles of evidence surrounding them.

Jake didn't answer right away. Instead, he rose and walked over to the trial evidence table. One by one, he picked up the bagged evidence.

The crime scene photos were among the most gruesome he'd ever seen and that was saying something. Ruby Ingall's head had been found in the cornfield behind her house. The rest of her was in the barn. Jake worked his way through the blood evidence, checking it against the lab reports.

Birdie joined him. She'd only just started organizing the physical evidence.

"Was any of it Hall's blood?" she asked. Jake held the report in his hand and skimmed it.

"No," Jake said. "It's all Ruby Ingall's. And there was a lot of it. She was exsanguinated inside the barn, basically.

Birdie held a copy of the autopsy report. She sank slowly back into one of the folding chairs as she read it. Jake went over to the table containing the collected evidence. He lined up the photographs taken at the crime scene. The location of each sample was marked with a yellow, numbered tag. These could be cross-checked with the lab reports. It looked like the largest concentration of blood had been found on the barn floor just in front of one of the empty horse stalls.

"It wasn't a clean cut," Birdie said, looking up from the autopsy. "Coroner said whoever killed her basically sawed her head off."

Jake wrinkled his nose in disgust. "Why, I wonder?"

"Why saw instead of chop?" Birdie asked.

"No, why cut her head off at all? That wasn't the cause of death, was it? I feel like I read somewhere the coroner said that it was done postmortem."

"That's right. Probable cause of death here was strangulation. And the theory is she was killed in the house then dragged out to the barn for ... um ... the rest of it."

"So he maybe thinks he's gonna chop her up and dispose of the pieces. I've butchered deer many times with Max. Even with good sharp knives, it takes a while. He gets as far as the head and either loses his nerve or panics. Heard someone coming?"

"Your guess is as good as mine. But this was brutal. Sadistic. Do you have any sense of Wesley Wayne Hall from meeting him? Looking him in the eye?"

Jake shrugged. "Birdie, I've known murderers who you'd think are the nicest guys on the block. So have you. I don't have some sixth sense by looking them in the face. And Hall has every reason to lie to me now. He knows he's got an expiration date."

Jake looked through the blood evidence markers. He ran his finger down the columns of the lab report.

"I really wish Ed would have let the experts handle all this," Birdie said. "I know there's no such thing as a perfect murder investigation. There are always mistakes. Human error. It's just ..."

"What?" Jake said, not looking up from the numbing rows of numbers.

"I don't think Hall's defense lawyer did him any favors either. You said Hall gave Ed a name? An alibi witness?"

"Scott Moore," Jake said. Something was missing. He set the lab report down and went back to the tagged photographs. Picture upon picture of little yellow triangles all over the barn and inside Ruby Ingall's kitchen.

"Well," Birdie said. "Moore was never called as a witness at the trial."

"Hall said that."

"I know," she said. "He mentions him in his statement to Ed when he interviewed him. Only ..."

"Only what?"

"Only I don't see any statement from Scott Moore in Ed's report. He never talked to him. Or if he did, he never documented it. I don't even see any narrative about attempts to contact him. It's like he just ignored it."

"Hall said that too," Jake said.

"What about Wymer, his lawyer?" Birdie said. "Do we have any idea whether he tried to track the guy down?"

"I don't know." Jake felt a chill go through him as he looked at the photographs from Ruby Ingall's kitchen. He picked up the blood evidence lab report again.

"Christ," he muttered. "Ed, you lazy son of a bitch."

"What?" Birdie said. She walked over and stood at Jake's shoulder.

"Look at this." He handed her the lab report. "Give me the tag numbers from the samples sent in."

It took her a moment, but Birdie then read off twelve tag numbers. Jake laid out all the photographs that showed those numbers.

"That's it?" he asked. "You're sure? I'm not missing anything?"

"That's it," she said. "What's the matter?"

"This," Jake said. He picked up two photographs taken in the kitchen. One of the tile floor near the refrigerator. The other on a counter near the sink. He threw them down in front of Birdie, his blood starting to boil.

She looked at the report. Then she looked at the two photographs.

"Those samples were never sent in," she said. "Ed only had the samples from the barn tested? Jake, that can't be right. Ed can be stupid, but he's not an idiot, right?"

Jake walked over to the far end of the table. The samples were there. Two vials in plastic bags. Their tags corresponded with the numbers in the kitchen photographs.

"Ed Zender doesn't track down Wesley Wayne Hall's alibi witness," Birdie said. "His girlfriend is now recanting her entire testimony, claiming Ed harassed her. Flat out threatened her to say she saw him coming home covered in blood. Ed never had BCI out there to process the scene. And he never sent blood samples from the kitchen for testing. Jake ..."

"I know," he said. "Dammit. I know."

"Nobody knows this," she said. "Do they? I mean, Hall's lawyer certainly never brought the blood evidence issue up at trial. Do you think it's possible Ed or Tim Brouchard never disclosed it? I mean ... Ed's Ed and Tim's Tim. But ..."

"But," Jake said. "I need to make a call. I need to talk to Mark Ramirez. Get his take."

"He could run those samples now," she said. "Jake. Are you sure we're the ones who should be getting involved in this? There are groups. The Innocence Project, maybe."

Jake shook his head. "No. Do you really want an outside agency traipsing all over this? Let it be us if it has to be anyone."

"This is going to have to be ... official," she said. "You know that, right? We've gone sooo far beyond the down-low here, Jake."

"I know."

"So now what? None of this means Ed got the wrong guy. You said yourself Allison Sobecki is problematic. We don't know why Scott Moore was never pursued as a lead. It doesn't have to be because of incompetence. What do you want to do?"

Jake ran a hand over his face. "The last thing I want to do is cause anybody distress they don't need. You're right. Ed still might have arrested the right guy. Odds are he did. It's just ..."

"Just," Birdie answered.

"Yeah. So I've got to pay a visit to Ruby Ingall's family. I've poked around enough to bring attention to this. I can't risk them hearing about it from some outside source. It has to come from me. It's time for me to go back to that farm."

Eight

At one time, the Ingall farm encompassed nearly fifteen hundred sprawling acres and took up much of Navan Township in the southern part of Worthington County. Though no one alive remembered it, a dispute over the naming of the township had divided families and ended in a near-fatal shooting between Sam Ingall's six times great-grandfather and George Navan, the very first county commissioner. The Ingalls had the last word though. Not a single Navan ancestor survived into the latter half of the nineteenth century while the Ingall farm still stood.

Jake hadn't had much occasion to come down this way since joining the Sheriff's Department. As a kid, he'd earned pocket money like many of the other boys his age bailing hay or picking corn. He never much liked the work though. And he'd never set foot on the Ingall farm until this very day.

It was impressive. Jake had to admit it. Over the generations, various members of the Ingall family had partitioned off some of the land. It now encompassed just under three hundred acres. Most of that was still devoted to the cornfields. They'd added new out buildings and new farming technology, but the original white, two-story farmhouse and big red barn still stood, lovingly restored to its former glory by Sam Ingall and his wife, Brittany.

A flock of chickens pecked in the grass as Jake slid off his sunglasses and got out of the car. The family was expecting him. Sam Ingall had been stoic on the phone when they spoke last night. He didn't ask what Jake wanted to see him about. He'd just politely told him to come after four, just before dinner.

A large white bantam hen screeched to a halt just in front of Jake and let out a loud cluck. Then she stuck out her neck and walked a circle around him.

"Cool your jets, Virgilene!" a female voice shouted. Its owner came around the side of the house carrying a basket filled with chicken feed. She looked to be about thirty years old. Pretty, with a curvy figure, bouncy brown curls, and bright eyes. She wore rubber boots and a daisy-print apron over a simple blue dress.

"You're the policeman?" she asked.

Jake smiled and extended a hand. "Detective Jake Cashen. Uh ... Just Jake."

She set down her basket and wiped her hand over her apron. "Nice to meet you, Just Jake. I'm Brittany. Brittany Ingall. You've come to talk to my husband?"

"Well, both of you, actually. The family."

Brittany had a firm handshake. "The whole family. You sure you know what you're getting into?"

A few of the chickens raced toward Brittany. She leaned over and scattered some feed on the ground. The chickens moved off.

In the distance, Jake saw a small pen filled with at least a dozen goats. Two horses grazed in the paddock behind the barn.

"It's beautiful out here," Jake said. "Tranquil."

Brittany laughed. "It's a complete circus. But it's our circus and we like it just fine. Come on in. Sam's just in the kitchen going through some invoices. He's been expecting you."

Jake followed Brittany up the porch. It was a big, wraparound affair, complete with cane rocking chairs. He paused, touching the intricately carved rails on one of them.

"These look ... old," Jake said.

Brittany smiled. "About a hundred and fifty years. We found them in the attic a few years ago. I restored them myself."

"It's amazing work." It was more than amazing. Jake knew something like that would be worth a lot of money.

"It's a hobby. Well, this whole place started out as a hobby. My father owns the farm adjacent to this one. I grew up there. Maybe you know him. Garth MacDonald?"

"Old MacDonald had a farm," Jake said almost under his breath.

"Don't let him hear you say that," Brittany laughed. "The old part."

"Sorry."

"That's how Sam and I met. We kind of grew up together. For most of that, he was a serious pain in my ass. A total stinker. But then ... well ... I fixed him."

He'd only known Brittany MacDonald Ingall for a few minutes, but Jake had a feeling she'd be capable of bending whatever man she chose to her will.

"Before we go in," she said, touching Jake's arm. "I know why you're here. We all do. We had a little family meeting about it last night."

"You do? I mean, you did?"

"Of course. You're here about Ruby."

"Yes."

"You like those rockers? Have a seat in one, Just Jake."

He complied. Instead of sitting, Brittany leaned on the porch railing right in front of him. She put her basket on the ground and crossed her arms. Her smile faded, but she still had a friendly twinkle in her eye.

"He's a good man, my Sam. But he's been through a lot in his life. You understand what I mean?"

"I'm not here to upset anyone. There're just some things that have transpired that I wanted to talk to you all about face to face."

"He found her. You know that, right?"

"I do."

"He was fifteen years old. I told you. Sam had been a stinker. Kind of a wild kid. But that was before all of that. After? Well ... he wasn't a kid anymore. I was there. I went to Ruby's funeral. My whole family did. And what I saw? Right before my eyes, I watched a boy turn into a man. Standing right over his grandmother's casket. And he's stayed that way ever since. This place? The rest of the family didn't want anything to do with it. Why would they? Sam found her right over there."

Brittany pointed toward the back of the house. Jake had to crane his neck a bit to see. But there was a small clearing in the cornfield. Right in front of it sat a massive cement bird bath.

"It had to have been awful for him."

"It was. And it ripped this family apart. You have to know that too. Ruby was the glue. Her son, Sam's dad, Larry? It killed him too.

He kept himself going as long as he could. Through the trial. But he had a massive heart attack the day the verdict was read. Did you know that?"

Jake swallowed past a lump in his throat. "I knew he passed away not long after his mother. I didn't know it was on that particular day."

"Sam was just shy of seventeen. He's the strongest man I know. He's had to be. But he's got people around him who love him. Me. His Aunt Loretta, that's Ruby's daughter. Her husband, Uncle Dan. They're part of this too."

"I understand," Jake said. "Again, I'm not here to upset anyone."

"Okay then," she said. "Let's go in. They're all in there."

"All?"

"Sam called Dan and Loretta. You might as well do this in front of everyone."

Brittany pushed herself off the porch railing. Jake rose out of the rocking chair. As he followed Brittany inside, he had the sense he was about to face the Ingall family firing squad.

As Jake walked into the house, his stomach immediately growled. The heavenly scent of freshly baked bread and fried chicken wafted to him. Pots clanged from deeper in the house.

Brittany led him down the hallway. The house itself was immaculately restored, from its gleaming, six-inch-wide hardwood floors to the high archways, coved ceilings, and fieldstone fireplace. The place should be in a magazine, he thought. All these ridiculous modern farmhouse design shows. This was the real deal.

Laughter and loud voices reached him. As they walked past the parlor, the hallway opened up to an immense kitchen. The heart of the home. Three adults sat at a long wooden table. An older couple, Jake guessed, was Uncle Dan and Aunt Loretta. The younger man, Sam, sat at the head of the table, his laptop open and a stack of papers beside him.

"Sam?" Brittany said. "This is Detective Cashen. Jake? This is my husband Sam, and my in-laws. Dan and Loretta Clawson."

Sam had a bushy head of dark hair. Clean-shaven, he wore a white button-down shirt with the sleeves rolled up and a weathered pair of blue jeans. He rose from the table and gave Jake a solid handshake. Dan and Loretta did the same. Dan looked to be about sixty years old with a gleaming bald head and kind eyes. He towered over his wife, Loretta. The woman had wiry, silver hair and a big smile. She couldn't be five feet tall. Jake half-remembered while reading the coroner's report that Ruby Ingall was about the same size. Loretta Ingall Clawson favored her mother enough to be eerie. Jake wondered if Sam thought the same from time to time.

"Thanks for agreeing to talk to me," Jake said. Brittany left the others and headed into the kitchen. Loretta quickly rose to help her.

"You're here about Ma?" Dan asked. He had a booming voice, but not unkind.

"Well, yes," Jake said. "I have some questions. But those can wait. There have been some developments in Ruby's case that I felt you should hear in person."

Jake became keenly aware that he was standing just a few feet from where Ruby Ingall may have died. Beaten to a pulp, then strangled and dragged out to the barn where even worse happened to her. The dining room opened into an alcove. The kitchen was just beyond that along with those wonderful smells of Brittany and Loretta's cooking.

The long dining room table looked handcrafted just like the rocking chairs outside. It had thick planks of wood and seating for at least twelve. On the wall beside it were floor-to-ceiling built-in shelves painted an olive green. The top shelf contained old cookbooks with well-worn spines. Several shelves housed family photos, some looking like they dated back to the building of the farm. Jake found himself moving closer to look. Sure enough, one faded black-and-white photo showed what looked like the groundbreaking. Two leathery-faced men in overalls held the handle of a single shovel, carved into the fresh earth.

"Bartholomew Ingall," Dan said. "He bought the land from the government. We've got an old deed in storage somewhere."

"That's something," Jake said. The rest of the shelves held figurines. Chicken. Dozens of them. Maybe a hundred. Some made of glass. Others porcelain. Some metal. All shapes and sizes. The largest was an impressive bantam rooster made of wrought iron. It towered over the other shelves as if surveying the scene.

"Those are Grandma's," Sam said. "She loved her chickens. A few of the live ones on the farm are descended from hers."

"You can talk and eat at the same time," Loretta said. She and Brittany came back to the dining room carrying heaping plates in each hand. Loretta set one down in front of Jake. His eyes widened. Two succulent pieces of fried chicken. A dollop of lumpy, homemade mashed potatoes, corn, and cornbread. It smelled delicious.

"You don't have to feed me," Jake said. Though his stomach betrayed him. His mouth watered.

"Nonsense," Dan said. "Loretta's the best cook in the county. You don't sit at the Ingall table without leaving with a full belly. That was Ruby's rule."

"It was also her recipe," Loretta said. "The coating."

Brittany put a plate in front of her husband, then went to get another for herself. She sat down beside him, putting herself between him and Jake.

"Well, I truly do appreciate it."

"You're Max Cashen's grandson?" Dan asked.

"I am."

"Good man. After Ma died, he came out here with some of the other men in town. Helped us do some restoration to the barn and the house. I'll always appreciate that."

"He told me the same thing," Jake said. He bit into a drumstick and nearly had an out-of-body experience.

"Good, huh?" Sam said, biting into his own drumstick. "Aunt Loretta makes it better than Grandma did. Nobody would ever say that to her face but even Grandma knew it."

They ate in companionable silence for a little while. To Jake it would have felt sacrilegious to bring up what he came here for while such good food was in front of him. Instead, he asked about the farm itself.

"It's amazing what you've done out here," he said.

"That was all Sam," Dan said. "He had the drive. The passion. The rest of us? We probably would have been content to let him sell it."

"I wanted to keep it in the family," Sam said. "It felt ... I don't know. Like a calling."

Loretta reached across the table and touched her nephew's hand. "It was Grandpa Sam. That's who Sam's named after. My father. He passed away when he was fifty-six. Same as my grandfather. Same as my brother."

"All of them?" Jake asked, incredulous. "They were all fifty-six when they died?"

"Yes," Loretta said. "We come from a long line of men with bad tickers. Everybody tried to get my mother to sell this place after my dad died. She wouldn't hear of it. She was only an Ingall by marriage but that was enough. She wanted this place for her son and grandson. She got her wish."

"I didn't do any of it alone," Sam said. "Brittany's father took me under his wing. Made me a proposition. A five-year plan. If I couldn't make a go as a farmer, he offered to buy the place from us at fair market value. And here we are. Ten years later and still going strong."

Loud thumping came from upstairs as three pairs of feet clomped their way down the stairs. A moment later, Sam and Brittany Ingall's children made their appearance. They lined up like the Von Trapp children. Brittany got up and ordered them all to wash their hands before taking their places at the long bench on the other side of the table.

"Sam the Third," she said, rustling the hair of the tallest boy. "He'll be eight on Friday. Then we have Henry, my chicken whisperer. Virgilene's got a crush on him. He's seven. And this wee lass is Charlotte. She's five."

"Pleased to meet you," Sam the Third said, displaying a toothless grin. Then the younger Ingall brood went off and did as their mother bid, washing their hands at the kitchen sink.

"Come on," Sam said. "We can finish our conversation in the living room."

"I'm sorry," Jake said. "I really didn't mean to interrupt your family's dinner."

"Oh, somebody's always eating around here," Loretta teased. "If you waited for them not to be, nothing would ever get done."

This earned her a playful swat on her behind from her husband. Dan looked up at his wife with love-misted eyes. She leaned down and kissed him.

Sam put his napkin on his plate. With a gesture from his wife, he drew Jake away from the table and into the other room. A moment later, Dan joined them. Like Brittany, Jake sensed a protective aura around him toward Sam. Sam Ingall had lost a lot in a short amount of time. He'd found his grandmother's body in the most grisly fashion. Then lost his father. It made Jake feel good to know he had an aunt and uncle who had stepped in for him.

"You might as well be blunt," Sam said.

"All right," Jake said. "I told you there have been some developments in your grandmother's case. I'm sure you're aware Wesley Wayne Hall has maintained his innocence."

"We don't say that name here." Loretta appeared. She walked in and took a seat beside her husband.

"I'm sorry," Jake said. "Look. The truth is, I'm not at liberty to divulge very much of the details. But some things have come to light that cast some doubt about the way the investigation was handled."

"You're saying you think he didn't do it?" Sam asked.

"No. I'm not saying that. I'm saying there are some ... anomalies with how the investigation was conducted. And they may well rise to the level of it being reopened. I just wanted to prepare you for that. Get your input."

"Our input?" Dan asked. "What do we have to say about it?"

Loretta walked fully into the room and took a seat beside her nephew. Brittany appeared, leaning against the wall with her arms crossed.

"A lot," Jake said. "I want to be sensitive to your feelings and your rights. I'm not looking to put any of you through something painful. But I understand it's inevitable."

"That man killed Ruby," Brittany said. "He came into this home and took out his revenge for her standing up to him. He was a thief. A liar. A murderer. If you ..."

"Brittany, please," Sam said. He held up a hand. His wife stood poised and ready to unleash her rage, but her husband stilled her.

Sam shifted in his chair and faced Jake. "Detective, this is my family. I would be lost without them. Truly lost. Probably dead. My wife? It's like she taught me how to breathe again. They want to protect me and I love them for it. I don't know you. But I've heard enough about you to believe that you're a good man. A good cop. Are you?"

Jake paused. "I hope so."

"I hope so too. So I believe you wouldn't have walked into my home. Into my Grandma Ruby's home. Into the very room where she was killed. Unless you didn't think you had a choice."

"No," Jake said. "No, I wouldn't."

"All right," Sam continued. "So if something happened. These anomalies. Could it mean that man would get exonerated? Or a new trial?"

"It's far too soon to know any of that. I'm just saying there's probably enough where this could get reopened. And if that happens, well, it's going to generate some publicity, I'm sure."

"There's an election," Brittany said. "This is political, isn't it?"

"No," Jake said. "But I can't promise certain people won't try to make it that way."

"They already are," Dan said. "Ed Zender's putting that monster's face in his campaign ads. We've had a few reporters sniffing around already. We didn't approve of that. Corrine Forbush. The lady in the commercial. She's a neighbor. We thought she was a friend."

"I'm sorry for all that. I really am."

"You came here," Sam said. "You said all this to our faces. I appreciate that. Ed Zender's people didn't extend us the same courtesy. Corrine Forbush didn't either. So it matters. I'm glad you know that. And I know you have to do what you have to do. But will you at least agree to keep us informed? In person?"

"Absolutely," Jake said. "You have my word."

Sam rose. Jake rose with him. Sam took a step toward Jake and reached for his hand. Jake gave it. They shook.

"I'll hold you to that," Sam said. Eye to eye, Jake knew he would do whatever he could to keep his vow to the Ingall family. Dan, Loretta, and Brittany closed ranks around Sam. They would take his lead, but they would also have his back.

They were a family. Broken. But strong. Ruby Ingall must have been a remarkable woman. Her legacy stood in front of Jake now and in the land around him. He just prayed that what he had to do next would all be worth it.

NINE

"How'd he take it?" Birdie stood in the doorway of his office. He glanced at the clock. It was after five. He'd worked two hours overtime catching up on a few cases that needed his attention. She looked ... awful. Soot covered her face and she had small cuts on her forearms.

"What happened to you?" he asked.

She pushed off the doorframe with her shoulder. "Long story. Served a couple of search warrants that got hinky. I ended up halfway up a chimney."

Jake frowned. "You shouldn't be doing that crap."

"Nobody else was small enough to fit. It's okay. Seized a kilo of meth, half a kilo of coke, half a kilo of fentanyl, and a whole cache of stolen guns. It was worth it."

"Not if you end up with asbestosis. Were you at least wearing your gear?"

"Simmer down, Granny. I know how to do my job."

"Except it shouldn't be your job. This should be your job."

"Well, from your mouth to God's ... er ... the county commissioners' ears. Though I'm pretty sure the conduit will close unless Meg Landry wins in a few weeks. You planning to head down to the thing? A bunch of us are going."

"The thing ..." Jake paused. "Oh. Crap. The town hall. That's tonight?"

"Starts in less than an hour. If you give me a few minutes to clean up, I'll walk over with you. I'm sure Landry would appreciate seeing your face in the audience."

"Yeah. Of course. Yeah." Though Jake could think of about a hundred things he'd rather do than sit in on a political function. At the same time, he wanted to hear how Ed Zender would handle it as much as anything else. Plus, he'd half promised Landry he'd be there.

"So how'd it go at the Ingall farm?"

Jake ran a hand through his hair. It needed a cut. He generally liked it only slightly longer than a buzz cut. He'd let it grow a little over the summer.

"It went. They're a nice family. That place is something else. Have you seen it? Sam Ingall restored the house and the barn. He took over all farming operations. It's pretty impressive. He's gotta be doing well. Some money went into those renovations."

Birdie smiled. "I mean, sure. Sam's making a go of the farm. But the money you're seeing didn't come from him."

"What do you mean?"

"You don't know?"

"I guess not. I didn't think Ruby Ingall was worth very much. I mean, the farm. Sure."

"That's not farm money, Sam. That's all Brittany."

"Brittany? I thought she stayed home with the kids. She said her dad owns the adjacent farm."

Birdie rolled her eyes. "You know, you should follow social media every once in a while. You're a Luddite."

She came further into the office and pulled her phone out of her back pocket. She swiped up then turned the screen so Jake could see. A video played. Brittany Ingall smiled at the camera.

"Howdy, fellow chicken mamas! Check out this gem Virgilene gave me today!" Brittany wore a blue apron with tiny pockets all over it. She reached into one of the pockets and pulled out an impressive egg.

Birdie clicked the screen closed and pocketed her phone. "Brittany Ingall is Farm Wife Life."

"Farm Wife Life?"

"She's got like a zillion followers. A couple of years ago, she started posting videos. Her best tips for raising backyard chickens. Gardening tips. A lot of it is just a day in the life of a hobby farm. She went viral. All these people with their modern farmhouse aspirations just eat this stuff up. She's monetized. Making a small fortune. She did a whole series on the renovation of the barn and main house. I heard a rumor she was being courted for a book deal and may end up getting her own show on one of the home and gardening channels."

"Wow," Jake said. "I had no idea."

"She tries to keep the history of the farm on the down-low. A few times she's had comments from people asking about Ruby's murder. She shuts that down pretty quickly. I imagine the family's not too thrilled about those ads Ed's running, dredging it all back up again. How'd they take the news you're sniffing around the case?"

"That explains a lot," Jake said. "Brittany was pretty protective of her husband. I didn't realize she's also trying to protect her brand."

"They threw you out?"

"Not even close. They made me dinner. They couldn't have been nicer. But Brittany laid down some pretty clear boundaries. I was vague. Didn't tell them about the missing alibi witness or the possible issue we have with the blood evidence."

"No reason to yet."

"They appreciated me coming out there in person. I can't imagine how tough that had to have been for Sam. Finding his grandma like that."

His mind drifted. *Finding his grandma like that.* Over thirty years ago, his own parents had died by violence. His sister Gemma had been the one to find them. She hadn't been too much younger than Sam Ingall at the age he found his grandmother.

"Do they understand what you're up against?"

"I think so," Jake said. "You were right. They were none too happy about Zender's ads. I promised them I'd personally keep them up to date on any new developments. They seemed satisfied with that."

"If this goes anywhere, you know you're going to have to go back out there. Maybe a lot."

"I know. But let's just see if anything comes of that blood evidence. I've got a call in to Mark Ramirez at BCI."

"You ready?" Deputy Chris Denning poked his head in. "We're about to head across the street."

"I'll be along in a few minutes," Birdie said. "I want to at least wash my face and change into my street clothes. Denning nodded and disappeared down the hall.

"What about you?" Birdie asked. "I'll come back and grab you. I just need about fifteen minutes. A bunch of us were thinking of heading over to Gemma's for a beer after."

"I'll come to the town hall," Jake said. "For as long as I can stand it. I kinda just want to head home after."

"Suit yourself," she said. "I'll see you in a few."

Birdie excused herself. Jake shut down his computer. More than anything, he wanted to call it a day. But he knew Birdie was right. Meg Landry would appreciate seeing friendlies in the audience tonight. She could handle herself against the likes of Ed Zender, but he owed her at least his moral support.

Jake grabbed his suit coat off the chair and made his way downstairs where he knew he'd find Birdie. Anxiety he hadn't expected made his heart rate jump. Meg *had* to have a good night. The race was closer than it should be. If she lost, Jake might never get to the bottom of the Ingall case.

TEN

"Meg Landry has run this office the same way Greg O'Neal did. The same old same old. Cronyism, favoritism. She's used her office like a blank check and the people of this county deserve better. They deserve someone sitting in that office who actually knows what real policing is."

Jake couldn't believe what he was hearing. He and Birdie walked into the Stanley High School auditorium about twenty minutes after the town hall started. They'd missed Meg's opening statement but heard enough of the tail end of Zender's to make the hair on the back of his neck stand up.

"Would you like to respond to that, Sheriff Landry?" the moderator asked. It was Bridget Woodbine, the town librarian.

"Indeed I would," Meg said. She stepped out from behind her lectern and walked to the edge of the stage.

"To be honest, I can't even believe what I just heard. Mr. Zender is accusing me of cronyism? I'm the first female sheriff this county has ever had. And I think Sheriff O'Neal, if he were here, would have a thing or two to say about that characterization. Going after a man who isn't here to defend himself is a cheap shot. That seems to be about all my opponent has lately."

"What about the internal reports that came out last summer about crime being on the uptick since you became sheriff?"

An older man in the front row held the microphone. Jake squinted. It was hard to tell who it was in the dim light. Meg herself shielded her eyes with her hand as she stared directly into the auditorium's hot stage lights.

"There are really two parts to that question and I'd like the opportunity to address both of them. First of all, you mentioned internal reports. That's important. The reports you're talking about, that were published in the *Daily Beacon,* were not meant for public dissemination."

"Oh geez," Birdie whispered beside him. He felt the same way. Meg was off her game. She'd just taken some obvious bait and was about to walk off with a hook in her mouth.

"I'm sorry," Bridget Woodbine said, taking the microphone back from the questioner in the front row. "You're saying you have a leak in your office? Were those numbers false? Or were you just not expecting them to be made public?"

"I'd like to know that as well," Ed said, smirking.

"That's not what I meant at all," Meg said. "The point I'm making is that my opponent has not been running a clean campaign. He has not answered how he managed to get a hold of those reports."

Meg's color drained. She knew the mess she'd stepped in.

"She's choking," Birdie whispered.

Another person walked up to the microphone ready with a question. Jake could only see her from the back. She had long hair and wore a business suit. But the second she started to speak, Jake recognized her voice as Bethany Roman, an investigative reporter for the local news.

"She's about to take a hit," Birdie said. "Look at Zender."

Sure enough, Ed Zender puffed out his chest as Bethany began to speak.

"Sheriff Landry," she started. "Since we're talking about potential leaks in your department. Can you comment on reports that you've authorized the reopening of the investigation into Ruby Ingall's murder?"

Meg's head snapped back. "Your information is wrong. There's been no reopening of any investigation. And this isn't a press conference, Ms. Roman. If you have questions you'd like to ask of my office about any ongoing investigation, or lack thereof, you can submit them to my press liaison."

"This is a matter of public interest though," Bethany said. "And this is a public forum. I believe the public has the right to know if you're using county resources to run opposition research."

"What?" Meg said. "Whoever your source is …"

"Jake," Birdie said, clutching his arm. "How in the world did Zender find out you've been asking questions? And please tell me you've given Landry a heads-up."

He gritted his teeth. "I wanted to talk to the Ingall family first. Who the hell talked to Bethany Roman?"

"This is outrageous," Zender shouted. "The Ingall family has been through quite enough."

"I never said …" Meg started.

"Sheriff, isn't it true that Detective Jake Cashen paid a visit to Wesley Wayne Hall under your orders?"

Meg spotted Jake in the crowd. She gave him a look that could have turned him to stone.

Shit. Shit. Shit.

She was trapped. Somehow, Bethany Roman found out about Jake's trip to Chillicothe. If Meg denied it, she'd look like a fool for not knowing what her own detective was up to. If she admitted it, she'd have to give a reason. One she didn't know.

"I'm not at liberty to discuss the specifics of any cases my detectives are working on, Ms. Roman. You know that quite well."

"So he is working on it?" Ed said. "This is unbelievable. This is exactly what I'm talking about. And it's why I have the endorsement of the county commissioners. Meg Landry has used her office to advance her own personal interests since the day she took office. It's time to put an end to that once and for all. And for the record, Wesley Wayne Hall and only Wesley Wayne Hall is guilty of the murder of sweet Ruby Ingall. For Sheriff Landry to use that case ..."

"Sheriff Landry?" Meg said. "If anyone on this stage has tried to profit off the grief of that family, it's you, Ed. That's your face on those billboards next to Hall's. Not mine."

"That's right," he said. "Because I'm a real cop. And that's what the citizens of this county deserve as sheriff."

Thirty merciless minutes later, the town hall was over. Jake wished the ground would open up and swallow him. From the flash of anger in Meg Landry's eyes as they settled on him, he realized she was, in fact, about to swallow him.

"My office," she mouthed as she took her place at the center of the stage and posed for a few pictures for the newspaper.

"You want me to come with?" Birdie asked.

"No," Jake said. "I'm gonna have to face the firing squad on this one alone."

ELEVEN

J ake had parked on the other side of the gymnasium. A further walk from the auditorium, but he thought it would afford him privacy on his way out. It did, but not in the way he had hoped.

Bethany Roman anticipated his plan. She parked her car right alongside his. She was waiting for him, leaning against the hood of Jake's truck.

"I'm not doing this now," he said. She didn't move. She just smiled at him. Almost full dark now, she stood in the shadows. Jake had also purposely parked under the one street lamp that had no bulb.

"Jake, when? You need to get ahead of this story and I'm the only one who's going to give you that chance."

"Ahead of what story? There's no story."

"Really? So you're going to lie to my face? Tell me you didn't go visit Wesley Wayne Hall on death row last month? Didn't have Erica Wayne pull the court files for the Ruby Ingall murder?"

"How did you ..." Jake put a hand up. "No. Never mind. No comment."

"I'm not even interested in any of that. Well, I am. But I'm more interested in why Meg Landry pretended like that was all news to her."

Jake went rigid. He wouldn't even give her the satisfaction of changing his facial expression.

"Or maybe she wasn't pretending," Bethany said. "Maybe, you've been doing this on the side. Without her authorization. Which is it? Is Sheriff Landry actually using her office to do opposition research on Zender like I asked her? Or does she not have a clue what her own detectives are up to?"

"What is this?" Jake said. "What are you trying to do?"

"It's a story. And it's what I said in there. A matter of public interest. I know the Ingall family was none too pleased Ed Zender started running campaign ads with Hall's mugshot on them. Taking a victory lap right over their grandmother's grave. I have to admit, even I thought that was pretty underhanded."

"I suppose you'd know," Jake muttered. He moved around her and opened his truck door.

"Jake, come on. I've asked the question. It's out there. This is a small town. I knew Deputy Wayne pulled those court files about five minutes after she did it. You had to know it was going to get out. I wasn't trying to play gotcha in there. It was a legitimate question. Never mind the political ramifications. Is Hall innocent?"

"I'm not doing this, Bethany," Jake said. "Not here. Not ever."

"Really? How long do you think you're going to be able to dodge me? And if it's not me, it'll be somebody else. I'll go see Hall if I have to."

"Do whatever you want," Jake said.

"Really? I'm giving you an opportunity here. It's bullshit what Zender is doing. Zender himself is bullshit. I know that. I can see what's happening, Jake."

"Then we don't have to talk."

"She's gonna lose!" Bethany said. "You get that, right? The polling's bad. Zender's outspending her. He's got a slicker campaign. Meg thought she was gonna win this one just by keeping her nose down and doing her job. The world doesn't work like that."

"Do what you gotta do," he said. "I'm done talking. I've got somewhere else to be."

He started to climb into his truck.

"Jake," she said, her voice cracking. Bethany grabbed Jake's sleeve. "I'm on your side. I know you don't believe me. But I am. I screwed everything up between us. I know that. I should have been more forthright that night when we met. I just ... I didn't plan on liking you as much as I do."

She smelled good. She did that night, too. He'd been tired and lonely and a little bit drunk. While all that was true, he went home with her because he was attracted to her. She looked up at him now, eyes shining in the dim light, lips slightly parted as if she wanted to kiss him. She leaned in.

"Good night, Bethany," Jake said. "I'm sorry. I'm not your story. There is no story. I can't help you."

She let him go. Fire lit her eyes. She took a step back.

"There's a story," she said. "The more you push me away, the harder I'm going to dig. At some point, you won't be able to help yourself."

Jake clenched his jaw. Bethany took another step back, moving out of his path. He started the truck and drove away.

J ake wanted to be anywhere but here. Birdie and the others were already at Gemma's bar by now. Sitting in a dark corner sipping a cold draft beer sounded like heaven. But he knew he'd never make it there. Besides, if he knew Bethany Roman, she wouldn't let anything go. She was probably already at the bar on the off chance he might show up, or hoping Birdie or one of the other deputies would let something slip. Jake knew Birdie wasn't that careless.

Jake walked as slowly as he could down the long corridor leading to Meg Landry's office. The door was slightly cracked, letting a sliver of light spill onto the hallway tile.

He raised a fist to knock. He never made contact. Landry swung the door open. If he thought Bethany's eyes had fire in them, Landry's were practically molten.

"Get in here," she said, her voice a low monotone.

She held the door open, then shut it tightly behind him, locking it.

He stood at attention at the end of her desk, not daring to take a seat. If he was about to get dressed down, let it be on his feet.

Landry walked around to the other side of her desk. She sat down hard.

"You wanna tell me what that was all about? Are you gonna make me beg?"

"I didn't ..." Jake started.

"Because it can't be what I think it was," Landry said, gesturing wildly with her hands. "It can't be that my star detective reopened a murder case that's been closed for fifteen years without telling me. A murder case that my opponent has been using as a wedge issue in his campaign against me. I know it's not that. Because my star detective would *know* how bad that could look. Surely, he'd give me a heads-up on something like that."

"Meg," Jake said.

"No," she snapped.

"Okay."

"Because a thing like that would absolutely blow up in my face. A thing like that is exactly the kind of thing a hungry reporter would use to grab a headline."

Jake stood with his hands behind his back, bracing himself for the rest of Meg's onslaught.

"A thing like that ... using county resources to run opposition research on another candidate ... I mean ... that's the kind of thing that sets off internal investigations. Inquiries by the attorney general even. Hell, that's the kind of thing that could get an elected sheriff recalled, never mind the impact at the polls."

She slammed her fist against the table. Jake didn't think he'd ever seen Meg Landry get this angry. Her face had gone pure white.

"Never mind the fact that we've got a victim's family out there. I mean, if they're hearing about this at the same time the rest of the town is, that could be very bad," she ranted.

Jake kept his jaw clamped shut.

"You," she shouted. "Now you talk."

"I ..." He exhaled and started over. "I'm sorry."

Whatever Meg had expected him to say, that seemed to throw her off guard.

"You're sorry?"

"Yes."

"Just ... sorry. You're not going to deny anything I just said?"

"Actually, I'm going to deny most of it. Well, not so much deny. More ... explain. If you'll let me. But I've seen that expression you've got on your face from my sister enough times and it usually doesn't get me anywhere if I do anything other than apologize. And I am sorry. I had no idea Bethany Roman was going to ask you that question. It was a cheap shot and I told her so."

"You *told* her so? You talked to her? Tonight?"

"Well, no. She followed me out to my truck."

Meg threw her hands up. "Oh. Well. That makes it okay."

"I didn't say a word. I told her no comment."

"That'll fix it."

"I'm sorry. I am. Do you want the explanation?"

Meg pressed her thumbs into the corners of her eyes. "Sit down."

"Are you sure?"

"Yes. Sit down. Quit standing over me. Sit."

He did.

"Okay. Talk."

"I got a letter," he said. "From Hall. He ... well ... there was enough in it that got me curious enough to pay him a visit. So I did."

"You visited him. And you didn't think giving me a heads-up at that point would have been wise?"

"I didn't think anything would come of it. I just ... he mentioned something that got my attention."

"Which was?"

Jake hesitated. He realized telling her about Hall invoking Rex Bardo would only make things worse.

"Hall's girlfriend has recanted her testimony. She's making claims that Ed Zender leaned on her pretty hard. Threatened her. Physically. Also, with violating her probation and messing up her custody arrangement. She was scared. Now she's saying she lied on the stand. Never saw Hall covered in blood the night of Ruby Ingall's murder. I don't know how familiar you are with the case. But the girlfriend's testimony was pretty crucial to the jury at the time."

"You believe her now?"

"Honestly? I don't know. But if it was just that, I'd have left it. Hall also claims he's got an alibi witness that Zender never ran down. So I wanted to look at the files. Erica pulled them for me at my request. That's where I'm at."

"Great. I should have known you'd drag Deputy Wayne into this. You realize that puts a target on her back too if Zender wins. Jake, why didn't you tell me any of this? You had to know it was going to get out."

"Because I wanted to make sure there was some there, there. Before anything official had to happen. The man's on death row. He's got a date with a needle next month."

"I know," she said. "Three days before the frigging election. If I didn't know better, I'd have thought Zender's campaign worked that out in advance."

"And I didn't think it was something you should know. Not yet. That's the God's honest truth. I don't know how Bethany Roman got the story."

"There are probably a hundred different ways," Meg said

"Erica was careful. She wasn't flaunting the fact she was pulling files."

"She wouldn't have had to be. We both know that. One off-handed comment from one of the clerks down there is all it would have taken."

"I honestly didn't think anything would come of it. I thought I'd make sure all the t's were crossed then move on."

"What are you telling me now?"

"Meg ... they're not. There are problems. Holes in Zender's investigation."

"Hall was convicted. He had a lawyer."

"A crappy one. His lawyer was disbarred a few years after his conviction for incompetence."

"He's had appeals," she said.

"Again ... crappy representation. He's a nobody. Broke. Wesley Wayne Hall has gotten the justice he could afford. Now maybe he's guilty. He probably is. It's just ..."

"Holes," she said.

"Yeah."

Meg gritted her teeth. She mouthed the F word.

"Yeah," Jake said.

"What do you want to do?"

"I've got a call in to Mark Ramirez. I was going to come see you tomorrow morning and lay this all out. I'm damn sorry it got out tonight. It's a mess. My mess."

She shook her head. "Except it isn't. You work for me, Jake."

"I work for the county. Like it or not, that means I also work for Wesley Wayne Hall."

"You see what this looks like?"

"I do."

"Jake, you've put me in a horrible bind."

"I meant my apology, Meg."

She sat back hard. "The thing is ... I know. And I know you wouldn't do any of this just to trip up Ed Zender. You don't play dirty pool."

"Thanks for that."

"Well ... shit, Jake."

"Yeah."

"If I told you to walk away from this, would you?"

He pursed his lips. "Except you wouldn't. Because you don't play dirty pool either. And you wouldn't let a man get executed for a crime he didn't commit just so you could win an election."

She closed her eyes and shook her head. "No. I wouldn't. So what are the odds he didn't commit this crime?"

"Honestly? My gut? He probably did it."

"But Zender screwed up."

"I think so."

"So we have to be sure."

"I think so."

She slammed her palm against her arm rest. "Dammit. Okay. Yeah. Okay. So we don't have a choice."

"No."

"Well, I appreciate your honesty. Even if it's a little too late, Jake."

He resisted the urge to apologize again. She knew he was sorry.

"Okay then. Work with Ramirez. I'll take whatever heat's coming. What the heck? I've always wanted to take up knitting. Or cooking. I'll have plenty of time after the election if things keep trending this way."

"It's still a long time between now and November," Jake said.

"Get out of here," she said. "I'd like to drown my sorrows in solitude for a while."

Jake rose. He hated leaving her like this. But there was nothing else he could say or do.

TWELVE

"I really appreciate you meeting with me."

Jake sat at another kitchen table in another farmhouse not far from the Ingalls. This one belonged to Garth MacDonald. Sam Ingall's father-in-law. Garth had a weather-beaten, tan face and kind eyes. He'd walked in wearing a John Deere baseball cap, but promptly took it off. He was of a generation that would never wear their hat at a table, no matter whether there was food on it or not.

Garth's farm was a fair bit smaller than the Ingalls'. He grew soy beans and had just two horses in the paddock behind it. He and his wife Lindy lived here alone now, though Brittany, their daughter, checked in on them almost daily.

"Sam filled me in on your conversation," Garth said. He had a deep, gravelly voice that Jake knew commanded attention at the local chapter of the Ohio Farmer's Union. Garth had served in a leadership position there for over a decade. He was a bit of an elder statesman among the local growers in Worthington County.

"He's a good kid," Garth continued. "And he's been through hell."

It was a statement, but also a warning, Jake knew. "The last thing I want to do is cause any more distress for the Ingall family. Which I know you're part of."

"You don't think Wesley Wayne Hall killed Ruby?"

The man was direct. Jake could work with that.

"To be honest, I haven't decided yet. But there are enough things about the way the investigation was conducted that cause me some concern."

"Pretty convenient if you ask me. Won't do much good for old Ed Zender to have you rooting around trying to pry out the crown jewel of his career."

"How well do you know Ed?"

Garth set his jaw to the side. Jake detected the slightest twinkle in his eyes.

"I know him well enough to know he's an idiot."

"Right," Jake said. "Well, I'll leave my opinions on that matter to myself. Ed's almost immaterial to this. And right now, I'm just trying to make sure every lead gets run down."

"You're saying it wasn't back in the day?"

Jake paused. He had a party line he knew Meg would prefer he used. It was an ongoing investigation. He couldn't go into detail. But Garth MacDonald was sizing him up. Judging his worth. It could bite him in the ass down the road, but for now, Jake decided to give him a straight answer.

"Yes. There were loose ends. They may amount to nothing. I actually hope they do. But they're loose enough that I can't leave them."

"What do you suppose I have to do with any of it?"

Jake pulled out his notepad. He'd written a name down. He slid the pad across the table so Garth could read it. Garth pulled a pair of readers out of his shirt pocket and slipped them on.

"Scotty Moore?" he said.

"Yes. You know I've talked to Hall. He has said that Moore was with him the night Ruby Ingall was murdered. As far as I can tell, nobody's ever talked to Moore. I'd like to. Hall said he and Moore did some work for you around the farm during that era. And that you may have kept in contact with him over the years."

Garth put the pad down. "Well, I'm afraid you may have wasted your trip. I haven't heard from Scotty Moore in a couple of years."

Jake suspected as much. But there were other things he hoped Garth MacDonald may be able to shed light on.

"Tell me about Ruby. How close were the two of you?"

"We were friends. My family's owned the land adjacent to the Ingall family farm for a very long time. Her husband, Old Sam, is the one who rented me the cornfields some forty years ago. Just a couple of years before he died. The Ingall men die young, in case you haven't heard. Old Sam was fifty-six. Same age as his son, Larry, Young Sam's father."

"I heard Old Sam's father also died at fifty-six. That's a hell of a coincidence."

"I told my son-in-law he better get himself a good cardiologist."

"Sound advice."

"When Old Sam died, Ruby was sure grateful the farming lease was already in place. It took a great load off of her. Though there was still plenty that needed to be done around her farm. She still grew a small amount of her own crops. What she put on her table and fed to her livestock. A lot of people told her she'd be better off selling, moving into a condo somewhere. But she wouldn't budge. She was a farmer's wife. That land has been in the Ingall family since before the county was established. She wanted to pass it on to her son. But those boys had no interest in it while Ruby was alive."

"That's what I've heard," Jake said. "It's kind of amazing to me how well Sam's doing out there. And I understand your daughter is a social media marketing genius."

Garth smiled for the first time since they sat down. "She's something, my Brittany. That's for sure. A hell of a lot smarter than her old man. But Young Sam? He's impressed me too. I would have understood it if he didn't want anything to do with the land after his father passed. Larry was just destroyed when his mother was murdered. See, that's the thing people don't see. They read about Ruby. The way she was found. They know about Wesley Wayne Hall. Boy, if that name doesn't sound like he was destined to be a killer, I don't know what. But her death damn near destroyed them. All of them. Sam was just a kid. Fifteen. And to find Ruby like that. God, he was a mess. Just broken."

Jake went still, allowing Garth MacDonald to plumb the depths of his own memories. His face hardened. Then he locked eyes with Jake.

"But I suppose you know a little something about family tragedy, don't you, son?"

The question shocked him a little. Garth MacDonald was in his early sixties. He'd lived in Blackhand Hills his whole life. His family had been here for generations. Of course, he would know Jake's own family history. At least what he would have read about in the newspapers.

"I knew your father a little," Garth said. "You're named after him."

"Yes."

"He was a couple of years younger than me. But I remember him pretty well. There were a few summers your granddad sent him and his buddies out here to do some work for my father. He was a hard worker, your dad. Kept to himself. But I knew my father felt he was one of the good kids. Reliable. No bullshit."

"I'm glad," Jake said.

"I didn't know your mother though," Garth continued. Jake felt his entire body go rigid. "She was from a different circle. An Arden. When I read about what happened, it always surprised me that somebody like Jake Cashen would marry into that family."

It was an odd thing to hear his full name used to refer to his father. An odd thing to see written on a headstone out in the small cemetery on his grandfather's land.

"Well," Jake said. "I can tell you that the Arden family was pretty surprised, too."

Garth let out a soft laugh. "No. I don't imagine they were too pleased by it. I've had plenty of run-ins with that group myself. I'm sorry. I know they're your mother's kin. But all the Ardens I've met are a bunch of rich, arrogant assholes who don't know what a hard day's work is."

Jake raised a brow. He couldn't fault the man's observation.

"Well," Garth said. "I don't mean any disrespect to your mama. If she saw something in your dad like I did, then she had more sense than most of her relations. I'm just real sorry for your loss."

"Thank you," Jake said. "But I don't remember much about either one of them. I was only seven when they ... passed away."

Passed away. What a ridiculous euphemism for what happened to his parents. They didn't pass. Theirs had been a brutal, violent end. His father had shot his mother, then himself. Jake shrugged off the memory of it.

"But you want to know about Ruby," Garth said. "About Wesley Hall and Ruby."

"Yes."

"Well, my experience with Hall was decent. There was a period of time. Maybe a year. Where he was one of the more reliable day laborers I had out here."

"Do you remember how you first came to know him?"

"This one," Garth said, tapping Jake's notepad. "Moore was doing some work for me. I had to redo all my fencing around the whole property. Moore had proven himself pretty reliable himself and I asked him if he had a friend or two he could bring out. That was gonna be too big a job for one man. He brought Hall. Then there were times I couldn't get a hold of Scotty Moore and I'd call Hall. There were a few of us. Landowners around here. We look out for each other. I knew Hall did work for Ruby. She knew he did work for me. We vouched for different people to each other. It still works like that around here."

"Of course. But then, I understand Ruby had a falling-out with Hall. What do you know about that?"

"Nothing directly. I know Ruby called me up one day and told me she caught Hall stealing gas from her. And she said he got real angry when she confronted him. Not many things scared Ruby Ingall, but she sounded frightened. She didn't want him around anymore. A day or two after that, he came here looking for work. Well, we had words. I told Hall if I ever heard he gave Ruby any more trouble, he'd have to answer to me. Ran him off. Made sure the other landowners around here knew what kind of an asshole he was. Then I heard later he was in town making some threats. Telling whoever would listen that Ruby was a liar. Crazy. That he wished he'd have just shut her up once and for all. Let's just say the kid didn't know how to read a room. I heard he got himself run out of more than one bar shooting his mouth off like that."

"That's what I heard as well."

"Then when we heard the news about what happened to Ruby, well, we all pretty much figured Hall might have had something to do with it."

"You went to the police yourself. I mean, of your own volition."

"You bet your ass I did. A group of us went. We told Ed Zender exactly what we knew about Hall and the threats he'd made."

"What about Scotty Moore? Did you talk to him about Hall at all? I mean, you knew they were acquainted."

Garth scratched his chin. "I did. Before Ruby died. After I ran Hall off. Moore was out here a few days after that. I told Scotty I didn't want Hall on my property again and that if he showed up, he was to let me know. Scotty told me not to worry about it. Told me he and Hall were no longer friends. Scotty pretty much confirmed what Ruby said, that Hall was a thief and not to be trusted. Well, I tore into Scotty pretty good after that. Cuz he vouched for Hall in the first place. Scotty swore up and down that Hall had changed. I gotta be honest. It made me think a whole lot less of Scotty after that. And again, this was even before Ruby turned up dead. This is why I don't get why Wesley Hall is going around saying Scotty Moore is his alibi. Last I knew, Scotty didn't want anything to do with Hall."

"Hmm," Jake said. "That's interesting. That's nowhere near the story Hall's telling today."

"Then you know what I know. Wesley Wayne Hall's a liar. Now,

Ed Zender's an idiot. But you can't convince me that Hall's innocent."

Jake picked up his notepad. "I promise you, I'm not trying to. But I really would like to talk to Scotty Moore. You don't have a number for him?"

"I don't. Like I said, it's been a few years since I've seen him. I heard somewhere he moved to Florida a while back."

"Do you know who you heard that from?"

Garth shook his head. "It was probably one of the other workers I've had out here. And I can't even tell you when I heard it. These guys, they kind of drift in and out over the years. For lots of reasons. Mostly it has to do with the economy. When it's good, I have a hard time finding day laborers. When it's bad, it's easier."

"Can you remember any of the guys Hall and Moore used to hang around with?"

"Sure," Garth said. He took the pad from Jake. He wrote down three names. John Macon. Jeremy Lynch. Lyle Luke.

"This was the crew I had around that time. Lyle's the only one I still call from time to time. He lives out in Maudeville. I can't say whether Lyle was close with either Hall or Moore. I'm just saying these were the guys I had overlap with during that time frame. One of them might have more recent information about Scotty Moore. And your best bet on that would be Lynch. Moore introduced me to him. I sorta remember some deal where Lynch didn't have a phone. So I used to get word to him through Scotty. I don't know if they were living together or not. But they were close."

"I really appreciate this," Jake said.

"You know, I don't have a big opinion when it comes to politics," Garth said. Jake suspected the opposite was true.

"But I sure don't like what Zender's doing. Dredging up this stuff about Ruby's murder. Sam's a good kid. He's strong. He's had to be. He'll tell you he's fine. That he's in a good place. A lot of that is a front. I was there, Jake. Finding Ruby like he did almost killed him, too. And it did kill his father. Larry kept it together long enough to make it through Hall's trial."

"Just long enough," Jake said, pocketing his notebook. "I understand he dropped dead the night the verdict came in."

"I was there," Garth said. "I mean, at the house. Sam found Larry face down, half out of the shower. God. He was a man by then. The stuff with Ruby made him grow up. He was only sixteen. And Julie ... his mother. She just couldn't take it. She wanted to sell their house in Stanley and move to Florida where her sister lived. Sam wouldn't go. He wanted to finish high school here. So she hung in there for two years. Miserable. Then, when Sam graduated, Julie had to move. She begged Sam to come with her. But by then, Sam had made up his mind. Ruby left the farm to Larry. Julie and Loretta wanted to sell it. Well, Sam wouldn't hear of it. He took a chunk of money he got from Larry's life insurance and bought Loretta out. He came to me. Eighteen years old. He asked me if I'd help him. If I'd teach him how to farm the land. When my lease ran out, he wanted to take over the farming operations himself. You could have knocked me over with a feather, Jake. Here was this kid. This broken kid who'd suffered and witnessed terrible things. But he'd made up his mind. He was gonna go to college. Get a degree in agribusiness. Carry on the family tradition. He got a scholarship from the Ohio Farm Bureau. And that was sure fitting. The night Ruby died. That's where we all were. We were at a fundraiser in Logan for the OFB. Ruby's whole family. Then Sam got himself a full ride from them."

"That's amazing," Jake said. "And you helped him."

"You're damn straight I did. Proudest day of my life when that lease ran out. He's had some ups and downs learning the business. But he's made a go of it. I love that boy like my own son. Now he *is* my son by marriage."

"He's lucky to have you. Definitely lucky to have Brittany."

"Not just us. Dan and Loretta really stepped up for him, too. They never had kids of their own. I think they tried but it just never worked out. Anyway, I don't blame Julie, his mom. She's a good woman. She just had too many bad memories here in Blackhand Hills, what with losing her husband. And Ruby. But Sam's all right. We've got his back. Forever."

Jake could see the love and pride written plainly on Garth MacDonald's face. Sam Ingall lost his father. But his aunt and uncle and his father-in-law had parented him, protected him, made him whole again.

"Thank you doesn't seem adequate," Jake said, patting his notepad. "I know you didn't have to talk to me. I know why you might think I'm doing something that could cause your family pain. I don't mean for it to."

"You gotta do your job," Garth said, rising. He held his hand out for Jake to shake. "But I also gotta do mine."

His handshake was firm. There was a promise in it. Garth MacDonald wasn't finished protecting the people he cared about. Jake knew this was a good man to have on your side. And a nightmare to have as your enemy.

Thirteen

S unday evening, as Jake made the slow, uphill walk to the big house for their weekly family dinner, he took the long way. He wound his way along the creek until he came to the one spot on Grandpa's land he never really liked to go.

Jake paused. The old man had been down here recently. Jake spotted tire treads from Grandpa's four-wheeler near the stone bench. Grandma Ava's headstone had fresh flowers in front of it. There were a few others buried here. His great-grandparents, Dorothy and Harold Cashen. Great-Grandpa Cashen had the largest headstone with a crucifix adorning the top of it. Over the years, Grandpa had remarked on it, saying his own father had wanted it there thinking it would ease his way into heaven. Grandpa Max felt certain the man was wasting his time. Though Max never got specific about just what sins Harold Cashen had committed to earn him a trip to the devil.

The smallest headstone was tucked next to Grandma Ava's. A simple, flat, rose quartz rectangle.

Fiona Rose Jarvis.

She had died the day she was born. Jake leaned down and ran his fingers over the engraved letters. His niece. Gemma hadn't told anyone she was pregnant until a few weeks before she delivered. She said Grandma Ava had known the whole time but never let on.

Jake had always regretted not realizing what was happening. He had been a self-absorbed sixteen-year-old with problems of his own. He'd only found out after the fact. Gemma never talked about it to him. Not once. He'd gotten a phone call from Grandma Ava. She'd been so matter of fact. And life moved on.

But none of that was why he came here today. Garth MacDonald's words stirred him more than he wanted to admit.

"I knew your father ... he was one of the good kids ...

No one ever wanted to talk about Jake Cashen Senior. Certainly not with Jake. They were being polite, perhaps. Thinking the pain of it would be too much for Jake. The awful thing his father had done in the last crazed, desperate moments of his life made him unworthy of remembering in any other way.

Maybe they were right. Maybe.

... he was one of the good kids ...

Jake placed a hand on the top of his father's headstone. His mother wasn't here. Not in this place. No. She had a monument in the town named after her family. Ardenville. A big, garish thing that you could see from the road. People rarely talked about her to Jake, either. And her family had shunned him and Gemma, as if their very existence was an affront to Sonya Arden's memory. But Jake knew better. He remembered a woman who loved him with all her heart. And loved his father, too.

Long before everything went so wrong.

Jake turned and headed back to the trail to the big house, leaving the ghosts behind him for now. At least, that had been the plan.

———

As he reached Grandpa's long gravel driveway, a pickup truck was heading down the other way. Jake stiffened. Its driver glared at him, then his pinched face broke into a smirk.

Dickie Gerald. He gave Jake a half-hearted salute with a mannerism that looked more befitting the middle finger. Dickie was at least smart enough not to go that far.

He rolled down his window. Jake braced himself.

"My aunt wants me to thank you," he said. "For going to see Wesley."

"I didn't do it for her," Jake said. And he didn't want anyone from the Gerald family thinking they owed him some favor. "You mind telling me what you're doing here?"

"Dropping off my son," Dickie said. Christ, Jake thought. He was alone in the car.

"Your visits are supposed to be supervised, Dickie."

Dickie smiled. "That's between Gemma and me. And *my* son."

Dickie rolled up his window and continued on down the hill. Jake made an effort to unclench his fists before he walked into the house.

Gemma was in the living room. Aidan sat in front of her talking a mile a minute about his trip to a reptile farm with Dickie. She listened only half-heartedly, running her fingers through her son's hair.

Checking for lice, Jake wondered. Or, God forbid, bruises. The thought of it made Jake's blood simmer. If Dickie ever laid a hand on Aidan, Jake knew he would kill him. The thought came to him not as some wild blood vow. It was just a simple fact. But even that sent a shudder through him in light of where he'd just been.

"Chili's on!" Grandpa Max shouted. It smelled delicious. As blind as Grandpa was, he could still work magic in the kitchen when it came to a few of his favorite dishes.

"Go on and help him set the table," Gemma told Aidan, kissing the top of his head. The boy was so happy, he forgot to squirm away.

"Saw Dickie," Jake said, waiting until Aidan was out of hearing range.

"Don't start," she said. "I'm doing my best."

"You're letting him take the boy alone?"

"Jake ..."

He put a hand up in surrender. "I don't want to argue. It's been a long week."

"So I hear," she said. "What are you gonna do when Ed Zender gets elected sheriff?"

"Who says he is?"

"She's in trouble, Jake," Grandpa called out from the kitchen. Jake and Gemma went to the table. Aidan had just finished setting out their bowls.

"There's still time," Jake said. "People will come to their senses."

"Heard you paid a visit to Garth MacDonald," Grandpa said. Jake stopped himself from asking him how that news got to him. This was Blackhand Hills. Grandpa knew everything. People also tended to have loose lips around him. As though his crappy eyesight also affected his hearing.

"I'm working a case, Gramps."

"Oh I know it. The whole town knows it. You really think Hall's got a shot at getting out?"

"What?" Jake said. "This isn't about that. I'm not trying to get the man exonerated. I'm just trying to make sure Ed Zender didn't screw up the investigation."

"How's that going?" Gemma asked, ladling chili into her son's bowl. Aidan reached over and grabbed two giant biscuits from the center of the table.

"It's going. I'm just trying to track down a witness. Once I do that, this'll probably be over. Depending on what he says."

"Scotty Moore," Grandpa said. He shook out his napkin and laid it over his lap.

"How the hell did you know that?" Jake asked. "Never mind. I don't think I want to know."

"You'd be right," Grandpa said, grinning.

"Did you know the guy?"

Grandpa shrugged. "Can't say as I did. He came around here once back in those days. Heard I needed some help clearing some brush on the trails. This was well after you left us."

Left them, Jake thought. He'd gone to college. Then took a job with the FBI in Chicago. Before her death, his grandmother had lamented his life choices and tended to take it personally. But he knew she had also been deeply proud.

"He did work for you?" Jake asked, spooning out his own chili.

"He most certainly did not," Grandpa said. "You know I never let riff-raff onto this property. It was your grandmother's idea. She got it in her head I was gonna screw up my back running a brush hog of all things."

"You did screw up your back," Gemma said.

"Agh." Grandpa waved her off. "Anyway. No. I shooed him away. But I knew he was doing work out at MacDonald's."

"Garth said Dad used to work for him," Jake said. "When he was a teenager. He said Dad was one of his hardest workers."

Gemma froze. Jake rarely brought up their father in front of Grandpa Max. Max looked thoughtful as he swallowed a mouthful of chili.

"Well, I hope so," was all he said. Things grew quieter after that. At least among the grown-ups. Aidan, on the other hand, launched into an excited recitation of his adventure at the reptile expo with his father.

"Can we get a bearded dragon?" Aidan asked. "My friend Trax has one. He's got a leash for it and everything."

"Trax?" Max said. "What kind of name is Trax?"

"Stop," Gemma muttered. This was an ongoing theme of Grandpa's to lament the names millennials inflicted on their children.

It was good though. The more Aidan talked, the less likely Grandpa would turn the conversation back to Ruby Ingall's murder.

As soon as everyone licked their bowls clean, Aidan was up clearing plates. Gemma never had to ask him. He was a good kid, that one. Eager to please. Smart. Jake prayed his good-for-nothing father wouldn't screw him up.

Later, Jake sat out on the porch. Grandpa and Aidan were inside watching a ballgame. The oak trees framing Grandpa's driveway had turned brilliant shades of red, amber, and brown.

Gemma came out and sat beside him.

"You okay?" she asked.

"What do you mean?"

"I don't know. You're quieter. Are you really worried about Meg Landry losing this thing? I mean, Ed Zender could be your boss. Is it wise for you to be chasing after this Wesley Wayne Hall thing?"

"How well do you know them? The Ingalls."

Gemma stretched her legs out on the porch. "I know Loretta Clawson a little bit. And Dan, her husband. Dan was a real estate agent for a while. Now he works for a mortgage company. Decent guy. Loretta's nice too."

"Garth MacDonald thinks the world of them. Especially Sam Ingall."

"It makes me happy he's out there working that farm. Not too many of our generation do it anymore."

"When he's old enough, you should take Aidan out there," Jake said. "Sam could teach him a few things. He could work in the summer like our dad did."

"That got to you, did it?" she said. "Whatever Garth MacDonald said. About Dad."

Jake shrugged. He picked up a fallen leaf. It had turned pure gold. "I guess. We just don't hear too many good stories about him."

"No. We don't."

"They took care of him."

"Of Dad?"

"No," Jake said. "Of Sam. He was fifteen when he found Ruby. I've seen the photos, Gemma. It was ... not good."

"No. I don't imagine it was."

"Garth though. And his aunt and uncle. Dan and Loretta. They took care of Sam. Surrounded him. Protected him. Made sure he was okay. As okay as a kid could be with that kind of baggage to carry around. Then later ... when his dad died. Sam found him too."

"That's awful," she said. "I didn't know that."

"They're good people."

Gemma nodded, her lips tightly pursed.

"I don't want to reopen old wounds for them."

"Then don't."

Jake twirled the leaf. "The thing is. I'm not sure yet. But I really think maybe Zender screwed this up."

"That's what your gut's telling you?"

"Yeah." It was the first time he'd admitted it to anyone.

"Gemma," he said. "I'm sorry that you've had to carry the baggage of Mom and Dad."

"What do you mean?"

"Finding them like you did. Sam was fifteen. You were twelve. Sure. We had Grandma and Grandpa. But they never ... we don't talk about this shit. And it's not like I wanna start. But seeing the Ingalls. I don't know. I just wonder how things might have been different if we had more family. You know. Aunts. Uncles."

"We did have more family," Gemma said bitterly. "It didn't help."

"No," Jake said. "It didn't." Instead of protecting them. Embracing them. Their mother's family blamed Jake and Gemma for being a product of a marriage they never approved of. They'd treated them both like dirt ever since.

Where Sam Ingall had come away from his tragedy with a singular purpose in life, Gemma had always struggled. She'd gone from man to man. Career to career. And Jake? He'd taken the first chance he could to get as far away from this place as he could. He didn't regret it. At the same time, he was sorry.

"I love you, you know," Gemma said. She pushed her shoulder into Jake's.

"Yeah. I love you too. Just … be careful. I mean with Aidan. With Dickie."

"I am. I promise."

"He's gonna find out his dad's a bum, you know that, right?"

He thought she would protest. Instead, she gave him that tight-lipped smile. "I know that. But it's not my job to tell him, Jake. It's my job to be here for him when he finds out on his own. Hard as that may be."

He put his arm around his sister. He'd been gone for so much of their adult life. But he was here now. And it would make all the difference.

Fourteen

"You know you're not winning too many popularity contests with this."

Detective Gary Majewski sat at the desk on the opposite side of the office. Majewski handled crimes to property for Worthington County. He made for the ideal office mate. He was generally quiet and kept to himself. Also, for the better part of the last year, Majewski had been on medical leave. Jake had always known him to mind his own business and keep his head down. So today's comment was a rarity.

"I didn't know I was in the running for any to begin with," Jake said.

"I suppose you're damned if you do and damned if you don't," Majewski said. "There are a lot of people around here who still have Ed Zender's back."

"Are you one of them?"

Majewski considered the question. "We worked out of this office together for a long time. I don't have a beef with the guy. We get along."

It wasn't really an answer.

"Look," Jake said. "I'm not trying to make trouble for Ed Zender. That's not what this is about. And I'm not *officially* doing anything."

Majewski smiled. "Unofficially officially. Got it. I'm just saying. Do you really think you're doing Sheriff Landry any favors with this?"

"Gary, I appreciate the advice if that's what you're trying to give. I really am just trying to do my job."

"Hmm. Well, I guess I can respect that."

He paused as if he were about to say something else. Instead, Majewski slipped his readers back on and turned his face back to his computer screen. It appeared what passed for a lecture was over.

Good talk, Jake thought to himself. He grabbed his suit coat off the chair.

"I'll be out of the office for a little while. I've got some interviews I gotta do."

Majewski looked up. "Where are you heading?"

Jake didn't want to answer. He did anyway. "I need to talk to Loretta Clawson."

Majewski took his readers off. "Huh. Unofficially officially."

"Something like that."

Before Majewski could pass any further judgment on the matter, Birdie appeared in the hallway. Majewski scowled when he saw her. Jake knew it wasn't from any dislike of Birdie. He imagined it was more that Majewski disapproved of Jake dragging her into what he clearly thought were shenanigans.

"Hey, Gary," Birdie said.

"Good to see you, Erica," Majewski said.

Jake hustled Birdie back out into the hallway and closed the door.

"What's that about?" she asked. "I don't know that I've heard Majewski say more than two words in months."

"He's chatty today," Jake said. "Full of opinions."

Birdie looked back toward Jake's closed office door. He took the lead and held the stairway door open for her. She stepped through it. When she saw there was nobody else coming up or down, she turned to Jake.

"Majewski's not the only one full of opinions. There seems to be a lot of it going around. I don't get it. I didn't realize Ed Zender had such a fan club around here."

"I don't think it's so much about love for Ed. I think it's more about distrust of me. Or maybe there's enough rank and file thinking they'll be better off with Ed in the big office instead of Meg."

They made it down to the parking lot. Birdie held her campaign hat in her hand. She slipped into the passenger seat of Jake's unmarked sedan.

"What do you suppose Ed's promising these idiots behind our backs?"

"Who knows? The county commissioners have come out and endorsed Ed. It might be more about that. People know where to find their bread and butter."

"People are still pissed Landry promoted you to detective so soon after you came here. It's probably got more to do with that than anything. Which is dumb. Everyone knows you're good at your job, Jake. And I don't think there's anybody else who really wants your job."

There was more to it. Birdie herself was the other issue. Jake had been pushing hard for her to be given a detective shield right along with him. Budgetary and political problems had stood in the way of that so far. But for as many people might begrudge Jake his shield, there were more that would begrudge it of Birdie. She was young, and she was a woman. Maybe the thought of having a woman sheriff as well as a woman detective was a bridge too far for some people. As far as Jake was concerned, it was well past time for those people to move the hell on.

"People are just gonna have to figure themselves out," Jake said.

"Does Landry know where we're headed today?"

"No," he said.

"Jake." Birdie turned in her seat. "She did give you the green light on this case, didn't she?"

"She didn't *not* give me the green light. She told me if there was something here, to let her know. I'm still trying to figure that out. A lot of it is gonna depend on what Ramirez finds with those samples we sent him."

"Is it wrong that I hope it's nothing?"

Jake made the final turn down Old County Road Seven. It was nothing but dirt now. The Ingall farm branched off to the south. But that's not where Jake was headed today. He turned down a hidden drive and made his way up to a brick ranch sitting on ten acres just to the north of the Ingall property.

Loretta Clawson was weeding her garden on the side of the house. She stood up and waved a gloved hand as Jake pulled up. Loretta's floppy straw hat blew off her head. Laughing, she picked it up. Two lively beagles heralded Jake's arrival with a chorus of howls.

"Don't mind them," Loretta said. "That's Gable and Mable. Mable's the fat one."

Mable waddled up to Jake on her stubby legs, sniffed his shin, then licked his hand as he leaned down to pet her. Gable gave Birdie the same treatment.

"Thanks for meeting me," Jake said. "Loretta, this is Erica Wayne. She's been helping me out with a few things."

Loretta pulled off her gardening gloves and shook Birdie's hand. "Come on in," she said. "I dressed too warm for the day. I read we're gonna be near eighty tomorrow. It's not good for peak fall colors. Feels like that comes later and later every year."

Gable and Mable ran off around the side of the house after a squirrel. Loretta led Jake and Birdie in through the front door.

They entered her living room. The house was cluttered, but not dirty. Loretta Clawson had picked up some of her mother's hobbies. Two curio cabinets housed various figurines. Where Ruby Ingall collected chickens, Loretta seemed to prefer glass doves.

Jake spotted a family portrait hanging just inside the doorway. He got closer. It was one of those cringeworthy studio sessions. Probably taken sometime in the late seventies. Loretta stood in the front wearing a purple blouse with a wide white collar. She had hair parted down the middle and feathered. She had been a pretty teen with wide blue eyes and straight teeth. Her brother, Larry, stood next to her looking like he wanted to be anywhere else.

Loretta's parents, Ruby and Sam, stood behind their children with their hands on their shoulders.

Jake had only really seen Ruby Ingall as an old woman. In this photo, she was probably in her late forties. She had a pleasing face with jet black hair. Old Sam's hair had already gone white and he sported a full beard, giving him a Santa-like appearance.

"He hated that picture," Loretta said. "Mom forced him into it. I'm glad she did. I honestly think it's one of the last ones we ever took. My dad died a few years after that."

"He was fifty-six," Jake said, remembering what Dan told him about the longevity of Ingall men.

"Yes," Loretta said. "Not a lucky age for the men in this family."

"That's so sad," Birdie said.

"She knew it," Loretta said. "My mom. She never said it out loud. But she was always in a hurry with my dad. Pushing him to finish projects. Get things in order. Like she knew she was only gonna have so long with him."

"Oh, you're here!" Dan Clawson came out from the kitchen. He wiped his hands on a red-and-white-checkered towel. "I just put a roast in the crock-pot for dinner later. I was just about to put another pot of coffee on. I know it's almost lunchtime. But maybe you'd like some?"

"I'm fine," Jake said, turning to Birdie. She waved off the invitation as well.

"Come on," Loretta said. "Let's go talk in the other room. The furniture's not as comfy out here."

They walked through the kitchen to a sunken family room. The furniture there did look more inviting. Big, overstuffed recliners and a long, L-shaped couch in front of a huge television. Dan had a news channel on. He clicked the screen off and turned on an overhead light. Birdie chose a seat at the end of the couch. Jake sat beside her. Dan and Loretta took the chairs.

"I really appreciate you letting us come out," Jake said.

"You promised you'd keep us in the loop on your little project," Loretta said. "Has there been something new?"

Jake had debated what he'd tell the family. He didn't feel comfortable telling them about the untested blood samples. Not yet. No reason to stir that particular pot if it came to nothing.

"I'm still trying to track down the man Wesley Wayne Hall claims he was with the night of your mother's murder. I haven't had much luck. He was another day laborer named Scotty Moore. I don't know if that name rings any bells. I don't believe he ever worked for your mother. I spoke to Garth MacDonald a bit. Moore did some work for him in that era and after. Garth lost track of him."

"These men come and go," Loretta said. "My mother was pretty particular about who she'd let on the farm though. I can tell you that."

"That's what I've been told. And look, it's probably going to be a dead end."

"But you have to be sure," Dan said. He reached over and touched his wife's knee.

"I didn't testify," Loretta said. She had a faraway look on her face. "I intended to go to court every single day. But I didn't make it past the opening statements. But Larry went. After he testified. He was there every day. I wish I could have found a way to stop him."

Jake's heart shredded just hearing about it. "Mrs. Clawson, I'm sorry. I really hate having to put you through any bit of distress."

She locked eyes with him. She wasn't crying. She didn't seem upset. She seemed detached. Jake knew it was her method of self-preservation. Loretta Clawson had just told him her brother had seen every horrible crime scene photograph that had been shown to the jury. He knew she believed it had ultimately killed him. She was right.

"We got a phone call today," Dan said. "Just a coincidence that it came the day you asked to come out and talk to us. It was from the prison. As Ruby's next of kin, Loretta has a choice. They allow a member of the victim's family to witness Wesley Wayne Hall's execution."

"You don't have to do it," Birdie said. "You don't have to put yourself through that."

"I know," Loretta said. "We've talked. I mean, the whole family. It's Sam I worry about most. He's lost more than any of us."

"She was your mother," Jake said. "You've lost plenty."

"I don't know how I feel," she said. "The death penalty, I mean. I don't know if it will make me feel better. Give me closure. I spent so many years hating that man. Fearing the name Wesley Wayne Hall. I'm not afraid of him anymore. I just feel … nothing. Numb. But if there's a chance. If you think there's a sliver of a chance that Hall isn't the one who did this. Well, that would be just awful. I don't know if I could live with myself if I didn't try to help you get to the truth."

Of all the things Loretta Clawson might have said, Jake wasn't expecting that. It humbled him.

"We don't feel hate anymore," Dan said. "None of us. Hatred is such a dark emotion. It eats at you."

"Yes," Birdie said. "It does." She, as much as anyone, understood what it was the Ingall family had to endure. She wouldn't even be sitting here had it not been for her own brother's murder. It was the catalyst that led to her moving back to Blackhand Hills to raise her nephew, Travis.

"What can we do?" Loretta said.

Jake let a beat pass. "Well, I'm just trying to get a fuller picture of what Ruby's life was like in those last weeks. Her routine. The people she saw."

"There wasn't much," Dan said. "Ruby had pretty bad neuropathy in her feet. She was having mobility issues in those last few months. Loretta and I would take her to her doctor's appointments. That's honestly the main thing she was leaving the house for in those days. We were trying to arrange for her to have more help in the house. A nurse's aide or something."

"Mom wouldn't hear of it," Loretta said, a sad smile on her face. "I would have preferred she sold that farm years before she died. It wore her down. Caused her stress she didn't need. Larry and I got into some arguments about that."

"Larry wanted her to keep the farm?" Birdie asked.

"Larry wanted whatever my mother wanted," Loretta said. "My brother wasn't interested in being a farmer himself. But he didn't stand up to her. Not ever. My brother was the original mama's boy. And I don't say that as a criticism. The two of them were just closer than my mother and I were. I was more feisty. I was more like my mother in personality and that made it harder for us to get along."

"Loretta's a Campbell, through and through," Dan said, his face filled with affection for his wife. "That was Ruby's maiden name. Pure Scot and the temper to go with it. Old Sam was much more even keeled. Larry favored him. Young Sam's like them too."

"Did she have any friends that called on her? Anyone else who might have come to the house that you didn't know about?"

"Dan," Loretta said. She reached back and touched her husband's cheek. "Do you think anything in those boxes would help?"

Dan's eyebrows went up. "Up in the garage?"

"Boxes?" Jake asked.

"Ruby's papers," Dan explained. "It's mostly junk. Well, to anyone else. Old farm ledgers. I think some of them were started by Old Sam's father. They did everything by pen and paper and Ruby was too stubborn to change."

"I just couldn't part with it," Loretta said. "It's strange the things you hang on to. My nephew wanted the farm. My father and grandfather's blood, sweat, and tears went into it. For me, the things I treasure most are smaller. Simpler. Her handwriting. My most prized possession is this little recipe box she kept. Most of it's just stuff she clipped out of magazines. But she'd add things. Notes. Annotations. Some of her personality, her thought process. You can see it. So I kept those. And the ledgers. Her checkbook and some old registers. They're in a couple of boxes."

"You're welcome to them," Dan said, rising. "If you don't mind helping me pull them down. They're on a shelf in the garage."

"That would be great," Jake said.

Dan gestured to him. Jake followed him down the hallway to the garage door off the kitchen. Dan had metal shelving along one wall in the garage. He took a folding step stool off a hook and pointed to the third shelf in front of them.

"Those two brown boxes," Dan said, pointing. Jake spotted two bankers boxes. They weren't labeled, but they were the only boxes on the shelf. Everything else was in plastic bins.

"Let me," Jake said. He took the step stool from Dan. He climbed up and pulled down the first box. It wasn't heavy. Dan took it from him. Jake pulled the second one. Some dust flew out, but again, it wasn't heavy.

"I really appreciate this," Jake said, climbing down.

"She's tough," Dan said. "But Loretta's hurting."

"I'm sorry," Jake said, holding the second box.

"It's not your fault. She meant what she said. If there's a ghost of a chance they convicted the wrong guy ... I don't think Loretta could live with herself if she didn't try to help you. Between you and me, I never liked Ed Zender anyway. Found him arrogant. Rude sometimes."

"He does seem to have that reputation."

"Doesn't mean he screwed up, though."

"No. No, it doesn't."

Jake set the box down. He popped the lid off of it. Just as Loretta described, it was full of ledgers. Jake took one out. In a meticulous hand, someone had written dates, times, and amounts.

"Feed," Jake said. "She's buying feed for the animals."

Dan looked over his shoulder. "Looks like."

Jake thumbed through a few more pages. It would take some going through, but these ledgers could help him build a chronology of Ruby Ingall's activities her last weeks on earth.

"No one ever asked for these?" Jake asked. He tried to keep his tone neutral. But inside, he felt his blood bubble, waiting for Dan's answer.

"No," Dan said. "Do you think they're worth anything?"

"Probably not. But I'd like to have a look just the same. You sure you don't mind me taking them?"

"Not if Loretta doesn't. You'll make sure you get them back to her?"

"Of course," Jake said. Dan hit the remote on his garage door. He picked up the second box and walked with Jake to his car.

"I'm glad you came out here," Dan said. "Between you and me, I'm not worried about Loretta so much. It's Sam we worry about. Always."

"I understand."

"He's like a son to us in a way. Those babies of his are more our grandkids than they are Julie's. I mean ... well, I don't mean it as anything against Julie, Sam's mom. It's just she only gets to see them a few times a year. Loretta and I are the ones doing the day-to-day grandparenting stuff. And we feel so blessed to be able to."

"Garth MacDonald said Sam's mom just couldn't stay in Blackhand Hills after Larry died."

"She felt like this place was cursed," Dan said. "I can't really blame her. Julie's a good egg. Sam thinks the world of her. We do too."

"Sam and Brittany are lucky to have you and your wife. You've been a stabilizing force."

Dan smiled. "That's family. You go where you're needed. It wasn't in the cards for Loretta and me to have babies of our own. We tried. Loretta had a few miscarriages. It was hard for her. But now, well, she'd do anything for Sam and Brittany's kiddos. So would I. In a lot of ways, this is the happiest time of our lives watching them grow up. Sam's amazing. That place? The farm? It *did* feel like it was cursed for a long time. But Sam just refused to let it be. He made it his. He turned it all around and made it into a place where we're happy again. That's a hell of a thing."

"It truly is," Jake said.

"If you need anything. Anything at all. Please keep doing what you're doing, Jake. Call me. I loved Ruby too. And Larry. But it's not as hard for me as it is for Sam and Loretta. Do you know what I mean?"

"I think so. She wasn't your mother. You didn't find her."

"Exactly."

"I really do appreciate this, Mr. Clawson."

"It's Dan. It's always Dan."

Jake put one box in his trunk. Dan put the other one in. He turned then and extended a hand to shake Jake's.

"I don't want her to go," Dan said. Jake cocked his head to the side, questioning.

"The execution," Dan said. "It would be a mistake. If someone has to go, it should be me. I'm trying to tell her that. There might come a time when I'll ask you to help me convince her."

"If I can, I will," Jake said.

"And I'm not sure I can do it either," Dan said. "So maybe, if it comes to it. If after you look through this stuff. Talk to who you need to talk to. If you believe Wesley Wayne Hall is the one who deserves that needle. I think maybe I could get the family to agree to let you go for us. To be a witness. Do you think you could do that?"

The question took him aback. At the same time, Jake realized why Dan was asking. It almost felt like a "you broke it, you bought it" proposition. If he was going to put the family through a possible reopening of this case ... if it ended up in the same place as Ed Zender left it ... let Jake be the one to bear witness.

"Yes," Jake found himself saying. "I think I could do that."

By the time he came around to the driver's side, Birdie had come out the front door. Loretta waved from the porch. Jake said goodbye to Dan and thanked him for the boxes again. He slipped behind the wheel. Before pulling out, he stared at the road.

"You okay?" Birdie asked.

"I don't know. I think I just agreed to be their witness to Hall's execution."

"Hooo, boy," she said.

Jake put the car in gear. As he drove back out to the dirt road, his text alert went off. He clicked the hands-free button.

It was Mark Ramirez. "Hey, Jake. I've got something for you. I'm heading down your way first thing in the morning. We can meet in your office if that works."

Jake felt a flood of apprehension go through him. Mark would have results on the samples Jake sent. As Jake made the turn back toward town, he wasn't sure what he hoped they would reveal.

Fifteen

Something was wrong.

Jake had known and worked with Agent Mark Ramirez on several cases over the past few years. He was a straightforward, unflappable guy. This morning, the man practically sprinted into Jake's office and bounced on his heels as Jake turned to shut the door.

Majewski was out investigating a theft at the Dollar Kart in Arch Hill. Birdie sat at his desk. She'd gotten here even before Jake did this morning. He wanted her to start going through Ruby Ingall's papers just as soon as possible.

Ramirez didn't wait for Jake to set him up. Mark grabbed a stack of papers on the table in the center of the room and pushed them aside. He pulled up a chair, took his laptop out of his bag, and gestured for Jake to get close to him.

"Whatcha got, Mark?"

Ramirez tapped his fingers on the table, waiting for his laptop to boot. He pulled a thumb drive out of his pocket and jammed it into the slot.

"This one's your copy," Mark said. He stood and pulled a file folder out of his bag. He spread out copies of the crime scene photographs Jake had sent him from the Ingall file. Every one of them were shots of the bloodstains. Some were from Ruby's kitchen, the others out in the barn near one of the workbenches.

Ramirez stood back. He ran his hand across his mouth.

"Okay," he started. "So I told you. We didn't process this crime scene. I wish to God we had. Part of me wants to throttle Ed Zender with my bare hands. Or break protocol altogether and get myself in front of a news camera. It's like he took a class on how *not* to collect and store blood evidence."

"Mark," Jake said. "What the hell's going on?"

"Okay. Okay. Here." Mark clicked his laptop. He pulled up a lab report. Numbers swam in front of Jake.

"So there was a lot of blood," Mark said. "I mean, a *lot* of blood. Of course there would be. Ruby Ingall was decapitated in that barn. Almost her entire blood volume spilled out on that floor there. Right there. In front of the workbench."

Ramirez jabbed a finger at one of the photos. A large, dark pool of blood made an oval pattern in front of the workbench. The machete used to cut her lay across it.

"Seven samples from the barn were processed. Zender sent them in. They were from the floor. Those were Ruby's. You see those here." He pointed to another crime scene photo. "But there was another sample, a smaller one taken from the workbench itself. That was matched to Hall. Then they tested the machete itself. No prints. But blood on the blade belongs to your victim."

"Okay," Jake said. "But that all came out at trial. It was to be expected."

"Sure, sure," Ramirez said. "Zender's theory ... and I'll be honest, without having this scene run by us ... I was skeptical. I've taken the approach to just remove Zender from the equation. His theory of the case. I wanted to just start from scratch, you know?"

"That's been my approach too," Jake said.

"Coroner said that poor woman was already dead by the time someone chopped off her head."

"Yes," Jake said.

"I don't think she was killed in the barn. She was taken to the barn."

"Right," Jake said. "And that was the crux of the testimony at trial."

"Right!" Mark shouted, raising a finger. "Blind squirrels find nuts."

Jake smiled. It was the exact analogy the Wise Men told him Frank Borowski had used about Zender when they worked together.

"I agree," Ramirez continued. "There was a struggle inside the house. In the kitchen. You've got broken dishes. Disarray." Ramirez brought the photos from the kitchen forward. He rooted through them for a moment until he found the one he had in mind. He slapped it in front of Jake. Birdie got closer, peering around Jake's arm.

"Here," Ramirez said. "Blood samples were taken from the kitchen floor. But Jake ... Zender never sent those in. You said it. I didn't believe it. I mean, Zender is Zender. I told you for years I didn't like how he ran his cases. But this? This isn't just sloppiness. This is blatant incompetence. Jake, these samples from the kitchen, from inside the house. They were never sent in."

"Okay," Jake said. "Tell me what you found, Mark."

"Here," Mark said, pointing to his screen with all the numbers. "I told you. Samples in the barn are a match for both the victim and your bad guy. Er ... your suspect, Hall. Hall's blood is on the workbench in the barn. Right next to the machete."

"I get that," Jake said. "What about the house though, Mark?"

"Here." Mark pointed to a photo of the kitchen floor. There was a large smear of blood leading to the back door. "The samples on the floor from this area, they're Ruby Ingall's."

"She was dragged," Birdie said. "She and the killer struggled in the kitchen. He hits her. Her nose was broken. She bled."

"She bled a lot," Mark said. "It's all down the front of her dress when they found the rest of her. My guess, she got dragged out of that kitchen face down by her ankles."

"Bleeding all the way," Jake said, his anger rising.

"But here," Ramirez said. He picked up another photo. This was blown up, showing a larger image of the kitchen tile. Jake squinted. He could see droplets of blood.

"These," Ramirez said. "These came from an elevated position. By a bleeder who was walking upright. They don't come from Ruby Ingall."

"Hall," Birdie said.

Ramirez shook his head. "I've got good news and bad news. The bad news is I can't tell you who this blood belongs to. The lab tried everything but blood collected and stored improperly in a dank, humid basement for fifteen years didn't help. No DNA. The good news, the lab was at least able to type the blood. So I can tell you who it *didn't* belong to."

"Not Ruby's," Birdie said.

"Not Ruby's," Ramirez agreed. "But not Hall's either."

Jake felt like his heart had turned to powder. It got hard to breathe.

"I can't pull DNA. But the samples in the barn. On the workbench. That hit positive for Hall. His blood type is AB+. That's pretty rare. Ruby Ingall, on the other hand is O+. That's pretty common. But this sample here in the kitchen, the droplets, it's from a subject with A- blood type. It's not Ruby. It's not Hall. I just don't know who it is."

Jake sat down hard in the chair behind him. "It never came out. Why the hell didn't Hall's lawyer make hay out of this?"

"Because he maybe didn't know. Jake, you're not getting me. It's bad enough we've got a third bleeder here in the house. What I'm telling you, this sample, this A- sample? It was never sent in fifteen years ago. It wasn't part of the evidence that was introduced at trial."

Jake's head spun. Beside him, Birdie went white. "Did Zender hide it? Fail to disclose it? Jake, if ..."

Jake put a hand up. "We don't know that."

"We know enough," Mark said. "Jake ... you understand I have my own duty to disclose this."

Jake nodded.

"This is appealable error for Wesley Wayne Hall," Birdie said.

"It's more than that," Jake said. "This is exculpatory evidence. Never mind the fact Zender had a duty to turn it over to the prosecutor, who had a duty to turn it over to the defense. This damn well could have exonerated Hall completely. At least in the hands of a half-decent defense lawyer."

"Jake," Birdie said. "If this was your case, you wouldn't have even made the arrest. Not at this point. Not until you had more."

He couldn't think that far. He could barely think at all.

"You have to take this to the prosecutor," Ramirez said. "Immediately."

"I know," Jake said. Now he was the one sweating. "Mark, thank you. You stuck your neck out for me on this one."

"You want me to go with you when you talk to your people?"

"No," Jake said. "I have to take this to the sheriff."

"She's running against Zender."

"She's still the sheriff. It's still her call. She told me to let her know if I found something."

"This isn't just something," Birdie said. "Jake, this is everything."

He squeezed his eyes shut. Since the moment he got involved in this case, he'd only wanted to make sure Ed Zender got it right. He never in a million years thought Zender could have done something almost criminal himself. Now, it was staring him in the face. In blood photographs and scientific reports and Allison Sobecki's account of her dealings with Zender.

But Wesley Wayne Hall might still be guilty. His blood was in the barn that day. He was either telling the truth. He wasn't there that day and it was old blood from a previous cut. Or he had told Jake an even bigger lie. He was there, and he'd had help.

Sixteen

"Maybe you should sit this one out," Jake said. He and Birdie stood outside Meg Landry's door.

"I'm just as involved as you are," she said.

"I know. But that could be a problem for you. Let me take the heat on this one. And if it ends up being ... credit ... I'll make sure you get that."

"Jake. When are you gonna get it through your granite skull that it's not your job to protect me?"

"If Landry loses ... if this blows up in my face, then Ed Zender's gonna be behind that door. You don't think the first thing he's gonna wanna do is get rid of anyone he thinks is an enemy? I'm sorry. But you'll be an easy target. You're one of the newest hires. You don't have the seniority, even with your military police and intelligence background."

Jake knew Birdie well enough to see her temper rising. The tips of her ears got red. At the same time, she knew he made a good argument.

"Zender's gonna try to fire or demote me anyway," he said. "No matter what happens with the Ingall case. Even if I'd never turned over this particular rock. He's gonna have it out for me. Tim Brouchard's gonna help him."

"You're right," she said. "I hate that you're right. But I know you're right."

"If this goes how I think it's gonna go, there will be plenty of stuff for you to do. For now … just trust me. Let me handle this. Let Meg be mad at me."

"The only person anybody should be mad at is Ed Zender."

"You two look terrible." Meg Landry walked up behind them. Jake and Birdie looked at her closed door, then back at her.

"Waiting for me?" She pulled her key out of her pocket and moved past Jake to open the door.

"I'll catch up with you after lunch," Birdie said. Jake gave her a grim smile and mouthed a quick thank you. Then he took a breath for courage and followed the sheriff into her office.

"I need you to make this one quick," she said. "I've got a meeting with the command officers in about ten minutes."

Jake shut the door behind him. "Yeah. You're gonna wanna cancel that."

Meg had a stack of mail in her hand that she'd picked up from the desk. Her shoulders dropped.

"Jake …"

"BCI got back to me on some evidence I asked to be reanalyzed in the Ruby Ingall case. It's a bit of a bombshell, I'm afraid."

Meg frowned. She picked up her desk phone. "Darcy," she said. "Is Boyd Ansel still in the building?"

She waited as Darcy answered. Meg nodded. "Can you have the desk sergeant grab him and tell him to come back up to my office?"

She gestured to Jake to have a seat in one of her office chairs. He really preferred standing, but Meg's expression was grave. He knew his matched hers and she knew how to read him.

"There was ..." Jake started. Meg put a hand up.

"Not another word. Not until Boyd gets here."

Two minutes later, Boyd Ansel, the Worthington County Prosecutor, walked into Meg's office. He was young, energetic, and so far had proven himself to be level-headed and confident. But he was also vulnerable in his own election next year.

Boyd saw Jake and immediately frowned. He had to intuit what this was about. The incident at Meg's town hall had started to grow legs with the local news.

"Sheriff?" Boyd said.

"Sit down," she said. "Jake has some information I think you're gonna need to hear as much as I will."

She gave him a look that said, "You're on."

"It's the Ruby Ingall case," Jake said. "It's about to get away from me a bit."

Meg buried her face in her hands. Boyd's frown deepened.

"I had some concerns," Jake said. "Particularly about how some of the evidence was handled. There were blood samples that weren't properly cataloged. Weren't sent for analysis in the package that got processed by BCI. So I asked Mark Ramirez to rerun them."

"On whose authority?" Boyd asked. "Meg, did you know about this?"

"I didn't. I wasn't ... not officially, no. But ... yes."

"There were droplets of blood in Ruby Ingall's kitchen that don't belong to Wesley Wayne Hall. As far as I can tell, Hall's defense team never knew that. It was never disclosed."

"Whose blood is it?" Meg asked.

"We don't know. It was too degraded for DNA. But BCI was able to type it. It doesn't match either Ruby Ingall or Wesley Wayne Hall. And it was mixed with Ruby's blood."

"Christ," Boyd said. He rose from his chair.

"Zender," Meg said.

"Stop!" Boyd shouted. "Not another word. I can't believe this. You understand what this looks like. It looks exactly like your detractors have been saying. If you've been using this office to ruin Ed Zender ..."

"She hasn't," Jake shouted back. "This has nothing to do with Landry. This has to do with me getting a letter from Wesley Wayne Hall. One that raised enough questions to get me to look at the damn file. It's a mess, Boyd. You need to review it. Zender cut corners. He didn't run down witnesses. He ..."

"I mean it, Jake," Boyd said. "Not another word. Not in front of her."

Meg still hadn't pulled her face out of her hands.

"She's the sheriff," Jake said.

"She's a political candidate," Boyd argued. "I'm sorry, Meg, but you can't be anywhere near this. You never should have been in the first place. Jake, you should have come to me. Only me."

"He's coming to you now," Meg said, looking up.

"Did you at any time authorize ..." Boyd stopped himself. "No. You know what? No. This conversation needs to end. Immediately. Jake, we need to talk somewhere else. Meg, you understand. You can't be involved in this. Not in any way. You have to be completely walled off. This isn't just about you or an election."

"Of course it isn't!" She leaned back in her chair. "My God. Boyd, I don't care about the election. I mean, I want to win. Yes. But not like this. And no, I have not used my office to make trouble for Ed Zender."

"I can't even be here," Boyd said. "You both understand that there will probably be an external investigation. The attorney general's office will end up demanding it. I don't want to sit in a damn deposition talking about what was said in this room today."

He got up and went to the door. He stopped, gripping the doorknob. "For your sake. For both your sakes, do not say another word to each other about this case. Jake, come with me."

"I mean what I said," Meg said. "Before you leave this room, you both need to hear it. If Wesley Wayne Hall is in prison for a crime he didn't commit, I don't care about my political future."

Boyd shook his head. "That's noble of you. I mean that sincerely, but this is now a giant stinking turd. You understand that."

Jake got up. He had more he wanted to say to Meg, but knew Boyd had a point. The last thing he wanted to do was make trouble for Meg. As much as Ed Zender was looking like the bad guy here, Meg's political future was also in jeopardy.

He followed Boyd out and led him down the stairs to the tucked-away storage unit he and Birdie had turned into their war room. Birdie was gone and Jake was glad of it. He knew his instincts were right. For now, Birdie's involvement needed to stay on the down-low.

Jake turned the light on and brought Ansel over to the table. He briefly outlined how far he'd gotten in his reinvestigation. With each new fact, each revelation of how Ed Zender had bungled this case, Boyd Ansel's color drained. By the time Jake was done, Ansel was sweating. He sank into a chair and squeezed his eyes shut.

"That son of a bitch."

"Pretty much," Jake said.

"Ramirez is going to have to report this too," Boyd said.

"He knows that. He's just as keyed up as you are. He's never been a huge fan of Ed's and it's because of stuff like this."

"I'm going to have to get a hold of the governor's office," Boyd said. "Hall's execution is set to take place in what, two weeks?"

"Yes."

"This is going to blow up in Landry's face."

"Why?" Jake said. "Zender's the one who screwed this up. Boyd, I can't prove it yet. But some of what happened ... I'm not sure it wasn't criminal."

Boyd put a hand up, as if shielding himself from any more bad news. "You can't prove it. Yet."

"That's right. So I'm not going to tell you everything I suspect might have happened."

"It's bad enough he didn't send these damn blood samples in. My God. Hall's been on death row for fifteen years!"

Jake sat down. "I need to get into this, Boyd. All the way. From top to bottom."

"Do you have any other leads? Be serious with me, Jake. What's your gut telling you? Never mind Zender's screw-up. Do you think Hall killed that woman?"

Jake picked up one of the crime scene photos from the kitchen. The bloody drag marks stretched across the black-and-white kitchen tiles.

"He still very likely could have," Jake said. "I still don't have a solid alibi for him. He is still the one on record making threats to Ruby Ingall."

"But none of that will matter," Boyd said. "Jesus, Jake. He needs his own lawyer. Did you tell him that?"

"He doesn't want one. Doesn't trust them. He had Barry Wymer. By all accounts, the guy was a train wreck. A hopeless drunk even back then. He screwed Hall over just as much as Zender did."

"This is different," Boyd said. "Because now I've gotta recommend to the governor that he stays Hall's execution while we figure out what the hell to do. If I were Hall's defense lawyer, I'd be filing charges. I'd demand an investigation into the sheriff's office."

"I know."

"All right," Boyd said. "What do you need, Jake?"

"Need? Time. And I need to be allowed to run this thing how I see fit. No interference from you. Certainly none from the county commissioners."

"They won't go for it."

"What's bad for the sheriff's office is bad for the county. They're not gonna want the attorney general's office involved any more than we do."

"All right. All right. I gotta figure out what in the actual hell I can tell the press. If there's some way to get ahead of this before it leaks. God. It's gonna leak. You know that, right?"

Jake wanted to reassure Boyd that he could keep a handle on all of it. But in his heart, he knew Boyd was right. For all they knew, somebody had already figured out why Agent Ramirez came to see him this morning.

"Yeah," Jake said. "We're out of time."

"Okay. Okay. I need you to be perfect, Jake. You understand? By the book. Everything. No surprises. No cowboy shit."

"I understand."

"Right. All right. God. The Ingall family. They have to be informed. They need to know that Wesley Wayne Hall is about to have a very good day. Dammit. If I were his lawyer, I'd demand he be released pending a new trial."

"I'm going to find out who did this," Jake said. "It very well may still be Hall."

"Fifteen years," Boyd said. "This case is beyond cold, Jake. Some of the witnesses are dead now. The rest? Good luck even finding them."

"You're gonna have to trust me a little, Boyd."

"What about the family? I need to head out there. Dammit. I should do that right now."

"Let me," Jake said. "Boyd, I've got a relationship with them."

"They don't hate you? They know you're the one trying to help Hall."

"No. I'm not helping Hall. To me this isn't even about Hall. It isn't even completely about Ed. It's about making sure Ruby Ingall gets real justice. The Ingall family knows that. I think. Please. I need you to let me talk to them."

Boyd nodded, though he still looked at Jake with doubt in his eyes. "Okay," he said. "But go now. Jake, you and I both know how this goes. By the time I walk out of this building, people are going to be asking questions. The media is gonna get a hold of this. On top of every other mess we've got on our hands, I won't be able to live with myself if Ruby Ingall's family finds out about this on the internet."

"I know," Jake said. "I feel the same way. I'll head out to the farm right now."

"And say what?" Boyd asked. He looked like he was about to be sick.

Jake paused. "I don't know. I guess the truth."

Boyd Ansel looked like he still needed a moment to collect himself. Jake left him staring at the wall as he headed back upstairs. Birdie was waiting near his office door. She held his jacket in her hand.

"Are we going to the farm?" she asked.

He was about to protest. Try to keep her out of it. Protect her. But the determined look on her face told him he'd be wasting his breath. So they walked out of the building together. And Jake was glad to have her by his side.

SEVENTEEN

S am Ingall took the news better than Jake expected. He sat at his grandmother's kitchen table, hands folded on top of it, and kept his eyes locked with Jake's. His wife, Brittany, had excused herself from the room, giving Jake and Sam a few moments of privacy. But Brittany's protective presence over her husband loomed. Jake could hear her in the other room, speaking gently to their children, tidying up after their morning playtime.

"He's getting out?" Sam finally asked after a moment of quiet contemplation, letting his brain absorb what Jake had just said.

"Not immediately," Jake said. "And maybe not for a while. But I believe the new evidence we've uncovered could be enough for Hall to get a new trial."

"His first trial killed my father."

"I know."

"And you won't tell me what new evidence?"

It was an odd thing. Jake sat just a few feet from where that blood evidence had been collected fifteen years ago. Sam and Brittany had renovated the kitchen, restoring it to what it might have looked like before Sam's grandparents had updated it to mid-century modern. The black-and-white-tile floor was gone. In its place was the original red oak hardwood.

"Right now, I have to treat this case as an active investigation. Because it is. Which means I really can't discuss the particulars. But I want to make sure that you and your family are in the loop every step of the way. As much as I can."

"I appreciate that," Sam said. "I'm just ... I'm trying to wrap my head around it all. It's not just that Wesley Wayne Hall might get out. But I think you're telling me he might not have been the one to do this? He isn't the one who killed my grandma?"

"I truly don't know, Sam. He very likely might have been. And I'm going to do everything I can to get to the truth once and for all."

"He hated her," Sam said. "He went around telling people he wanted to hurt her. Or that he wanted to make sure she got what he thought she had coming to her."

"Sam, there's a victim's advocacy group I think might be helpful to you and your family. I can put you in touch with one of their social workers. I know this is a lot to process."

"No. I know. I appreciate that, Detective. I do. It's just, we put this all behind us. We've moved on. I've moved on. I don't know if I can go through all of this again. My kids? They know about their great-grandmother. But they know the person she was. They know this house, this farm is part of their heritage. They don't know what happened here. It's taken me a decade to reclaim this farm. What you're telling me ... it's all going to be blown to bits again."

Jake's gut twisted. It was everything he never wanted to do to this family. Only there was no help for it. In that moment, his hatred for Ed Zender grew. And he could say nothing about it. Not here.

"Sam, I'm sorry. I truly am. I wish I had better news today."

As Sam sat in silence, Jake felt like an intruder. He understood what Sam said about reclaiming this space, this farm. Painstakingly washing away the crime that had happened here, literally, and spiritually. Now Jake was put in the position of having to reopen every old wound and bring the devil back in.

Jake said an awkward goodbye. Sam remained at the kitchen table, shell-shocked in his own way. Brittany stood at the front door. Jake barely wanted to meet her eyes. He knew she blamed him for some of this. Jake knew the blame lay at Ed Zender's feet. But telling her that would serve nothing. Not now.

"Keep in touch," Brittany said and that surprised him.

"Of course. I'm glad Sam has you."

Brittany gave Jake an unexpected smile. "So am I."

He left it at that. There was nothing he could say to her or to any of the Ingalls that could make this better. Not until he could give them the answers they needed.

As Jake walked out to his car, he felt the ghost of Ruby Ingall following him that day. Her family believed they had laid her to rest fifteen years ago. Now everything was a mess.

E ighteen hours. It was two o'clock on Thursday afternoon. At ten a.m. the next morning, Boyd Ansel would hold a press conference and let the media know he'd spoken to the governor's office. He would seek a stay of execution for Wesley Wayne Hall. Hall himself didn't know yet. Boyd didn't want to tell him anything until he had an answer from the governor. The cruelest thing would be to get his hopes up only to dash them.

Only Jake knew there was no way they were putting a needle in Hall's arm next month.

He stood at the end of a new, empty table Birdie had brought down to their war room. Jake picked up the two boxes he'd taken from Loretta Clawson's garage.

Birdie came in with a giant mug of coffee. Jake had already drank enough to keep him awake for two days if he needed to be. He was wired, and he knew it had nothing to do with the caffeine.

Birdie set her mug down. Jake pulled out a plastic zippered bag containing stacks of Ruby Ingall's check registers. She had meticulously dated all of them. They went back five years before her death.

"What do you want me to work on?" Birdie asked.

"Maybe start with those ledgers. Sam's grandfather kept handwritten almanacs on everything he planted. Suppliers he used. Ruby kept it up after he died."

"How far back do you want to go?"

Jake shrugged. "Maybe let's start with the last year before she died. I wanna build a list of the people she routinely had out at the farm."

"You think some supplier would have had a motive to kill her?"

"No. I don't know. I just know Ed Zender didn't do any of this. He zeroed in on Wesley Wayne Hall right away and never looked back. If nothing else, I want to try to build a list of new witnesses. See if there's consistency about what people remember."

Birdie looked skeptical, but she found the most recent ledgers quickly enough.

"Scotty Moore," Jake said. "If we can find him. If he'll say what Hall thinks he'll say, it could exonerate him once and for all."

"If he's credible," Birdie said.

"And to be honest, I'm not looking to exonerate Hall. I'm not his defense lawyer. I'm just trying to do what Ed should have done from square one."

"It's not going to be easy. In fact, it might be damn near impossible, Jake. Fifteen years is a long time. How well do you remember your daily routine and who you talked to on a regular basis fifteen years ago?"

"Fair point. But we have to start somewhere."

Birdie quietly began combing through the ledgers. She had a notepad beside her. From time to time, she'd write down a name or a date.

As Jake looked through Ruby's check registers, a picture began to emerge. Ruby Ingall lived an ordered life. She paid her bills on time. She preferred local small businesses to big box stores. She was generous with her children and grandson, never missing a birthday. And she was charitable to her church and St. Jude's, the Red Cross, and the Ohio Farm Bureau.

"Finding anything?" Birdie asked.

Jake told her his impressions. "Sam told me and his Aunt Loretta confirmed it. Ruby didn't easily accept help. She didn't really accept getting older with much grace."

"I can respect that," Birdie said.

"Me too. It's how my grandpa is."

"This is pretty straightforward." Birdie slid one of the ledgers closer to Jake. "It looks like she's writing every little thing down. Every expenditure. Her accountant must have loved her."

"She didn't use one," Jake said. "Dan told me she did her own taxes. The old-fashioned way. Pen and paper and mailing everything in."

"She had a good head for numbers then," Birdie said.

"I get the impression Ruby was the business woman. Sam, her husband, was the farmer."

"Sam the younger has followed the same pattern, it seems like."

Jake smiled. He hadn't thought of it that way, but Birdie was right. Brittany Ingall might be just like Ruby. For Sam's sake, that made Jake happy.

"I don't see her writing down any individual names in the check register," Jake said. "But what I'm seeing ... all the entries going back about two years before she died, she's taking out cash at regular intervals."

"She's paying her workers under the table," Birdie said.

"Right."

"What dates are you looking at?"

Jake wrote a few notes down. "First of the month," he said. "Like clockwork. She's writing herself checks to cash for a thousand dollars. And it's not for groceries or anything. She wrote checks to the stores for that."

"Here," Birdie said. "She's writing it down here in the ledger. See?"

Jake took the book from Birdie. Sure enough, on the fifth and nineteenth of every month, Ruby Ingall began writing down cash payouts to various individuals. Jake flipped the page to the last few months of Ruby's life.

"Hall said he started working for her about a year before she died," Jake said. He found the first payment in the ledger. Two hundred dollars. She wrote his full name out in her precise cursive. After a few months, she abbreviated it to WWH.

"These are the other names I found on a consistent basis," Birdie said. She slid her notepad over to him. He skimmed it.

"Any of them sound familiar to you? People Hall might have mentioned?"

"No," Jake said. "He mentioned Scotty Moore. But he said Ruby never had him come out here. Hall said Ruby's place was his own honey hole. And that was pretty typical for some of these guys. And that they respected each other's hustle in that regard."

There were other names though. None Jake recognized except for one.

"Jeremy Lynch," Jake said.

"Who's he?"

"Probably nobody." Jake pulled out his own notepad. He flipped to the pages he'd taken after talking to Garth MacDonald. Macdonald had given him four names of the day workers he used in that time frame. One was Scotty Moore. But another was Jeremy Lynch.

Wesley Wayne Hall and Jeremy Lynch had been paid by Ruby Ingall on four different occasions during the same pay period.

"Did Hall ever mention this Lynch guy?" Birdie asked.

"No," Jake said. "But like I said, Garth did. Moore and Lynch worked together sometimes at the MacDonald farm. If I can find Lynch, maybe I can find Moore."

"Zender never interviewed Lynch?"

Jake slammed the ledger shut. "There's no mention of a Jeremy Lynch in Zender's report. No witness statement. He didn't know about him."

"Jake. It's not that he didn't know about him. It's that he never bothered to find out about him. It took us what, twenty minutes between us once you got a hold of Ruby's papers? It is mind-boggling to me that Ed never asked to see these records. It should have been one of his first questions to Larry and Loretta Ingall."

Anger roiled through him. He let himself indulge in a single fantasy in his mind. In it, he wrapped his fingers around Ed Zender's neck and squeezed.

Eighteen

In two hours, Jake knew he'd have to stand next to Boyd Ansel in front of a bank of microphones and be ready with answers for the million questions lobbed his way. Answers he couldn't give. Not yet.

Is Wesley Wayne Hall guilty?

How long has the Sheriff's Department sat on exculpatory evidence that could have freed Hall?

Had Sheriff Landry used her office to reopen Zender's crowning achievement for political reasons?

And the most important question of all. Who in the hell killed Ruby Ingall?

Jake stood at his kitchen sink. He had drunk almost an entire pot of coffee already. He wore his best suit and gave himself a close shave this morning. He wanted to be anywhere other than the press room today. This was generally Meg's wheelhouse. For four years, she'd allowed him to do what he did best, mostly without interference. He solved cases. Put bad guys away. He wasn't a political creature. Hated talking to the media. But now, he had no choice.

He poured the dregs of the coffeepot down the drain and washed out his mug. He left his cell phone on the charger in the bedroom. He almost walked out without it, but his text chime went off. He doubled back to grab it.

The text came through from Virgil Adamski. Odd, that. Virgil wasn't one who liked to text.

"Turn on the local news," it read.

"What's going on?" Jake texted back.

"Just turn it on. In about five minutes, your day's gonna get pretty bad. Landry's will get worse."

Shit.

Jake hunted for his remote control out in the living room. He rarely watched television at all. He preferred to unwind in the woods. It was bow season. There was a trophy buck out there he kept picking up on his trail camera. One of these days, he knew luck would be on his side.

He found the remote and clicked on the set. It took a moment for him to find the local news channel. When he did, the cameras were pointed at an empty lectern outside Ed Zender's campaign office.

Jake felt the tension in his shoulders tighten. He stood there, holding the remote in one hand and his phone in the other. Thirty seconds later, Tim Brouchard stepped up to the lectern. Zender was at his side.

"Thank you for coming out here on such short notice," Tim started. "I promised I wouldn't keep you waiting. And I promised it would be worth your while. If you'll let me explain what we've learned this morning. Then I'll take a few questions."

Zender looked like he might be sick. He sported a new haircut. A fresh shave of his own. He wore a navy-blue suit with a red tie, an American flag pinned to his lapel. Brouchard looked slick. He wore his hair long now, greased back into a long ponytail. He towered over Zender.

"As you may recall," Brouchard said. "A question was raised at last week's town hall between Sheriff Landry and Detective Zender. It involved the arrest and conviction of Wesley Wayne Hall for the murder of Ruby Ingall. A case that Detective Zender was intimately involved in. Through his tireless efforts fifteen years ago, Ed Zender found the man who perpetrated that heinous crime and made sure he was brought to justice.

"It has come to my attention that Sheriff Landry is now trying to unravel Detective Zender's hard work and let a murderer go free. All for her own political gain."

"You son of a ..." Jake muttered. How the hell had Brouchard found out? The moment he asked the question of himself, Jake knew the answer. From the very beginning, since before Zender announced his candidacy, Jake and Landry had suspected he had someone working for him from the inside. Some old crony with a beef against Landry. But this? Nobody but Jake, Birdie, and Landry were supposed to know he'd been poking around the Ingall case.

"In about an hour," Brouchard continued, "my successor at the prosecutor's office, Boyd Ansel, a man whose loyalty to Sheriff Landry seems clear at this point, will issue a statement. He is seeking a stay of execution for Wesley Wayne Hall."

There was a murmur among the reporters. Cameras flashed. Questions were already being shouted. Brouchard made a downward gesture with his hands, trying to quell them.

"Make no mistake," Brouchard said. "What's going on is nothing more than political gamesmanship. Wesley Wayne Hall murdered Ruby Ingall. Period. Ed Zender arrested the right man after a thorough investigation. There is no reason for this stunt other than to impact your vote for sheriff. It is a travesty of the highest order. But this is the sheriff you have right now. Meg Landry has proven she will stop at nothing, use any dirty trick to try to keep herself in office. I can assure you, I will be speaking to the attorney general's office today. I am going to demand a full investigation into Meg Landry's conduct. Her blatant abuse of her office. In the event she is reelected, she will have to contend with the findings of that investigation. I sincerely hope it's not too late. She doesn't belong in that office. I believe her conduct might even rise to the level of a crime."

Jake's phone started to ring. He quickly put it on silent.

"Now," Brouchard said. "I know the allegations I've raised are serious. You know me. I'd been a public servant for this county for decades before I got involved in Ed Zender's campaign. I know you're going to say I have a vested interest in Wesley Wayne Hall's guilt. I was the one who got him convicted in court as the prosecutor during that era. So it's not just Ed Zender's integrity that has been called into question. It's mine too. And you better believe I'm going to fight like hell to defend it. I didn't want to stand out here today. I didn't want to have to make these claims. I was hoping that Meg Landry would conduct herself ethically and in keeping with the oath she took when she was sworn in as sheriff. She hasn't. I was also hoping that Detective Jake Cashen would honor his own duties as a law enforcement officer. He hasn't. Instead, he's nothing more than an implement for Meg Landry's political ambitions."

Good, Jake thought. Make it personal, Brouchard. This was a fight that had been spoiling between them for years.

"What the citizens of this town need to know," Brouchard said, "is what might have seemed like a question aimed at a legitimate public interest in that town hall was anything but. It has come to my attention that the reporter who raised that question, Bethany Roman, has had a personal relationship ... a romantic relationship with Detective Cashen for the better part of a year. She became privy to the inner workings of the Sheriff's Department through her sexual liaisons with Jake Cashen. She was fed these disgusting lies about the Ingall investigation through pillow talk and then weaponized them against Ed Zender for the benefit of Meg Landry."

Jake's vision clouded. His heart thumped behind his rib cage. He threw the remote control across the room. It hit a couch cushion. If it had made contact with the wall, the thing would have shattered.

Jake's phone vibrated again. He looked at the screen. Boyd Ansel was calling. Jake walked over to the television and turned the thing off. He wanted to rip it straight off the wall.

"Cashen," Jake said, tight-lipped as he answered the phone.

"You're watching?"

"Yeah."

"I need to know one thing from you right now," Ansel said. "Are you screwing Bethany Roman?"

Jake swallowed hard. Answering this question went against everything in him. His personal life should be nobody's business but his own. But he knew he wouldn't have that luxury now where Bethany was concerned.

"Once," he said. "Almost a year ago. I didn't know she was a reporter at the time. It was a bad decision after a bad night. And before you ask your next question ... I didn't ...."

"No," Ansel cut him off. "I don't have any other questions for you right now, Jake. You might want to talk to your union rep sooner rather than later."

"This is bullshit, Boyd. I know you know it. This is Zender trying to cover his ass. I don't know how Brouchard found out about your plans to call the governor's office. It wasn't from me. It couldn't have been from Bethany Roman. I don't talk to her. I have no relationship with her."

"Jake, you get that none of that is going to matter. This looks bad. Awful. For you. For Landry. Now, for me."

"It's all crap! You'll notice that Brouchard didn't have a single cogent thing to say about what's really going on with the Ingall case. He conveniently failed to say anything about the blood evidence Zender mishandled. I now have a list of witnesses about as long as my arm that Zender never followed up on. This was a ploy. Brouchard's feeble attempt to get out in front of this thing before your presser later this morning. I don't know who tipped him off."

"You and Landry should have come to me the second you had suspicions about the Ingall case! Instead, you interviewed Hall on your own, Jake. It looks bad. It looks exactly like what Tim Brouchard is saying it looks like."

"I don't care what it looks like," Jake shot back. "I care who killed Ruby Ingall. And I'm damned sure going to find out who did."

"You may not get the chance," Ansel said. "This may be taken out of your hands. Rightfully so, maybe."

"No. No way. I've made a promise to Ruby Ingall's family. They trust me. Fifteen years ago, they trusted Zender and he screwed them all over. Larry Ingall died because he breached that trust. Ed's got blood on his hands. I'm going to do my job and I'm not going to let Zender, Brouchard, you, or even Meg Landry stand in my way."

"Jake," Ansel said. "You're too attached. You've let this become personal."

"You're damn straight I have. That woman was butchered on her own farm. If Hall did it, I'll make sure he stays right where he is. But if he didn't, then there's somebody still out there. Somebody who got away with it. I won't let that stand, Boyd."

Boyd let out an audible breath. "Look, I don't want anybody else coming in and taking the case from you. I'm telling you we may not have a choice."

Jake went silent.

"I'm telling you that whatever you have to do, do it quick. The best way to shut Brouchard up and keep control of this is if you come back to me with proof positive of who committed this crime, Jake; the clock's ticking. I can stall. A little. Not much."

"I don't need much time," Jake lied, but adrenaline coursed through him.

"Good," Boyd said. "Because you don't have it. And neither do I."

Jake clicked off. He saw his reflection on the black television screen. His face was cold, hard, determined. And he knew what he had to do.

Nineteen

Boyd Ansel got through his press conference. He managed to make his prepared statements, then all hell broke loose. Jake watched the whole thing unfold from the annex next to the press room. Boyd didn't want Jake on camera. He didn't want his picture on the front page of tomorrow's paper. The story was supposed to be about Ruby Ingall and Wesley Wayne Hall. Only Jake knew it wouldn't be.

By the time Ansel got done, he pulled at his collar and loosened his tie. Jake shut the door to the annex.

"That went well," Jake said.

"Don't start," Boyd said. "I need you to do me a favor. Try not to put your face in front of any cameras for a while."

"That's not a favor," Jake said. "That's a life goal."

"Fine. Just be careful who you talk to. You know what? Don't talk to anybody. Not even Landry. Especially not Landry. I need the two of you to stay as far away from each other as humanly possible."

"That's gonna be a little harder. I work for her, Boyd."

"You work for the county," Boyd snapped. "With any luck, you're going to be able to *keep* working for the county after this whole thing's over. I meant what I said though. Get yourself a lawyer. At least talk to your union rep."

"I haven't done anything wrong."

"Fine. Sure. Like that'll matter."

"We done?" Jake asked.

Boyd's face fell. "Jake, have I given you the impression I'm your enemy?"

Jake felt something loosen in his back. He felt like an ass. "No," he said. "I know you're doing the best you can. I am too."

"Good. Just ... I don't know. Try to lie low for a while. Try not to make any more news."

"How'd it go with the governor's office?"

"Hall's getting his stay. But I imagine by the end of the day, some of these online groups will be calling for his release. What I need from you is a reason I can give the court of appeals to keep him right where he's at."

"I'll do what I can," Jake said. "If he's guilty, I'll prove it. Hall can sit tight for now."

Boyd's cell phone started to ring. Whoever was on the other end, Boyd's color drained. Jake decided to leave him to it rather than get dragged any further into the headache that was Boyd Ansel's life. Jake had plenty of pain of his own.

He kept his head down for most of the rest of the day. Birdie had the day off, which was for the best. The accusations hurled by

Brouchard were only going to piss her off. Birdie tended to shoot from the hip when someone made her angry. Boyd was right about one thing: they couldn't afford any more surprises or drama today.

Meg stayed sequestered in her office. Jake couldn't imagine the kind of calls she was fielding. He felt bad. Like he was abandoning her in her hour of need. But it wouldn't do any of them any good to be joined at the hip today. Jake was getting enough sidelong glances from the other cops in the building.

So, he kept his head down. Worked on a few other cases cluttering his desk. Helped Majewski run down some witnesses on cases he had. Then, when four o'clock rolled around, Jake managed to slip out without being seen. He probably should have gone straight home. But it was Friday. He had the next two days off, thank God. And he'd promised Gemma he'd hang out with Gramps at the bar tonight. Keep him out of trouble.

It was a good enough plan. But when Jake got to the bar, he had people waiting for him. Virgil, Chuck, and Bill had helped themselves to Jake's dimly lit corner booth. They motioned him over and poured him a beer.

"Rough day?" Virgil started.

"How'd you know Brouchard was going to pull that this morning?" Jake asked.

"Ed and I still have a few mutual friends. One of 'em called and gave me a heads-up. I wanted to make sure you didn't miss the show. Though I had no idea the crap Brouchard was going to spew."

"Jake," Chuck said. "We get you can't let us in on an active investigation. But what's your gut telling you? About Hall?"

"I wish people would stop asking me that."

"Fair enough," Chuck said. He poured Jake another beer from the pitcher in the center of the table.

"What's your gut telling you?" Jake asked the three of them. "About Ed?"

Chuck, Virgil, and Bill passed a look. Jake got the impression the trio had already been discussing this very issue at length.

"Frank was worried," Bill said. "I think we told you that. He was starting to see things he didn't like about the way Ed was running his cases. Too aggressive. Too hard ass. Like he had something to prove. Trying to make a name for himself in the wrong ways. I know it came to a head. I don't know what Frank said to him. Or what he did. But Ed finally eased off. Went in the other direction. Got lazy."

"You're sure Frank had nothing to do with the Hall investigation?" Jake said. "Not even off book? Because his name's nowhere in that file."

"He was gone," Chuck said. "Like we told you. Frank used to pool his vacation time in those days. Ed was one hundred percent solo on Hall."

"Which means he didn't have anybody checking his work," Jake muttered.

"Jake," Virgil said. "Ed hasn't won himself any points with that stunt he pulled today. Certainly not with any of us. There are plenty of people who don't like Meg Landry for whatever reason. But anybody with a brain in their head knows you'd never get careless about some girl you were screwing."

"And it's nobody's damn business anyway," Bill barked.

"Thanks," Jake said. But he was starting to feel eyes on him. And he was starting to think coming to Gemma's bar was a mistake.

Friday night at the end of the day shift and it was filling up with other cops. Most gave him looks of support. A thumbs up here, a lift of the chin there. But Jake knew he was the main topic of conversation in hushed whispers around the room. As the drinks started to flow, things would become less hushed.

"Jake," Virgil said. "Look. I have a pretty good idea how you're gonna answer this. But I have to ask. *We* have to ask. Because we all know you well enough to recognize what we see."

"What are you talking about?" Jake asked.

The men were cagey. Looking uncomfortably at each other. Jake got the impression Virgil had drawn some sort of short straw before Jake even sat down.

"Are you too close to this?" Virgil asked. "You've spent a lot of time with the Ingall family. It's easy to get sucked in. We've all been there. We all have those cases where it just leaves a mark more than it should."

"I'm fine." Jake bit out his answer.

"No, no. Yeah. I know," Virgil continued. "But you know, maybe it's not the worst idea to just let BCI run with this one. Take a step back."

"You think I can't be objective?" Jake said. "Because of Ed? Yeah. I'll admit it. Right now, I pretty much hate the guy. That doesn't mean I'd hang him out to dry or purposely try to ruin him because of it. I know what I'm doing."

"It's not your feelings toward Ed we're talking about," Bill chimed in. "It's your feelings about the Ingalls."

"I know how to do my job."

"Not a man here doesn't know that," Chuck said. "We're just ... we don't wanna see you dragged down by their tragedy. That's all. And I know you know what we mean."

"I do," Jake said. "And I hear you. But I'm telling you. I've got a handle on this. And I'm close. I can't say more than that." But even as he said it, Jake knew it was a lie.

"Okay then," Virgil said.

"I appreciate the beer and your ears," Jake said to the men. "But I think if I'm gonna make good on my promise to Boyd Ansel to lie low, I need to get on home."

"We've got your back, Jake," Chuck said. "Don't ever doubt that, okay?"

It was good to hear. He knew it. But it was good to hear, just the same. Jake said his goodbyes. He stopped briefly to say hello to his grandfather and his cronies. He waved to Gemma over the bar. He could tell she wanted to pull away from whatever she was doing. He found himself glad her bar business kept her occupied. He wasn't in the mood for either a lecture or a hug from her. Jake just wanted to be alone.

He slipped out the back. By the time he drove up his long gravel driveway, it had gotten dark. He was tired. Worn out. One last stiff drink and the comfort of his own bed sounded like heaven.

He parked and started up the walk. A flash of movement and a glint of light to his left. His hand went instinctively to his side arm.

"Relax," a female voice said. Bethany Roman rose from one of the rocking chairs Jake kept on the porch.

Jake looked back. He hadn't seen a car in the driveway.

"I took an Uber," she said. "I didn't want to risk anyone seeing my car parked in your driveway."

"So some Uber driver just knows you're here," Jake said. It was then Jake noticed the wine bottle in Bethany's hand. Her gait was a little unsteady.

"Yep," she said, noticing where his gaze fell. "I started without you. It's been that kinda day."

"I'm not in the mood for you right now," Jake said. He walked up to the porch and pulled out his keys.

"Well, that's too damn bad. It seems you and I are stuck with each other no matter what we do."

Jake went very still. Bethany came up to him and put her hand on his arm. "You know what they're saying about me?" she asked.

"The same thing they're saying about me."

"I doubt that very much, Jake. That's never how this works."

He turned to her. "How does it work?"

She smiled. "Aw, come on. You gonna make me say it? Poor Jake. When the dust settles, you're gonna be a hero. Again. The man who saved the day. Or Ruby Ingall. Hell, maybe even Wesley Wayne Hall. But me? I'm just the whore who couldn't get a story unless it was on her back."

"Nobody should say that."

She plopped herself back down in the rocking chair. "They suspended me."

"What?"

"With pay. That's my consolation prize. Pending the outcome of some internal investigation that's just gonna be a sham. My news director just wants to save face. Make it look like he took this all seriously. That he's not in this for the amount of clicks we get on the website."

"I'm sorry," Jake said. "However you got your scoop, I know it wasn't through me. Or any relationship people think we have. I'll be happy to tell anyone who will listen."

"Nobody's going to listen, Jake. And nobody's ever going to believe anything else about me."

"How did you find out?" Jake asked. "About the Hall case. You asked that question at the town hall. Who tipped you off?"

She pointed an index finger at him while she still gripped her bottle of wine. "You're not quite that cute, Jake. You know I can't reveal my sources."

"Never mind," he said. "Birdie pulled the court files. It wasn't exactly a secret."

"Birdie," she spat. "You like her."

Jake grumbled. "You're drunk."

"I'm not nearly drunk enough. And not nearly as drunk as I'm going to get. Relax though. I called myself another Uber. I know how to take care of myself."

Jake went to her. He sat in the rocker beside her. "You know, I'm sorry. Tim Brouchard screwed you over today. You didn't deserve it. He just figured out a way to use you to get back at me. There's been a thing coming between Brouchard and me for a long time. I don't like that you got caught in the middle of it."

Bethany turned sideways and flung her legs over the arm of the chair. Jake couldn't help thinking they were nice legs. Great ones, actually. If he were being honest with himself, it's what first caught his attention when he saw her at a bar what felt like eons ago.

"And that," she said, "is exactly like you. Do me a favor, Detective Cashen. Don't do that."

"Do what?"

"Be nice. Be chivalrous. Be ... decent."

"You'd prefer if I were an asshole?"

"Yes, actually. I would. It would make my damn day. But instead, you have to be a nice guy. Because you *are* a nice guy. Despite all your attempts to make people think otherwise."

"Well ... I'm sorry?"

Bethany took a swig of wine. She then tilted the bottle, offering it to him.

"I'm good," he said. "Something tells me one of us should keep a clear head."

"The thing is," she said. "I like you. I still friggin' like you. I've tried not to. But it's done me no good. I'm still gonna be branded the bad guy. The slut in all of this."

"You're not," he said. "But Bethany, let's not pretend you were the good guy, either. You came here that night under false pretenses. You knew I thought you were somebody else. That you weren't a reporter. You let me think it. You should have told me the truth." The night he and Bethany Roman had their one-night stand, Jake thought she was another cop from a different department. She let him believe it. It was only the next day he found out she was a reporter.

"Maybe I should have. But see, that's the thing. I spotted you a mile away. A nice guy. The rare honorable cop."

"We're not that rare, Bethany."

"Says the guy who's about to expose Ed Zender for what he really is."

"This isn't about Ed. It's about justice for Ruby Ingall."

"Right." Bethany saluted. "We all want that. Only now, who knows if she'll ever get it? Tim Brouchard is good. I gotta hand it to him. Let me give you a piece of advice, Jake. Whatever this thing is between you and Brouchard? He's going to win."

"The election?"

"No. Who knows? Who cares? But you. He'll find a way to destroy you. Because he fights dirty, Jake. And he doesn't seem to care who gets in the way. I'm a shining example of that. Collateral damage. Roadkill. He waited for his chance. Bided his time. I don't know how he found out you and I had our little fling. I didn't tell anybody, Jake. Did you?"

"No," he said. "Nobody that would have used it against me."

"Well, he found out somehow. And he figured out a way to use me to get at you."

Jake knew she was right. It didn't make him feel any better about the whole situation. But it was exactly the kind of thing Tim Brouchard would do.

"He's got powerful friends, Jake. You almost destroyed him. Cost him his job as a prosecutor. His wife, if the rumors I heard are true. To me, this feels like Act I for Tim Brouchard. He still wants higher office. More power. You cut off his immediate path to get it. He's carving another one. Right over my back, this time."

Headlights turned down Jake's driveway.

"I'll say it again. I'm sorry. If there's any way I can help you, I'll try."

Bethany rose. She set her nearly empty bottle of wine on the ground. Coming to Jake, she surprised him by straddling his lap. He had to grab her by the waist to keep them from both toppling off the chair. It was quick, but she leaned in and kissed him. Jake was almost too stunned to react. Almost. In spite of himself, he felt a stirring. She was still sexy. Even though he knew she was trouble, and a road he had no interest in going down again. Too much had happened.

He carefully helped her back to her feet. Her ride rolled up the driveway.

"Good luck, Jake," she said, waving at him over her head as she sauntered down the porch steps.

"Yeah," Jake whispered. "Good luck to you too, Bethany." He meant it. He watched as she climbed into the car. As her driver made the turn, he had to swerve to the right to avoid another car coming up. Jake rose.

It was Birdie's car. She parked, got out, and watched Bethany's ride make its way back down. Birdie frowned as she turned back to Jake, answering his unasked question whether she recognized who she'd passed on the way in.

"It's not what you think," Jake said, realizing how stupid that sounded.

"You know what," Birdie said. "I'm not even sure I care. And it's not why I'm here. I know you're having a bad day. I'm not sure if this is going to make that better or worse."

Jake got a sinking feeling. Birdie walked up to join him on the porch.

"Jeremy Lynch," she said. "I think I found him."

She handed Jake her phone. She'd pulled up a photograph. A mug shot. Jake quickly read the caption beneath it. He caught Birdie's eye.

"Christ," Jake muttered.

Birdie gave Jake a tight-lipped nod. "Exactly."

TWENTY

"It's a common enough name," Birdie said. "There were ten Jeremy Lynches in the state, Jake. Hundreds in the country."

The next morning, he and Birdie came into the office. It was Saturday. Jake didn't even bother asking to have the overtime approved. He no longer cared.

Jake had printed out the mug shot and rap sheet for one Jeremy Lynch, born 12/18/78 in Cuyahoga County. Currently serving for aggravated burglary and attempted murder.

"Garth MacDonald's on his way in," Jake said. "He was having breakfast over at Papa's Diner. He'll be here in ten minutes."

"What are you going to tell him?"

Jake took a breath to answer, then stopped himself. He realized he had no earthly idea.

"You can't show him that mugshot," she said. She went to Jake's computer. A minute later, she'd printed out a copy of Jeremy Lynch's most recent driver's license photo.

"Good," Jake said. Though the photograph was older than the mugshot. Lynch had been arrested in Marvell County six years ago. The mugshot was from last year. The driver's license photo was nine years old. The man had aged considerably, which didn't surprise Jake. He was doing hard time and it showed.

"This will be closer to what Lynch would have looked like when Macdonald knew him. If it's the same guy."

Lynch had thinning brown hair in his driver's license photo. In the mugshot from last year, he'd put on maybe thirty pounds and shaved off what hair he had left. Still, he had cold, gray eyes. There was no mistaking this was the same man.

There was a soft knock on Jake's office door. Marie, one of the part-time weekend clerks, poked her head in. "Hey. Jake, your appointment is here. Do you want him in the conference room?"

"That's perfect, thanks Marie."

Birdie folded the printout of Lynch's driver's license photo, then the two of them crossed the hall where Garth MacDonald was waiting.

He was chatting up Marie. Marie's husband also farmed. They were friends. She asked about Garth's grandkids, Brittany and Sam's brood. Marie touched Garth's arm as Jake and Birdie walked in.

"We'll talk again soon," she said. "We'll have to have you out. Ernie's got a new tractor he wants to show you."

"Looking forward to it," Garth said, beaming. He was casual, easy.

"Sorry to interrupt your breakfast," Jake said.

"Aw, no worries. I told you before, anything you think I can do to help, I'm happy to."

"How are things out at the farm?" Birdie asked. "I know this has to be pretty stressful for your daughter and her family."

Garth's smile faded just a touch. "They're managing. We're all managing. Brittany just handles things. Not much fazes her. And Sam is Sam. He doesn't say too much. He's worried. I know that. The sooner he can put all this behind him again, the better. So that's why I said it. Whatever I can do to help with that process, I'm glad to do it."

Jake stepped forward. Birdie handed him the piece of paper with Lynch's photo. They could have done this over the phone. Jake wanted to. But when he called Garth and found out he was just across the street, Garth wouldn't hear of it. So here he was.

"You gave me some names the last time we spoke. Men you remembered hiring as day laborers around the time Ruby was killed. One of them was a guy named Jeremy Lynch."

"Sure. Quiet guy. Can't remember how I got this name. But you said you were more interested in finding Scotty Moore."

"I still am. But could you take a look at this photo and tell me if you recognize the man in it?"

Jake put the paper down. Birdie had blacked out the name on the photo. Garth picked it up.

"That's Lynch," Garth said without hesitation.

"You're sure?"

"Course I'm sure. Jeremy Lynch. He was a good worker. Kinda rough around the edges. Had to have some words with him about his language. My other grandkids were maybe eight and ten back then. They're grown now. But Lynch liked the F bomb as I recall."

"How many times did you have him out? Do you recall?"

Garth handed the paper back. "Not sure. I wanna say maybe a dozen times. We were rebuilding one of the barns back then. Lynch was a good carpenter, if I recall. That's the main reason I had him out."

"Did you recommend him to Ruby or anybody else?" Jake asked.

"I might have. I don't remember specifically."

"But he stopped coming out," Birdie said. "Or you stopped asking him to. Do you remember why or when?"

Garth shook his head. "Not really. These guys come and go. That's just how it is. I wanna say Lynch was laid off from his factory job. That's a pretty common scenario. He probably got recalled. Like I said, he was a damn good carpenter. They're hard to find anymore."

"So to your recollection, there wasn't any negative reason why he stopped working for you?" Jake asked.

"Nope. We finished the barn rebuild in maybe July of that year. The project ended. So I didn't have a use for his particular skill set. I can check my records, but I don't think I used him on the next building job. But I can't say there was a specific reason other than I probably called him up and he couldn't come out."

"Thanks," Jake said. "That's helpful."

"Did he do something?" Garth asked. "You think he has some involvement with what happened to Ruby?"

Jake couldn't tell him. It surprised him a bit that Garth hadn't heard through the grapevine about Lynch's later crimes. At the same time, his major arrest came years after Garth's dealings with him. Well after Ruby Ingall's killer was presumably convicted.

"I'm not sure," Jake answered as honestly as he could. "But from what you told me before, he was tight with Scotty Moore. I'm just hoping if I can talk to Lynch, he might have more recent info on where to find Moore. I just wanted to make sure I had the right guy."

Garth stood up. "Well, I'm sorry I don't remember more than I do. I'm happy to check my records. I can tell you exactly the last time I had Lynch out at my property."

"Thanks," Jake said. "It's not critical. But you never know where something might lead."

"Happy to do it. You call me if you think of anything else."

Jake thanked him. Garth said his goodbyes. He closed the conference room door after him. Birdie leaned against the wall.

"They're all just so ... helpful," she said. "We're blowing up their lives again and all they want to do is cooperate."

"Yeah," Jake said. "I don't even know what I'm hoping for anymore. That Hall is guilty or he isn't."

Birdie looked at the photo of Lynch. "So what's next, boss man?"

Jake gave her a wry smile. The day he could boss Birdie around, he'd know the end of the world was coming.

"I make a phone call. Lynch was arrested in Marvell County. That's Detective Dave Yun's territory. There's a good chance he was involved in the case. He owes me a favor or two. I'm just hoping he didn't have hard plans today."

Birdie smiled. "Looks like I better cancel mine."

Jake felt bad. He hadn't even considered the disruption in Birdie's life.

"It's fine," she quickly said. "That is, if you're okay with me tagging along."

"I'm more than okay with it." Jake pulled out his phone. He made a quick call to Dave Yun. His Marvell County counterpart answered immediately. As soon as he understood what Jake needed, Yun told him he'd meet him at his office in an hour.

TWENTY-ONE

"Lynch was a bad dude," Dave Yun said. The Marvell County Sheriff's Department was smaller than Worthington County's by a good margin. Yun was a one-man band, much like Jake, but he had far fewer deputies working alongside him.

"So he was your case," Jake said.

"You bet." Yun had brought up a box containing the Lynch case file. He started spreading out crime scene photographs.

"My victim, Gloria Garcia, was a saint. She lived alone in the house her grandfather built. Soybean farmers. Though they sold off the tillable land years before. Gloria still kept some chickens, a couple of goats, and an ancient mule named Guillermo that used to try to bite your face off. Gloria let that old bastard live on her front porch. Then I heard rumors that she even brought him into the house sometimes when it got really cold."

Jake picked up one of the photos. Gloria Garcia sat in one of her kitchen chairs, her face covered in blood, her left eye swollen shut.

"Left her for dead," Yun said. "That's actually what saved her. Lynch stabbed her in the back but managed to miss anything vital. Gloria lay there, still as stone, while Lynch went through her house and cleaned her out. Soon as he left, she managed to crawl to the phone on the wall and call for help. She tried to refuse medical treatment at the scene. I damn near had to knock her out myself to get her into an ambulance. Mild concussion, broken cheekbone, broken arm, eighteen stitches in her back. Thank God Gloria was just as stubborn as that old mule."

"What did she say happened?" Jake asked.

"She hired Lynch to build an addition off the back of her house. They got into a dispute about what she was gonna pay him. Gloria wasn't satisfied with the job he was doing. Started getting suspicious that he was on drugs. Then she realized there was some money missing from a tin she kept on the counter. There was a confrontation and Lynch went ballistic. Attacked her. Went through the house and stole a few stashes of cash she kept inside. Her engagement ring. He took off, thinking she was dead. She, of course, ID'd him right away."

"She was so lucky," Birdie said.

"She was," Yun said. "That old bat was hard to kill, that's for sure. Until breast cancer got her. She passed away two years ago. She didn't have a will. There was some drama there over it that just got resolved in the probate court. Her next of kin was a cousin who lived in Alabama. That house should have been on some historical record. Gloria's grandfather built it himself. Well, the cousin tore it down and parceled off the property. Now there's three or four of those awful black-and-white, cookie-cutter modern farmhouses out there. Gloria'd be spinning in her grave. But I guess you can't blame anybody but her. She could have written out what she wanted done."

"Did Lynch confess?" Jake asked.

Yun shook his head. "Wouldn't talk. Got a lawyer out of the gate. But it wasn't much of a trial. One day. The jury was back within an hour. Gloria took the stand and that was it. Slam dunk. I don't know what his lawyer was even thinking. A PD. Young kid. In over his head."

"Seems like a pattern," Jake said. "Wesley Wayne Hall's lawyer didn't do him any favors either."

"You think Lynch could be connected to what happened to Ruby Ingall?" Yun asked.

"I think I can't rule it out yet. I have a record of Lynch being on Ruby's property a couple of months before her murder. We've got a blood sample that doesn't match Hall's blood type. DNA's a no go. Do you know what Lynch's blood type is?"

Yun thumbed through part of the file. "It wasn't part of the case. Only Gloria's was found at the scene. But Lynch has been in the system for years. Seems like a phone call or two and we should be able to find that out."

Birdie made a note. Jake knew she'd have that information as quickly as humanly possible.

"The MOs are pretty similar," Birdie said, looking over Jake's shoulder at the crime scene photos. "Only, he didn't kill Gloria Garcia. If it's a pattern, you'd expect him to escalate, not deescalate. Ruby Ingall was decapitated. She was murdered in the home, then taken to the barn to be … um … disposed of."

"It's hard to say," Jake said. "Maybe something spooked Lynch, if it was him. I'd like to try to figure out where he was when Ruby was murdered. Garth MacDonald said he hadn't seen the guy for a couple of months prior to Ruby's murder. Ruby herself hadn't had him out to her place since earlier that summer either, if her

records were up to date. It's similar enough to keep pursuing. Only
..."

"Jake, it never occurred to me to reach out to Worthington
County or any other jurisdiction when I was clearing the Garcia
case. Ruby Ingall wasn't really on my radar."

"Why would it be?" Jake asked. "As far as anyone knew, Ruby's
killer was already collared and on death row. Jeremy Lynch wasn't
even connected to Ruby's case until now."

Yun made a noise low in his throat. "How'd you put them
together?"

"Ruby's family had records. Ledgers. Check registers. Lynch's
name popped up. And I talked to her neighbor, another farmer.
He listed Lynch as one of his day workers during that time frame."

"So why the hell didn't Ed Zender do that?"

Jake went quiet. Yun frowned. "You've got a real mess on your
hands, don't you?" Yun asked.

"You could say that."

"Well, if there's anything I can do, you just let me know."

"This was plenty," Jake said.

Yun frowned and chewed his lip. "Jake. I just need to put this out
there. Of course, I'm following the local elections. It doesn't look
good for Sheriff Landry. I know you know that. God forbid if
Zender wins. Are you safe?"

Jake's first instinct was to brush off Yun's question. It was
something he didn't really want to think about. "Probably not,"
Jake finally said.

Yun nodded. "Well, if Zender wins and does something
unbelievably stupid like shit can you? You need to know you've got

a job here in Marvell County. The sheriff mentioned it to me himself."

It unsettled Jake to think about the Marvell County Sheriff's Department talking about his predicament.

"I appreciate that, Dave. Truly."

"I can send copies of whatever I have to you this week."

"I appreciate that too."

"Once we know whether Lynch's blood type is a match, that could change things," Birdie said.

"What's your next step?" Yun asked.

Jake stared at the crime scene photos. Among them, he picked up Lynch's original booking photo. Those cold, dead eyes stared straight through him.

"I want to talk to him," Jake said. "If he didn't do this, he still knows Hall's alibi witness. He and Hall overlapped out at Ruby's farm. He should have been questioned back in the day. I'm not sure what good it'll do now, but I need to sit across from this asshole."

"Let me make a call for you," Dave said. "I'll get you on the list. Whether he likes it or not, Lynch is gonna sit down with you."

Jake tossed Lynch's photo back on the pile. It landed right next to the one of Gloria Garcia, looking fierce, defiant, and bloodied.

TWENTY-TWO

Sunday afternoon, Jake fulfilled another promise he'd made. One of the hardest ones. He went back to Ruby Ingall's farm. As he pulled up, he noticed a new feature out on the road. Someone had staked a "Re-Elect Meg Landry for Sheriff" sign. It was perhaps a simple thing to some. But Jake realized with a hard lump in his throat that this was more about him than Meg, perhaps.

They knew what Ed Zender had done.

Jake brought a small file with him. He'd let Birdie take the day off. He knew the next couple of weeks he'd need her more than ever. She'd canceled more than one date with her new boyfriend. Keith Ingram wasn't someone Jake liked very much. Though he didn't get a vote.

He came at two o'clock, not wanting Sam or Brittany to feel obligated to feed him. Even so, the heavenly scent of fresh cinnamon rolls wafted to his stomach as Loretta opened the front door. He was glad the whole family was here. One less trip to make.

"It's good to see you, Jake," Loretta said.

Jake smiled. "Under the circumstances, I doubt that."

"Nobody blames you," she said, her face registering legitimate concern. "I hope you don't think that."

"I think if it weren't for me, maybe you'd have a little more peace in your life."

Loretta's eyes danced over him. "Oh, Jake. This is hard. I can't lie about that. But we know you want to make sure Mom gets to rest easy. Just as much as we do. Now come on in. Brittany put a fresh pot of coffee on. I was just teaching her how to make one of my secret recipes. Pumpkin spice cinnamon rolls."

Loretta showed Jake to the kitchen. Brittany's youngest, Charlotte, sat at the table coloring a picture of a donkey. Not a mule, but it conjured the memory of Gloria Garcia's infamous Guillermo.

Brittany was at the oven, pulling out a tray of Loretta's rolls. She had a bowl of white frosting on the counter. "These will need to cool a little. But the first batch is good to go."

"They look perfect," Loretta said. She quickly plated four cinnamon rolls as big as Jake's fist and carried them over to the table. She'd already set smaller plates out. Wielding a pair of tongs, Loretta served one roll to Jake and another to Charlotte.

"Honey," Loretta said. "Why don't you take that in the basement? We're gonna have a bunch of boring grown-up talk. I'll call you up later and let you lick the frosting bowl when your mama's not looking."

Loretta gave her niece a quick wink. The child scooted off her bench seat and scampered out of sight.

Deep laughter came in from the side door as Dan and Sam walked in from outside. Each man dutifully removed his boots in the mudroom just beyond the kitchen. Sam walked up to his wife, put his hands on her waist, and kissed her neck. Brittany blushed as she wiped her hands on her apron.

Jake felt like an intruder. No. Worse than that. He felt like a ghoul. A wraith of doom ready to pierce this family's hard-earned happiness. He didn't know Ruby Ingall. But he could feel her in this room. The light. The love. They honored her by living their lives here in her kitchen. Carrying on.

"Hey, Jake," Sam said.

"Sam," Jake said. Dan reached across the table and shook Jake's hand. Then he took a seat opposite him and grabbed a roll for himself.

"I don't wanna keep you long," Jake said. "I just wanted to bring you up to speed on what's happening." Brittany closed the oven door. Sam had taken a seat at the head of the table. She came to stand behind him, resting her hands on his shoulders.

Loretta brought in another plate of rolls and set them on the table. She sat beside her husband.

"Whatcha got, Jake?" Dan asked.

"Questions," Jake answered. He pulled out two pages from the file he'd brought. They were photocopies of Ruby Ingall's ledger. Jake had highlighted the entries for Jeremy Lynch. He'd found six of them from May to August the year Ruby was killed. He slid a third sheet of paper beside the ledger pages. This was the copy of Lynch's driver's license photo.

"Do any of you remember this man? Or remember Ruby talking about him?"

Loretta and Dan took turns viewing the pages. Dan then handed them to Sam.

"I know you were just a kid, Sam," Jake said. "But you did work for your grandma when she had other handymen around, didn't you?"

"Not a lot," Sam said. "I mostly handled stuff around the yard. Weeding. Mowing. Edging. In the winter I'd come out and shovel for her."

"He looks a little familiar, I guess," Loretta said, her brow furrowed. "I just don't know. I never spent a lot of time out in the barn. When I came, I'd visit with Mom in the house."

"She didn't have that much help," Dan said. "Or she didn't like to. We've talked about this. Getting Mom to get people out here was a constant fight."

"I wish Larry were here," Loretta said, the distress in her voice clear. "He's the one who ran interference with Mom on this stuff. He's the only one who could talk her into getting help out here. And that was limited. I didn't know the people she hired. Larry handled all of that."

"Begrudgingly," Sam said. "Dad was worried all the time. I remember that well enough. He was always upset. Grandma would turn people away he sent out to help her. Either she'd say she could do it herself. Or she'd say she could hire her own people."

"If you came at my mother telling her she couldn't do something she used to be able to do, she'd fight you," Loretta said, though the memory made her smile.

"You couldn't tell Ruby anything." Dan laughed softly. "Stubborn old woman."

Just like Gloria Garcia, Jake thought. The similarities only seemed to grow.

"If she wrote it down in the ledger," Sam said, "then Lynch was out here. Though I couldn't tell you what he did."

"I have reason to believe he was a pretty capable carpenter," Jake said. "Brittany, your father told me he helped build one of his barns."

Brittany nodded. "Sounds about right. He had a bunch of workers out there that summer. He fired a bunch of them, too. I was fifteen or so. Just starting to blossom, as they say. I got some catcalls when I'd go out to get Brat, my horse. Dad overheard and he ran a few off. But I don't recognize this guy as one of them. But I couldn't swear to it."

"Do you think he had something to do with what happened to my grandma?" Sam asked.

"I don't know yet," Sam said. "But it's a lead. Possibly."

"Have you talked to Wesley Wayne Hall?" Loretta asked. "Is he … is he trying to get out of jail?"

"I'm not sure if he's hired a lawyer. I'm sure the prosecutor will fight any motion he makes for release. And he hasn't been granted a new trial or anything like that so far. He's just gotten a stay of execution. This will be a long process."

"He came out here," Dan said. "Boyd Ansel. Nice enough guy. Real apologetic about everything."

"I'm glad," Jake said. "He should continue to keep you informed of everything going on with the legal end of things."

"Do we need to get a lawyer of our own?" Brittany asked.

"Brit," Sam said, patting his wife's hand. "Not now."

"Well, we have rights too," she said. "And if Ed Zender messed this case up this badly, shouldn't there be some recourse for us?"

"I can't counsel you about that," Jake said. Though he doubted Brittany Ingall was truly asking his opinion. It felt more like a shot across the bow. Ed Zender's mistakes were the gift that kept on giving.

"We really do appreciate you coming out here," Dan said. "We know you don't have to. It means a lot."

"I won't keep you," Jake said. The specter of Brittany Ingall was strong. She might seem abrasive to some. But she really did remind him a lot of his sister, Gemma. Fiercely protective of those she cared about. To a fault. The withered look on Sam's face reminded Jake of one he sported himself when Gemma got her back up about something.

"Take a cinnamon roll to go," Loretta said. "For your grandpa. Mom always liked Max."

"He liked her too," Jake said. Loretta was up like a shot. She produced a small plastic container and popped two rolls in it.

"Thank you," Jake said. "I'm heading to my grandpa's for Sunday dinner after this. It'll be his dessert."

"Oh, then let me pack you more," Loretta said. She grabbed four more rolls and filled the container. Then she walked him out to his car.

"Don't pay any attention to Brit," she said. "She's just a lioness when it comes to Sam. My mother was too. And about Larry. She and my sister-in-law used to lock horns all the time over it. Nobody was good enough for her son."

Jake smiled. "I've got a sister like that, myself."

"Yes, you do. Say hello to Gemma for me, too. She used to be the only one who could get my color right back when she was doing hair. I haven't found anybody as good."

"I'll tell her."

Loretta touched his cheek. It was an intimate gesture, almost maternal. Loretta's eyes misted. "I remember your mother, too. She was like a princess. Always so put together. Kind. She'd be proud of you, I think."

Jake pulled away faster than he meant to. He hadn't expected to have his mother invoked like that. It stung, somehow. As if Loretta Ingall had pierced the thin membrane of his objectivity. He couldn't afford it. The Wise Men's warning echoed through him. He thanked her again and walked away.

He had one more stop to make on his way to Grandpa's. Gemma had texted him, saying Gramps was out of milk and coffee. Jake pulled into the Dollar Kart parking lot.

Loretta Ingall Clawson was on his mind. She knew his mother. They wouldn't have traveled in the same circles. Loretta was a country girl. Not that Ardenville was some big city, but the Ardens weren't farmers. His mother had lived in a big, fancy house. She would have had the finest clothes growing up. Wanted for nothing.

Most of the members of his mother's family had thumbed their noses at anyone they felt was inferior. Poor. Lower class. But not Sonya Arden, his mother. She fell in love with his father. A Cashen from the wrong side of town. His people had worked out at the clay mill for generations. Laborers. While Sonya's father had gotten a college deferment and had connections to the governor, Grandpa Max had been drafted and sent to Vietnam.

"She was a princess ... so kind ..." Loretta's words blazed within him. He found himself envious of her memories of his mother. He had so little of his own now.

He was thinking of it. Trying to push it out of his mind when a shadow crossed in front of him. He felt a whoosh of air. Instinct kicked in and Jake ducked just before Ed Zender's blow would have made contact with the side of his head.

Jake whirled around, assuming a ready stance. Fists up, legs wide apart.

"Who the hell do you think you are?" Zender spat. His face was purple. His teeth bared.

"You really wanna do this here?" Jake asked.

They were alone in the parking lot, but Jake knew the Dollar Kart had surveillance cameras. Part of him hoped Ed would take another swing.

"She's got you doing her dirty work for her because she knows she has no business in that job. The only reason she got it is because Greg O'Neal had a bad heart and a hard-on for her. Rumor is she knew exactly what to do with that second thing."

"Get in your car, Ed. Go home. Before you do something stupider than usual."

"You proud of yourself?" Ed said. "If Wesley Wayne Hall walks, it'll be on your head, Jake. He killed Ruby. Plain and simple. Now you've got that family thinking he didn't."

"I don't have them thinking anything. But this? This is on your head, Ed. You didn't do your job. You made a snap decision and now I've got no choice but to clean up your mess. Wesley Wayne Hall was an easy target. You put blinders on and never considered looking at anyone else for killing Ruby."

"You better watch your back, Jake. Consider yourself warned."

Jake felt his anger rise like hot lava. He took a step forward and got in Ed's face. "Or what?"

"You don't have as many friends as you think you do. You've coasted by sucking on Meg Landry's teat. Well, that's about to dry up. I know all about you. The FBI kicked your ass out so you had to come crawling back here, tail between your legs. O'Neal didn't want you. He did your family a favor. He knew exactly how worthless you really are. He never would have let you do anything beyond writing traffic tickets. You're a liability. A nut job just like your old man. I'm not the only one who thinks so."

"You're full of crap, Ed. Now get out of my way before you have a stroke."

Jake shoved him. Not hard enough to hurt him, but hard enough to make Ed's eyes widen with fear. Jake turned his back on Ed Zender. Part of him wished ... no ... prayed that Zender would try to take another swing at him. Just one.

He didn't. Jake quaked with fury as he walked into the store. The two cashiers closest to the door stood there, slack-jawed. They'd seen the whole thing. Jake wondered how much they heard.

TWENTY-THREE

"He doesn't get too many visitors anymore," Corrections Officer Mitt Frederick said. "He had a lawyer for a while but that petered out."

Jake sat in the CO's breakroom slugging down piss-poor coffee, before heading down to his meeting with Jeremy Lynch. He needed to find out as much as he could about the guy's personality.

"My understanding is he didn't have much of a defense to the crime he was convicted of. His victim identified him. Had total recall of everything he did to her. How's he managed in here?"

"He's got this crazy vibe. A dead-eyed thing. Early on, he picked a couple fights with people you don't pick fights with. He got lucky in that he didn't get dead over it. It was strategic on his part. After that, I think most of the guys in here decided Lynch just isn't worth bothering. So he keeps to himself. Doesn't cause too much trouble. Every once in a while he's gotta show his muscle. But he's not somebody we worry about too much."

"No family? A wife? Anything?"

"Rumor is he's got a kid. A son. I don't know about the mother. He hasn't had any girlfriends visit him. He gets letters. Keeps a picture of a little boy under his bunk. The kid in the photo is maybe two years old but he's had it since he got here. So maybe the kid is eight or nine by now. Not sure. I asked around. The kid's name is Lennox. Or that's what Lynch calls him," Frederick said. "He's got a sister who lives in Arizona. She visited him once in the five years he's been here. That was in the beginning. His mother was elderly. I think the sister came to appease her. But his mom died a few months after Lynch got here. Your visit will probably be his big excitement for the year."

"Do you have any idea where the kid lives?" Jake asked.

Frederick looked through the file. "No. But Lynch put in for a transfer to Cuyahoga a couple of years ago that got denied. He was extra ornery after that. Assaulted another inmate in the laundry room. Did three months of solitary for it."

"How long's he got left?" Jake asked.

Frederick looked through Lynch's file. "He's not eligible for parole for another six years. He's serving twenty. He'll get out eventually. Unless he screws himself over. Which is entirely possible."

"Well, I appreciate your insight," Jake said. "Is there anything else you can think of that might help me out?"

"Just don't believe anything he says. Lynch is smarter than he lets on. And mean. You're not gonna get any remorse out of him if that's what you're looking for."

"Appreciate the heads-up," Jake said. He and Frederick rose.

"I've got you set up in a private room. Lynch will be shackled, but it's private. No cameras. I can put one of my guys in there with you."

"That won't be necessary," Jake said. "I'll do better one on one with him."

"Suit yourself," Frederick said. He led Jake down the hall and directed him to take the elevator down one floor. One of the guards would show him to the interview room. Jeremy Lynch was already waiting.

Jake thanked Frederick and started down. He carried just a thin file folder with him. He opened it and leafed through the contents, not even sure he'd end up using it today. If Lynch was as cold as Frederick warned him, Jake had very little leverage. But he'd worked with far less and gotten big results. He could wing it if he had to.

The guard opened the door. Lynch sat with his back to the wall, wearing a blue jumpsuit with orange stripes down the side. His wrists were shackled through a loop on the table.

"Sorry," he said, his voice hard. "I can't get up."

Jake said a quick word to the guard and ignored Lynch. He let the man wait for a moment, curious about why Jake was here. Finally, Jake walked to the table and sat down. He pulled out a pen and pad of paper along with his business card. He slid the card across the table so Lynch could read it.

"Jake Cashen," Lynch read. "Worthington County. Well, that's a real shithole." Lynch flipped the card back toward Jake.

"Thanks for talking to me," Jake said.

"It took some doing. Clearing my schedule and all."

"Right. You wanna guess why I'm here?"

Lynch sat back. "I don't have to guess. I know who you are."

"Really? What have you heard? Nothing that could hurt my feelings, I hope."

Lynch smirked. "You made some big moves. Pulled some pretty tight strings. Word is you took a needle out of Wesley Wayne Hall's arm."

"For now. You know Hall." It was a statement, not a question. Lynch didn't take the bait. He just stared at Jake, his face blank.

"You crossed paths with Hall. I already know that. Did some work for some of the same people out in my neck of the woods. That's what I want to talk to you about. Among other things, I'm trying to find somebody. Word is you might be able to help me."

Jake took a page out of his file folder. It was an old driver's license photograph of Scotty Moore. He showed it to Lynch.

"Friend of yours?" Jake asked.

Lynch leaned in, squinting at the photo. "Sorry," he said. "My eyes aren't what they used to be."

"Take your time."

"Maybe," Lynch said. "Though I can't think of a single good reason why I should tell you anything."

"I understand you worked with Scotty Moore," Jake said, tapping the photograph. "I'm interested in finding him. I thought maybe you could tell me the last time you talked to him."

"It's been a while," Lynch said. "I've been kinda busy the last few years."

"Right. But before that. You both did some work for Garth MacDonald. Out at his farm. He said the two of you showed up together quite a bit. Same truck."

"I crashed at his place sometimes," Lynch said. "But that was a million years ago. That guy? Scotty Moore? He had issues. If you told me he's still alive, that'd be a shock. He had some pretty bad habits when I knew him. That's probably why Old MacDonald fired him."

"MacDonald never told me anything about that. He didn't strike me as the kind of guy who would have tolerated that from somebody who worked on his property. Macdonald had young grandchildren around during that time."

Lynch shrugged. "Maybe he was just too stupid to notice. Why the hell are you asking me all this?"

Jake let his face fall. "Look. I could sit here and pretend. Give you some song and dance about how I'm just following up on a few leads. Tying up loose ends. But you already know who I am. Even in here, I know you follow the news. I'm in the middle of a real shitstorm in my county. I work for one sheriff who probably shouldn't be in that job. And there's another one about to get elected in her place who is a real problem for me and a lot of other people. Because of it, I've got a bunch of idiot politicians, including the governor, breathing down my neck to make sure everybody else did their job. So here I am. Asking you ridiculous questions we both know the answers to. But when I'm done, I'll be able to check your name off a very long, very bullshit to-do list. So. If you could do us both a favor and just tell me you haven't seen or heard from Scotty Moore or have any earthly clue where he might be today, I'll leave. You'll never see me again. And I'll go back to the shit-shoveling job I've got to do."

Lynch smiled. "You still haven't answered why I should care about any of your problems."

"No. I suppose you shouldn't. Except you're in here. You're not exactly some model inmate. You have a reputation for shit-stirring from time to time. Now, maybe it's warranted. Maybe you're just defending yourself. But some day in the not-too-distant future, you're gonna sit in front of a parole board. You're gonna try to convince another panel of useless bean counters why you deserve not to be here. They'll look at your file. They'll see you tend to use your fists to solve your problems. They're gonna look at this ... and they're gonna decide you're not fit to see real daylight."

Jake took out a copy of one of the photos of Gloria Garcia, bloodied and bruised. Lynch barely looked at it.

"Or," Jake said, "they might also see a letter from me telling them how you cooperated with me and helped me find a material witness to one of the worst crimes in Worthington County."

"Doesn't interest me," Lynch said.

"You were tight with Scotty Moore," Jake said. "You ran in the same circles for years. Garth MacDonald said you always knew how to get a hold of him when nobody else could. Well, I've got a strong hunch you still can. Or you can put me in touch with somebody who can. That's all I'm asking for. In exchange, I'll make sure the parole board knows you're interested in improving your situation."

Lynch regarded him. Those cold eyes Mitt Frederick talked about stared back at Jake. Were they the last thing Ruby Ingall saw?

"They're not gonna let me out of here," Lynch said, no emotion in his voice.

"Gloria Garcia is dead now," Jake said. "She didn't have any close family. Nobody that'll speak for her at a hearing. You've got nothing to lose by helping me. And you've got something to gain."

"I told you," Lynch said. "Odds are, Scotty Moore is long dead."

"Only you know he's not. And I think you know why I'm asking about him. It was you, Scotty, Lyle Luke. John Macon. Fifteen years ago, you made pretty good money out at MacDonald's place and a few others. I know how it worked. How it still works. You guys all relied on each other to get work. Vouched for each other. Word of mouth. Just tell me who might still know how to find Scotty Moore. I know it's been a minute since you talked to him. If it doesn't pan out, I'm not gonna hold that against you."

"Yeah. I don't care about your problems. You think some dusty old letter in a file somewhere is gonna help me? I'm not a snitch. Word gets out that I am. That does me more harm than anything you think you can help me with."

"What about Lennox?" Jake said. It was there. Just a flicker. But he sensed a reaction.

"He's pretty far away, isn't he?" Jake guessed. "You write to him. Do you think your ex is reading your letters to him?"

"I think we're done."

"You're right," Jake said. "Odds are, you're not gonna get paroled anytime soon. Maybe never. But you could be closer to your son."

Lynch went still as stone.

"Look, you wanna be at Cuyahoga? You help me out, I can maybe facilitate that. This case I'm working on? It's a way bigger deal than Gloria Garcia. A way bigger deal than you. So the way I see it, right here, right now, it's the only time you're ever gonna have any leverage, Lynch. You've been in here a long time. You might as well be nobody. So here it is. You help me find Scotty Moore. You answer my questions about a few things that might have happened down in Worthington County, and I'll work on getting you that transfer. I can't get your ex to bring him here, but at least distance won't be the barrier."

Lynch started to squirm in his seat. Jake knew the look. The temptation. The desperation.

"Scotty has a sister. She and I used to hook up every now and again. That's how I could get a hold of Scotty. He'd always answer his phone for her. But I don't know if that's still true. Scotty burned a lot of bridges back then."

"Her name," Jake said. "Her number if you can remember it."

"I need to see my kid," Lynch said. "If you can get me a transfer to Cuyahoga ..."

"Her name."

Lynch grabbed the pen. Jake shoved the pad of paper in front of him. Lynch wrote down the name Camilla Newbern. An address in Cincinnati.

"Cami is a nurse. She works at Good Samaritan. It's not the kind of job you leave. Plus, she's got a couple of kids of her own. I can't promise she'll talk to you."

"You leave that to me," Jake said.

Lynch slammed the pen down. If he expected Jake to leave, they were far from over.

"Now, tell me about Ruby Ingall."

Lynch made a face. "Never heard of her."

"Nah. No good, Jeremy." He took another sheet out of the file folder. This was a copy of Ruby's ledger with Jeremy's name in it.

"You worked for her. Same summer you worked for Garth MacDonald. But Scotty never did, did he? You remember why?"

"I told you. Scotty was using at the time."

"Did you bring him out there? To Ruby's? Is that what happened?" It was a bluff. Meaningless. Jake meant to throw Lynch off.

"No. That was something to do with Wes and Scotty. They were always at each other's throats, those two. I stayed out of it."

"What do you remember about Ruby Ingall?"

"Why you asking me about that old lady? I told you what I know about how to find Scotty Moore."

"Ruby didn't trust too many people. She trusted Hall though. And you?"

"I never had anything to do with her," Lynch said. "Wes was weird about that."

"What do you mean?"

"He called me up. Told me he was working a job and needed an extra set of hands. Didn't tell me whose place it was but texted me an address and told me when to show. So I did. Shocked the hell outta me that it was the Ingall place. That was Wes's honey hole. He made that real clear. Told me not to expect it to be a regular gig. Made sure I never talked to the old lady one on one. He was a real dick about that. Paranoid. I think he figured I'd try to poach work from him. I didn't need it. I wasn't planning on sticking around in Blackhand Hills for long. Wes was welcome to it."

"You're telling me Wesley Wayne Hall got you the job with Ruby Ingall?" Hall never mentioned it. The multiple times Jake asked him who else worked out there when he did, Hall never brought up Jeremy Lynch.

"Yeah. That's what I'm telling you. And it was two or three days. She paid me in cash. Actually, she didn't pay me. She gave the money to Wes. I didn't even know she knew my name. Wes must have told it to her."

Lynch was out at Ruby's farm. He admitted it. Put himself there. At the crime scene. Along with her ledger, it was proof positive.

"Jeremy, I need you to think real hard for me. Start trying to remember where you were the night Ruby Ingall got her head cut off."

Lynch reared back. All at once, he realized what Jake was truly after. "No. No, man. No. I had nothing to do with that old lady. I wasn't there."

"Fifteen years is a long time. You went out there. You saw the sweet setup Ruby Ingall had. And there was Wes reaping all the benefits of it for himself. Ruby wouldn't even give you the time of day, huh? That's disrespectful."

"You can go to hell. I gave you what you asked me for. Ruby Ingall? That's not me."

"Jeremy, what's your blood type?"

Lynch gave Jake the middle finger. "Get a warrant, man."

"I plan to."

"We're done in here!" Lynch shouted at the top of his lungs.

A moment later, the door opened and two guards came in to take Jeremy back to his cell. Jake rose. He watched Lynch as he left. Gloria Garcia's battered face swam in front of him. Ruby Ingall's severed head.

Did he do it? The warrant for his blood would be easy to get. But Jeremy Lynch had the motive and opportunity. And he'd proven himself capable of it with Gloria Garcia. He'd been easy to find.

Too easy. Once again, Ed Zender's mistakes rose like an evil specter in the room.

Except for one thing. Jake now knew Wesley Wayne Hall had lied to him.

TWENTY-FOUR

Paige Landry looked like her mother, a fact that caused her an untold amount of frustration. Jake knew better than to mention it. Paige stood in the doorway, looking him up and down. Just shy of her seventeenth birthday Paige was starting to look like the woman she would later become, even as she fought against it. She'd recently dyed her hair jet-black and cropped it short. She wore heavy black eyeliner and Jake thought he could notice a hole in her nostril. A new piercing that he knew would drive her parents to the edge. Jake knew better than to mention that, either.

"Hey, Paige," Jake said. "She home?"

Paige popped her gum. "You've gone rogue, I see?"

Jake smiled. "Looks like you have too. How much trouble'd you get into for this one?" He decided to go against his better judgment and tweaked Paige's nose.

"I'm grounded until I'm forty. But what else is new?" Paige opened the door and let Jake in.

"She's out back. My dad's off getting us takeout. He always panics and over orders so if you're hungry, there'll be plenty."

"I don't think it's good if I stay that long," Jake said.

Paige looked around him out the door. "You parked down the street? Good idea. Though it's gonna make it harder for you to make a quick getaway."

"I'll take my chances," he said, tousling her head. "How you holding up, kiddo?"

"Oh, you mean with the fact my mother's about to lose her job?"

"Election's not over yet."

"Oh, she'll lose. Of course she'll lose. Then they're gonna make me switch to yet another school and restart my life just when I'm starting to feel like I have one."

"Keep the faith," Jake said.

"Well, like I said. She's out back. She cracked a bottle of wine. You want a glass?"

"I'm good," Jake said.

"Suit yourself," Paige answered, then she disappeared upstairs. Jake made his way through the Landrys' kitchen. Meg was sitting on the patio staring at a small koi pond Phil Landry had built last summer. He had half a dozen fat, colorful fish swimming among a group of lily pads.

"It's supposed to be soothing," Meg said. She didn't turn, but must have heard Jake talking to Paige.

"Yeah? How's it working?"

"Not as good as the wine. You want?"

"No. Paige already offered me some."

"Great. My minor daughter is serving as a bartender inside my own home. I should put that in my next campaign ad."

"Might work."

Meg finally turned to him. She was dressed casually in a pair of black sweatpants and an Ohio University tee shirt.

"It must be pretty bad that you're here willing to fraternize with me."

"It's not bad. I'm just not so great at following rules."

Meg smiled. "That, my friend, is the understatement of the year. Have a seat, Jake. It's looking like we're gonna go down together, huh?"

"What's with all the nihilism? You haven't lost anything yet."

"The thing is," Meg said, pointing with her wine glass. "People aren't blaming Zender for Wesley Wayne Hall's stay of execution. You gotta give Tim Brouchard credit. He's managed to make people blame me for all this happening on my watch. At the same time, he and Ed are the ones who screwed everything up fifteen years ago. I mean, that's talent. If I weren't on the business end of it, I could marvel at it."

"You got new poll numbers?"

Meg gave Jake a thumbs down and blew a raspberry.

"Election's still a couple of weeks away. And I'm not done yet. That's what I came here to tell you. Never mind Boyd Ansel's embargo, you're still the sheriff. And I don't work for him."

"Damn straight," she said. She took another sip of wine. Something told Jake she wasn't on her first bottle.

"Wesley Wayne Hall's been lying to me," Jake said.

"Are you surprised?"

"No. He swore up and down he didn't bring anybody else out to
the property. Well, he did. He brought Jeremy Lynch there. Turns
out Lynch beat the hell out of a different elderly farm owner a few
years later. He's doing twenty years for it. He cleaned her out. The
MO fits."

Meg put her wine glass down. "He killed Ruby too?"

"Maybe. I'm getting a warrant for his blood and DNA."

"The mystery blood sample. Jake, even if the type matches with
Lynch, that won't prove he was there. You said Ramirez told you
the sample was too degraded for DNA."

"At least it's something," Jake said. "A lead. And it means if Hall's
not a murderer, then he might be an accomplice, definitely a liar,
and a probable moron. Maybe all three."

"I don't even know what to hope for. Am I supposed to be rooting
for Hall to be innocent or guilty?"

"I want him to be guilty," Jake said. "I want to think that Ed
Zender wasn't actually capable of letting a guy rot in prison for
fifteen years. Or take a needle in his arm."

"Because at the end of this, he might still be your boss."

"Meg," Jake said. "I don't care what Ansel says. I don't care what
anybody says. And I don't care what the voters say. Ed can even fire
me if he gets your badge. This thing isn't going to be over until I
prove who killed Ruby Ingall once and for all. It's bigger than you
now. It's bigger than me."

Jake heard Meg's garage door open. Phil was home with the
takeout.

"I'm sorry I didn't come to you in the beginning," Jake said. "That's the only regret I have in this."

She turned to him. "You know. I was really mad at you about that. I got some advice about it. Certain people counseled me to fire you. Said it was the only way I could save myself."

Jake smiled. "Well, thanks for having my back. I think. Hell, maybe I'd be better off if you did fire me. Put me out of my misery."

"Nah," she said. "Then what would you do with yourself? Bus tables at Gemma's. You know, I wouldn't mind seeing that."

"It'd be a hell of a lot less stressful. That's for sure. Plus, I wouldn't have to deal with your bullshit anymore." He smiled. Meg knew he was teasing.

"You'd be nothing without me," she said. "You never would have made it long in field ops. You'd have lost your damn mind."

"Probably."

She reached for him, grabbing his hand. Meg's eyes were a little misty as she looked at him. "I'm glad you took me up on my offer though. If I accomplished nothing else, promoting you was a good decision."

"Now I know you're drunk," Jake said. "And as I recall, you didn't promote me so much as conscript me. I don't remember having much of a choice."

"You have one now." She turned serious. "You could drop this. Stop making waves. Hand this thing over to BCI or even the attorney general's office. Get out of the way of the freight train barreling straight at both of us, Jake. There's no way we both come out of this unscathed."

"Unless I go public with what I know so far," Jake said. "Hall's girlfriend is willing to make a statement. Tell the world Zender roughed her up and threatened to take away her kid if she lied about Hall the night Ruby died. He committed a crime, Meg."

"It's not enough. Brouchard and his cronies will destroy that girl. You know it. Until and unless you can prove who really killed Ruby, you'd be feeding her to the wolves."

"I suppose you're right," he said. "But I'm close, Meg. I can feel it. I just need a little more time."

"If he wins," she said. "He's going to take all of this out on you. In a big way, I have the least to lose. My job, sure. But I'll just find another one. Maybe not here in Stanley. But I'll land. Somewhere. You? This is your hometown. You could leave too, but you won't. Not now. You have your grandpa, Gemma. Your roots. Ed will keep coming after you. He's a puppet, sure. But the people pulling his strings have real reasons to hate you. You could get hurt, Jake. Maybe you should back off. Let somebody else pick up the torch."

Jake considered her words. A large white-and-orange koi swam in a zigzag pattern in the pond near his feet. Smiling, he turned to Meg.

"Now, does that sound like me? Letting somebody else fight my battles?"

"It's not just you," she said. "Zender knows who you care about. Brouchard does too. They'll punish Erica. I won't be there to stop them. They'll have her writing traffic tickets the rest of her career if she stays."

"Erica can take care of herself," Jake said. Though he knew it made him a hypocrite. Birdie'd been pushing back against Jake's attempts to protect her ever since she moved back to town.

"Are you sure?"

Jake knew she wasn't just asking about Birdie.

"I'm sure," he said. "And I know what I'm doing."

On that, he was less sure. To Meg's credit, she didn't call him out on it. But he took her point. She was giving him an out. A chance to salvage his own career if the election went against her. But as they sat there that evening, Jake knew he wouldn't take it. He'd rather crash and burn than work for Ed Zender anyway. Meg could read the decision in his eyes. Letting out a huff, she smiled.

"So what's next?" she asked.

Jake answered without missing a beat. "I need to have another conversation with Wesley Wayne Hall."

TWENTY-FIVE

A different Wesley Wayne Hall walked into the interview room as Jake sat waiting. His eyes lit up with hope. He blinked back tears as he took his seat and waited for the guard to thread the irons around his wrist through the loop in the table.

"You saved my life," Hall said, his voice cracking. "I'm getting calls from all over the country. Advocacy groups. Reporters. But I haven't talked to any of them yet. I wanted to talk to you first. Whatever happens, I don't want to screw anything up."

Jake's head throbbed. He realized he'd clamped his jaw so tightly he could feel the pulse there. He took a quick mental five count. Keeping his temper would be the challenge for the next half hour.

"You've been lying to me," he said.

Hall's face fell.

Jake pulled the copy of Jeremy Lynch's driver's license photo out of his portfolio and slid it to Hall. Hall looked at it. His expression stayed neutral. Jake expected some recognition. Some new agitation out of Hall. But he was just blank.

"What is this?" he asked.

"You tell me."

"Am I supposed to know who this is?"

"Yeah, Wes. You're supposed to know who that is. Look again. And think very carefully about your next answer. Tell me about him. The truth."

Hall squinted and brought the photograph closer. Like the one he'd shown Ruby's family, this picture had Lynch's name redacted. He wanted to give Hall another chance to lie. If he did, Jake was ready to get up and walk out of the room.

"He's familiar. It's been a while. I think he was one of the dudes I worked with on some of the farm jobs back in the day."

"His name?"

"Is he the one? Do you think he was out there? Killed the old lady?"

"His name!"

"I don't remember. Uh. Jason? Jamie? No. Wait. It was Jeremy. Is that right? Jeremy?"

"He knows you, Wes. Filled in some details for me that you conveniently left out. I asked you if you'd ever brought anybody else out to Ruby's. You told me no. You told me Ruby was particular about who she'd have on the property. But that's not what I'm hearing from some of the other farmers in the area. I'm hearing it was you and him."

Jake jabbed a finger on the photograph.

"It's been a million years," Hall said. "I didn't lie. I swear."

"You've had me chasing ghosts for you, Wes. Scotty Moore. This guy? You wanna know what Garth MacDonald told me?"

"I don't care what he said," Hall shouted. "Whatever he told you about me, it's not true. Ruby lied to him about me. Told him I was a thief. So whatever he thinks he knows, it's bullshit."

"Lynch was on Ruby's farm when you were. You worked together. You were the one who brought him out there. Vouched for him. Isn't that right?"

Hall sat back. "I might have. I don't remember it all. I did stuff for her for almost a year."

"You want me to believe that you just conveniently forgot to tell me about some other guy who was out on the property in the same time frame you were? You, who's been swearing you're innocent? Now here's this other day worker you just failed to mention."

"Did he do it? Shit, Jake. You have to tell me. Did Lynch hurt Ruby? Did you talk to him? If he's saying I had something to do with it, then he's a liar, too."

"I'm not Jake to you. Got it? We're not friends. I'm not on your side. I'm not your damn defense lawyer. I'm Detective Cashen. Lynch says he was tight with Scotty Moore. That you knew that. And yet again, you don't see fit to give me his name. So I have to ask myself, why? He's a lead. Somebody who could maybe point me in the direction of your missing alibi witness. Somebody who was out at Ruby's place. Knew the lay of the land. Maybe had dealings with her. But you don't bring it up. Seems to me there's only a few plausible explanations for that, Wes. One could be that you're a complete moron. But I don't think that's true. Or you lied because you didn't want anyone to connect you to Lynch. So why would that be? Huh? Did you bring him out there? Look the other way?"

"Did he hurt her?" Hall asked. "Do you have proof that he hurt her? You must. It has to be him, then."

"Why's that?"

"Because I *know* it wasn't me! Christ. I forgot, okay? Lynch? I don't remember how many times he was out there. Once? Maybe twice? Barely. And I don't remember it being anywhere around the time Ruby got herself killed. Last thing I knew, Lynch moved away somewhere. Got a factory job. Something steady. I don't know."

"All of a sudden you remember an awful lot about him, Wes."

"I didn't kill her! Why the hell won't anyone believe me? Are you gonna be just like Zender? He made up his mind that I did this thing. That was it. It didn't matter what I said. I told you the truth. Same as I told him. I hated Ruby Ingall for what she said about me. I've never denied that. She ruined my life. Made it so I couldn't get work. I was about to get evicted. Allison left me. All because Ruby Ingall couldn't calm down for two seconds and listen to me about a stupid five-gallon jug of gas. Did I shoot my mouth off when I shouldn't? Hell, yes. That's always been my problem. But that's all it is. I've got a big mouth. But I did not ... did *not* kill that old bitch."

Jake curled his fist. Hall's face had turned purple with rage. He trembled. His wrist and leg irons rattled.

Was he telling the truth? If so, it meant he was stupid. Not to have mentioned Jeremy Lynch when he could have helped exonerate him if he was innocent.

"Lynch is in prison," Jake said.

Hall dropped his head to his chin.

"He's doing time for aggravated burglary, Wes." Jake pulled a second photograph out of his portfolio. It was the worst of Gloria Garcia after the beating she took.

"He did that?" Hall said, his eyes taking on that hopeful light again. "Are you telling me Jeremy Lynch did that to this lady?"

"Yeah," Jake said. "That's what I'm telling you."

"Then why the hell are you busting my balls? When? Before Ruby?"

"No. It happened about seven years ago."

"I've been in here fifteen, Jake. You know I had nothing to do with this. This proves it. Jeremy Lynch must have killed Ruby. I didn't know him very well. I swear to God."

"I need you to think real hard, Wes. No more lies."

"I haven't told you one lie," Hall said, his voice losing all emotion.

"How did you meet Lynch? When?"

Hall shook his head. "I don't remember, man. I swear. Guys like him come and go. If you talked to MacDonald, I bet he told you that. Sometimes there wasn't enough work. So people would move on. Go to another town. Then drift back in if word got out there was something going on. If you're saying he did a lot over at the MacDonald farm, I don't remember that."

"Did Ruby ever ask you to bring help out?"

"Maybe once or twice, yeah. Not a lot. I told you. She was real funny about asking for help. And about who she'd let out there. She was one of those people who always assumed the worst of people. Always thought somebody was gonna steal from her. I wouldn't have put up with it at all, but she paid good. And she paid on time. I'm telling you. I don't really remember Lynch. But she had this fence she wanted repaired. It was a big job. One that was gonna take me weeks if I had to do it myself. I never called this guy Lynch. I'm telling you, until you showed me this picture just now, I didn't even remember his name. But there was one month in the summer when I asked Scotty if he had a buddy he could send out. I think it was him. Lynch. We hardly talked. He just showed up. I told him where he needed to get busy. And off he went."

"Did Ruby talk to him?"

Hall shook his head. "I don't know. He would have been working on one end of the property, me on the other. She had this little four wheeler she'd ride around in. She could have driven down to Lynch's end and talked to him. It wouldn't surprise me if she had. I told you. She was suspicious of everybody all the time. But I don't know. I didn't see her talking to anybody else. When I was out there, I tried to keep my head down and finish whatever she wanted so I could get paid and get the hell out. That was it. That's all I remember."

Jake wasn't sure whether it was better to believe Hall or not. It still seemed like a pretty huge omission to make.

"Why didn't you ever tell Zender about Lynch?"

Hall lifted his hands. The cuffs would only let him spread them so far. "I don't know. Like I said, this would have been a long time before Ruby died. I wouldn't have thought it was important. Because I *knew* where I was the night that old lady got murdered. And I knew Scotty Moore could back me up if he wanted to. I didn't think it was gonna be such a problem finding him. That all came out later. So that was my focus. Finding Scotty. Getting him to tell Zender I was with him. I told you. He said he would. I just don't know where he is anymore."

Jake debated telling Hall about Lynch's story. That Moore had a sister and he knew where to find her. In the end, Jake kept that detail to himself. No matter what else had happened, Wesley Wayne Hall was still the main person of interest in this case. On that, Ed Zender had gotten it right.

"I'll be in touch, Wes," Jake said, rising. Hall looked up at him desperately.

"Do you believe me?"

"This isn't about belief. Your blood was on the workbench. Right where the machete was found."

"I already told you. That was from at least a month before. I cut myself sharpening a damn mower blade. I told you, I explained all of that to my piece-of-shit lawyer and he didn't do anything about it. So I am asking you. Do you believe me?"

Jake didn't have an answer for him. He got a text instead. It was Birdie. The warrant for Lynch's blood and DNA had come through. She was coordinating with the prison to get a sample from him.

Jake said none of it to Hall. Whether it was to spare him potentially false hope, or to punish him, Jake wasn't sure. He left Hall staring after him as he summoned the guard.

Twenty-Six

C ami Newbern had a blessedly less common name than her brother. It had still taken Birdie the better part of a day to track her down. The address Jeremy Lynch had was woefully out of date. But she tracked Cami to an apartment complex just north of Cincinnati. She worked third shift at Good Samaritan Hospital, just like Lynch had said. Jake waited outside her apartment door. Just after eight a.m., a woman pulled up in a beat-up Dodge Durango. The license plate matched Cami's.

She wore her hair pulled back, dyed coal black. Her over-plucked eyebrows matched. She balanced a grocery bag on her hip as she fumbled with her keys. Jake pulled out his badge and carefully approached her.

"Ms. Newbern?"

She froze, key still in the lock. Jake got the distinct impression Cami Newbern was used to police officers approaching her like this. She had a fairly mild rap sheet of her own. Some petty theft in her younger days. A couple of shoplifting charges. She'd been popped for marijuana possession in the days it was still illegal. But for the past ten years, she'd kept herself out of trouble.

"I'm sorry to just show up at your door like this. I'm Detective Jake Cashen. I work down in Worthington County. Do you have a few minutes to talk to me?"

"What's he done now?" Cami didn't turn to face him. Her shoulders dropped with resignation. Then she rallied, turning to shove her bag of groceries into Jake's chest. He caught it. Cami fiddled with her key and opened the apartment door.

"Well," she said. "Don't just stand there. You might as well make yourself useful while you dump your bad news on me."

Jake walked in. Her apartment was sparsely furnished with two couches and a flat screen on the wall. Her kitchen was immaculate. No dishes out. Not so much as a single fingerprint on her stainless steel appliances. A tabby cat darted between Jake's legs and disappeared behind a coat rack in the corner.

Jake put her grocery bag on the counter. Cami reached into it and pulled out a jug of milk. She put that in the fridge and slammed the door shut.

Resting one hand on the counter, she glared at him. "So, what is it this time?"

"I'm sorry," Jake said. "I don't know what you're expecting. I understand your brother is Scotty Moore. He used to live in my county a while back. I was ..."

Cami's entire demeanor changed. A shudder went through her and her face turned ghostly white. "No," she whispered. "No. He isn't ... please don't ..."

"No!" Jake put his hands up. "No. No. Nothing's happened to

him. Not that I know of. I'm just hoping you can put me in touch with him."

She stood frozen, processing Jake's words.

"Ms. Newbern, can we sit down for a minute?" Jake gestured to the small kitchen table she had against the wall. Still mute, Cami walked over to it and plopped herself down in one of the chairs. Jake joined her.

"Scotty," he said. "Look, I'll cut to it. I'm investigating an old murder down in Blackhand Hills. I don't think your brother was involved in it or anything. But I believe he may have some information about someone who was. I just want to talk to him. But I've had a devil of a time finding him. I was given your name by an old acquaintance of Scotty's who said you're usually pretty good at getting a hold of him. That's it."

"He's not dead?"

"No. Not that I'm aware. How long has it been since you talked to your brother?"

"You mind?" Cami asked. She had a pack of cigarettes and a lighter on the table.

"It's your house," he said.

Cami lit a cigarette and took a long drag. It seemed to settle her nerves immediately.

"What murder?" she asked.

"Ruby Ingall," Jake answered. He decided to be direct with her. Either she'd help him get in touch with her brother or she wouldn't.

"Ruby Ingall? Why does that sound familiar?"

"It got a fair amount of publicity at the time. She was murdered on her farm fifteen years ago. I understand your brother was a frequent day worker on some of the farms in that region during that time frame. I promise you, I'm not interested in him for having some involvement in the actual murder. But I'm hoping he can clear up some other information I have."

"Scotty hasn't been in that area for years. Gosh. I bet over a decade."

"Were you close with him when he was?" Jake asked.

"He's my kid brother," she said. "He's had some tough times in his life. When did you say this murder happened again?"

"Fifteen years ago."

Cami let out a chuff. "Good luck getting Scotty to remember anything that happened fifteen months ago, let alone fifteen years. Detective Casher, is it?"

"Cashen."

"Cashen. Look, Scotty's clean and sober now. He's got a steady job at Serenity Farms. Can you believe that? It's a horse rescue place outside Cleveland. When Scotty was in rehab, he started doing equine therapy there. It turned into a regular job for him. He's happy. Content. It doesn't pay a lot, but it keeps him steady, you know?"

"That's great," Jake said. "And I'm not looking to upset him. I just need to talk to him. Do you think you could call him? Give him my number?"

Jake reached into his suit coat pocket and pulled out a business card. He handed it to Cami. She picked it up and tapped the corner with her finger.

"Scotty doesn't like talking to cops."

"I can understand that. But he really isn't in any kind of trouble. Not from me. This is about Wesley Wayne Hall."

Cami's eyes flicked to Jake's. She recognized the name. She put Jake's card down on the table.

"Do you remember Hall?"

Cami's nostrils flared. "Yeah. I remember him. He and Scotty did jobs together. Shit ... Ruby Ingall. That's why that name sounded familiar. She's the old lady who got her head cut off. Who Wes killed. Jesus. Look, you better leave. If you're trying to drag my brother back into Wes Hall's life ..."

"I'm not," Jake said.

"I thought Wes was headed to the chair," she said.

"He was ... er ... they don't use a chair anymore. But yes. Hall's been on death row for Ruby's murder. There have been some new developments in the case. I think your brother has some information about them. I just need to have a conversation with him. That's all. I swear, he's not in trouble over any of it."

"Wes Hall is toxic. Just ... bad news. He was using, you know that, right? He and Scotty. A lot of alcohol, but harder stuff, too. I was happy when Scotty finally got away from that guy. I wasn't exactly surprised when I found out what happened to him."

"Did you know Wes to be violent?"

"I didn't know him well at all. Maybe saw him one or two times when Scotty was crashing with me. Wes came to pick him up sometimes. Not very friendly. But then I've never been one to pretend with anyone. Wes seemed like trouble. Then it turned out he was. I'm not sure how I feel about passing your name along. Not if it's to do with Wes."

"Serenity Farms," Jake said. "I'm sorry. But I have to talk to him. It's non-negotiable."

"I can't stop you."

"No, you can't. But you can definitely make it easier. Do you really want me showing up at Scotty's job? You think that'll go over well? Even though I'm not there to cause any problems ..."

"No," she said. "No. You can't go there. You can't. I told you. He's happy there. He's clean. I should have kept my damn mouth shut."

"Well, you didn't. All I can do is reiterate what I said. I'm not looking to cause problems for you or your brother. It's just a conversation. A phone call to start with. That's it. Will you tell him? Give him my number?"

Cami rose. She walked over to her purse. Her cell phone was poking out of a compartment in the side. With her back turned to Jake, she punched something in. Then she slipped the phone into her back pocket.

"I understand Wes and Scotty worked together a lot. As day laborers. Scrappers."

"Wes always had some scheme he wanted to rope my brother into. Every time Scotty had a lead on a steady job. You know, the kind with health insurance. Real benefits. Wes would always talk him out of it. Saying all kinds of bullcrap about why should he work for the man when they could set their own hours. Scotty was gullible. A follower. Wes was one of these guys who thinks the world owes him something. Just ... trouble up and down."

"I get it. I do."

"Scotty wouldn't listen to me until he finally did. I got him an interview with a friend of mine who does concrete. High-end stuff. It was good money. I mean … real good money. And Scotty has a talent for that kind of thing. It was all lined up. Scotty had a future there. But Wes just dragged him down. Went nuts when Scotty told him he was done scrapping. Tried to cut Wes off. Well, Wes just managed to worm his way back in. Screwed things up. Got in Scotty's head. You ask me? Wes was jealous. Scotty was about to get his shit straight once and for all and Wes didn't want that. Next thing I knew, Scotty quit the concrete job. I was livid. Just furious. Then it wasn't long after that Wes got arrested for that murder. I was sad to hear about that lady. But I'll be honest. I was hoping it meant Scotty would finally be able to just walk his own path."

Cami's phone buzzed. She pulled it out of her pocket. She shot off a quick text and put her phone on the counter. Without a word, she picked up Jake's card and wrote something on the back of it.

"I should have just kicked you out," she said. "But he wants to talk to you. I didn't tell him why. Maybe he already knows. So here. I hope I don't regret this."

She handed Jake back his card. She'd written a phone number on it.

"Thank you," Jake said, rising.

Cami Newbern was done with him. She never even said goodbye or showed him out. She just kicked off her shoes and headed into one of the back rooms.

Jake pocketed the phone number and let himself out. By the time he slid behind the wheel, his phone rang.

"Hey, Birdie," he answered.

"You headed back?"

"Yeah. Got lucky, I think. I've got Scotty Moore's phone number and now I know where he works. Sounds like he's willing to talk to me. I'll call him as soon as I get back."

"Good timing," she said. "Ramirez called. He's gonna have some lab results for us the day after tomorrow at the latest. He'll come down with them."

"Good work, Birdie," Jake said. For once, he hoped Ramirez's news was conclusive. He just wasn't sure he knew what would count as good or bad.

TWENTY-SEVEN

The Serenity Farms Ranch sat on forty sprawling acres just outside of Cleveland. Though Cami Newbern hadn't wanted Jake to go anywhere near the place, Scotty Moore had a different idea. He felt safe there. It was quiet. Private. He told Jake to meet him in the picnic area to the east of the entrance. Signs marked the way.

Two ranch hands walked a pair of palominos with young riders. They waved to him. Jake waved back.

The picnic tables were empty when Jake got there. He parked on a gravel lot and walked under the pavilion. Checking his watch, he was five minutes early.

A crisp fall wind picked up. Jake selected a table in the corner. If anyone else came through, he and Moore should be tucked away enough to still have a conversation away from curious ears.

At ten minutes past ten, Jake worried Moore had gotten cold feet. He checked his last text. Moore had given no indication he might balk. Jake wondered if Cami had warned him off. She was a protective older sister. Jake knew the type. He knew Cami and Gemma would get along great.

A few minutes later, a beat-up green pickup pulled up and parked right alongside Jake's car. He'd driven his unmarked sedan. He knew someone like Moore would pick it out as a law enforcement vehicle in two seconds. He wanted no misunderstanding with Moore about who he was or why he was here.

Moore got out. He was smaller than Jake thought. Five foot two at most with wisps of blond hair under a Cleveland Browns baseball cap. He wore weathered work boots, a pair of jeans, and a red-and-black flannel shirt with a patch on the front with the ranch's logo.

Jake rose to meet him. "Thanks for meeting with me. I'm Jake Cashen."

Moore rubbed his hand on his jeans, then shook Jake's hand. He slid quickly onto the bench opposite Jake and took his cap off. Jake sat down. He brought nothing with him. Just the notepad in his pocket. But no photographs. Nothing to upset or intimidate Scott Moore. If Wesley Wayne Hall had told the truth, there'd be no need for any of it.

"You know what I want to talk to you about," Jake said. "You've read about the recent developments in the Ruby Ingall case."

"Yeah," Moore said.

"You were friends with Wes Hall."

"No," he said. "Not friends. We just kind of tolerated each other. Worked together. Wes didn't have any friends. Not real ones. He was too much of a bully."

"Okay." Jake felt a knot form in his stomach. A bully. If Scotty Moore felt threatened by Hall, that would cause a whole new set of problems. "Why don't you tell me about that? What was your relationship with Hall like fifteen years ago? How did you meet?"

"We both used to hang out at Chappy's Bar. A lot of us did. If you were looking for work around Worthington or Marvell County, that's where most of the guys hung out. The farmers knew that. They'd come in and put the word out when they had jobs. And if you had questions, like if you wanted to know who to work for, who to steer clear of, Chappy's was the place to put your ear to the ground. I was sorry to hear it burned down."

"Got it."

"I don't know exactly when I met Wes. But it was at Chappy's. I think somebody introduced me to him or him to me. I don't even remember. But we started hauling scrap together. I had a truck and needed somebody to help me out. So we started doing that. Split stuff 50/50. I didn't think that was fair. It was my truck. I was paying for the gas and the wear and tear. But Wes always seemed to know where to find jobs. And the good shit. So I went along with it."

"You didn't just haul scrap though. You were a day laborer at some of the local farms? I know you worked out at Garth MacDonald's."

"Mac was one of the good ones. If you kept your head down. Didn't bother him or the family. Showed up on time. He always had work for me. Sometimes it was real grunt work. Baling. Mucking out stalls. But like I said. If you proved yourself, he'd start having you help with harvesting. Then the pay was better."

"And in between, you'd haul scrap?"

"Yeah. I had a job at a stamping plant in Logan. I got laid off in 2006. That's when I started working a side hustle. It wasn't good for me. Not having the structure of a full-time gig. I started using again."

"Tell me about the fall Ruby Ingall was killed. How heavily were you using then?"

"Some. I had my good days and bad days. I was in rehab that August. Lasted a few weeks. I had a relapse around Christmas."

Jake sat back. "You're saying you were sober that fall? When Ruby died?"

"I sure was. And I think that's part of what happened between me and Wes. If I was using, he could get me to do whatever he wanted. Go along. Eat shit. When I had my head straight, I could see how much of a dick he became. He was cheating me out of stuff on the scrap hauling side."

"Okay. Scotty, you know why I'm here. Wes is telling me you have something to say about the night Ruby died. I need to hear it from you. Do you remember that night?"

Moore tapped his fingers on the picnic table. "Yeah. I remember. How the hell could anybody forget that? Not after what happened."

"What do you remember?"

"Wes got a lead on a big scrap job up near Bluffton. This lady's husband died. He was some kind of machinist. Had all kinds of equipment. Copper scrap, aluminum, stainless steel. Her kids didn't want anything to do with it. She just wanted it gone. I couldn't believe it. Some of that stuff you can sell for a lot of money. The kind that was gonna make that long of a trip worth it. So Wes called me up. I didn't wanna go. I had a job interview out in Dayton. Cami set it up for me. But this was gonna be easy money, so I blew off the interview and went with Wes."

"Do you remember the timing?"

"Wes was working at some odd job that day. He was getting off around six, I think it was. He wanted me to pick him up at his place. I got there right when he got home. Then we drove to Bluffton."

"That's what, a three-hour drive?"

"Yeah. About that. Or it should have been. It was late when we got there. Pitch dark. I thought it was stupid. Like why couldn't we wait until the next morning during daylight? So we could really see what the hell she had. But Wes insisted. He said if we didn't get out there, somebody'd beat us to it. That the lady was a real pain in the ass and wanted it taken care of that day. So we went. Then we got there ... it was bullshit."

"What do you mean?"

"First, Wes had crappy directions. We got lost. It was close to eleven at night before we even got there. And when we did, the lady wouldn't come to the door. She was gone or sleeping or something. She had a side yard where all the stuff was supposed to be but it was behind a locked chain-link fence and she had two Rottweilers guarding the place. Mean sons of bitches. So we pulled my truck up and turned on the headlights. You know, so we could at least see what she had. And it was nothing. Crap. All picked over or something. Or maybe Wes was wrong and she never had anything at all."

"What did you do then?"

"Well, I was hot. I blew off that interview to go out there cuz Wes insisted. And it was just a big fat nothing. Man, Wes was pounding on that lady's door. He was so mad he wanted to bust a window. I stopped him from doing that. Figured if she had Rottweilers out there, who knew what she might have in the house? Plus, I'm not

into that. Burglary. So we left. I was pissed. It was close to
midnight and I was gonna have to drive over three hours back. I
thought about leaving Wes by the side of the damn road. He
wouldn't shut up."

"What time did you get back?"

"That's the thing. We made it about an hour south. Then my
truck broke down. Turned out I had a bad alternator. We were in
the middle of nowhere. No cell service. I ended up having to walk a
mile to a gas station. Wes was just bitching at me the whole time. I
was damn lucky to find a guy with a used alternator."

"But Wes was with you?"

"Yeah. Took us two hours to get back on the road. So it was, I
don't know, six or seven in the morning before I dropped his ass
off at his house. Swore that was the last time I was gonna go out on
a job with him. Cost me two tanks of gas and he didn't pay me a
dime. It had been coming for a long time. I told you. He was a
bully."

Jake studied Scotty Moore. There were no outward signs that the
man was lying. The story was consistent with what Wes told him.
And yet, Moore just admitted Wes was a bully. How could he
know whether Hall intimidated him into giving him an alibi?

"You knew Wes was arrested for killing Ruby Ingall. It was big
news. You're saying he was with you that night. The whole night. I
find it real hard to believe you wouldn't come forward."

"We got into a pretty bad fight that night. Out there on the side of
the road. Wes blamed me for my truck breaking down. I blamed
him for screwing up my interview over nothing. It had been
coming to a head for a really long time between us. He took a
swing at me. Or I took a swing at him. I don't know. I really did
just wanna leave him out in the road that night. But I'm not that

big of an asshole. So I figured I'd drop his ass off home, and I'd be done with him for good. I told him that. And that's what I did. The next day, I left town and went to stay with my sister. Wes called me a day or two after that but I didn't answer the phone. He kept calling but I blocked his number. When I said I was done, I meant it. I didn't know anything about what happened with Ruby Ingall until a long time after that."

"When did you next talk to Wes?"

"It was years later. I packed my stuff up that next day. I told you. I was trying to stay clean. I went to stay with Cami. I don't know how long. Maybe a week or two went by. Then she got me a line on a job working a rig up in Alaska. She had a boyfriend at the time who was in that industry. She called in a favor. Thought it would be good for me to just get the hell out of Ohio for a while. So I did."

"But you did start using again," Jake said.

"Yeah. Alaska wasn't for me. I had some real rough years after that. But I got clean. I've been sober for nine years."

"What about Wes?" Jake said.

"I didn't know about Ruby. I told you. I left town after that night. Put Blackhand Hills behind me. I didn't hear about Ruby until a long time later. Wes was already doing time for it. A buddy of mine told me he was on death row. I knew Wes had a hot temper. And it seemed like it was getting worse. I had no idea they were saying this happened the night we had our fight. I just assumed it was some time later. And I gotta be honest. I believed it. I figured Wes just finally snapped. And I figured it was a good thing I cut him out of my life. But then I got a letter from him. This was maybe eight years ago. After I was already sober for good. He told me he needed my help. I swear to God, I had no idea anybody wanted to talk to me as some kind of witness."

"Would you have? Talked to the police?"

Moore put his hands flat on the table. "I don't know. I just don't know. Blackhand Hills had a lot of bad associations for me. I wasn't keen on going back. And I'm not saying I think Wes Hall is a good guy. But ... I do know what happened that night. October 4th. It was a Friday. I remember it because that's the day of that interview I missed. I still have an email about it. I'm not good about deleting that stuff. I know where Wes was. And if that's the night Ruby got killed, then I know Wes wasn't there."

"Scotty, this all sounds really compelling. It's a good story. But my problem is, why in the hell haven't you come forward? When you finally did know, you could provide an alibi for Wes. Why'd you stay out of it?"

Something changed in Moore's face. He lost some color. His brow furrowed in anger. "What the hell are you talking about?"

"If you say you knew the truth. That you could have potentially cleared Wesley Wayne Hall. A man who you knew was gonna eventually get the needle for a murder you don't think he committed. Why am I the first cop you're telling this story to?"

Moore shook his head. "You're not, man. I don't know what you're talking about."

"What do you mean?" Ice filled Jake's veins. It was as if he knew what Moore would say before he said it.

"I mean, I went to the cops. Eight years ago. I went back to Blackhand Hills. I walked in there and asked to talk to the detective who handled Ruby Ingall's case. I sat down with him just like I'm sitting down with you. And I told him all this. Every word. I gave him names. Dates. All of it. I even printed out the email confirming that job interview I'm talking about. I gave it to the dude."

"Who did you talk to, Scotty?" But Jake already knew the answer.

"Zender," he said.

"You're sure?"

"Hell, yes, I'm sure." Moore reached into his back pocket and pulled out an overstuffed wallet. He rummaged through it. Then he pulled out a frayed, faded business card and threw it on the table. Jake picked it up.

DETECTIVE ED ZENDER
CRIMES AGAINST PERSONS
WORTHINGTON COUNTY SHERIFF'S DEPARTMENT

"He gave me that," Scotty said. "Told me he'd be in touch if he needed anything else from me."

"And you walked out? You didn't follow up?"

"I told you. Blackhand Hills and me? It's not a good mix. The dude said he'd call me if he needed anything else from me. I took him at his word, man. What else was I supposed to do?"

What else? God. Zender knew. As long as eight years ago. He knew he'd arrested the wrong man. But he'd let him rot on death row anyway. Just to save his own skin.

Twenty-Eight

It was past four o'clock by the time Jake got back to the office. He hoped he'd find it deserted. Day shift should have already clocked out. Landry was out of town at a conference. He expected and welcomed quiet solitude while he decided his next move.

Ed Zender wasn't just incompetent. He wasn't just lazy. His actions had risen to the level of a crime. He'd intimidated Allison Sobecki. Failed to pursue Scotty Moore's statement. Failed to properly process the crime scene. Then, when finally confronted with a credible alibi witness for Hall ... a man serving on death row ... Zender had looked the other way.

Jake walked into the office feeling like a zombie. It took him a second to realize he wasn't alone. Birdie sat at Gary Majewski's desk. Standing beside her was Boyd Ansel, wearing a waxen expression, much like Jake's.

"Jake," Birdie said, rising. "We've been trying to get a hold of you for two hours."

"I met with Scotty Moore. I suppose it's good you're both here. Boyd, you might as well hear what he told me. You'll have a formal report from me on your desk by the end of the day tomorrow."

Jake gestured to the table in the center of the room. Looking skeptical, Boyd sat down. Jake leaned against his desk. Birdie swiveled Gary's chair to face him.

"Wesley Wayne Hall has an alibi. He was with Scotty Moore the night Ruby Ingall was murdered. Couple that with the problems we already know about, Boyd, I think you gotta do more than just stay Hall's execution. He's been telling the truth. He didn't kill Ruby."

Boyd's face fell. "Christ, Jake."

"There's more. Scotty Moore claims he came here eight years ago and told his story to Ed. He showed me Ed's business card. Now why the hell would Scotty Moore have an old business card of Ed Zender's unless he's telling the truth?"

"He knew?" Birdie said. "My God. You're saying Ed knew for at least eight years? Moore could blow a big fat hole in his case and he sat on it?"

"That's what it's looking like," Jake said. He wanted to punch something. He regretted not taking the opportunity to punch Ed.

"Why?" she said. "Why in the hell would he do that?"

"Why not?" Jake said. "Wesley Wayne Hall was the feather in his cap. It's the reason Greg O'Neal probably gave him a pass for all the later bullshit he pulled. And he had Frank Borowski to cover his ass all those years and handle all the real police work."

"Until you got here," Birdie said.

"You have to go public with this," Jake told Boyd. "People need to know who Ed is. This isn't about politics anymore. He's a criminal. You have to file charges. You're the lawyer, but I gotta think fraud is some kind of exception to any statute of limitations in a case like this."

"It is ... er ... it can be."

"This can't come from us," Birdie said. "If we're the ones going to the press with Ed's misconduct, it's just gonna look like Landry had a hand in it."

"Landry wasn't here," Jake said. "She's got about as clean hands as anybody. People are gonna go to the polls in ten days. They need to see Ed Zender in cuffs and a perp walk. Tomorrow!"

"I need to call the AG," Boyd said. "Erica's right about one thing. I have to be really careful how I handle this. You have a statement from this Scott Moore character?"

Jake tossed a flash drive on the table. "He let me record his statement. It's all there. He'll testify if it were to come to a new trial. But it shouldn't. It never should have come to trial in the first place. Hall never should have even been charged."

Boyd pressed his fingers to the bridge of his nose. Jake had a similar urge as his head began to throb.

"Somebody has to tell Landry," Birdie said. "She's in Columbus today."

"I'll call her," Jake said.

"No," Boyd said. "This should come from me. I meant what I said. The two of you need to be walled off from each other. Even with all these new developments, we cannot have even the hint of an appearance that Meg is using this office to go after Zender."

"She is using her office to go after a murderer, Boyd," Jake said bitterly.

"I know. But you need to trust me. I know how to handle this."

"You do?" Jake said. "Because I sure as hell don't. And I don't know if he acted alone at this point. Tim Brouchard was the prosecutor on the Hall case. If the AG launches an investigation, it should be into your office as well as this one. I'm sorry. I know that's not something that helps you. But ..."

"It will," Boyd said. "They'll have access to whatever they need. Full cooperation. Total transparency."

"As it is, Zender's exposed this department to a massive lawsuit. Hall will ask for compensation. Fifteen years. Fifteen damn years!"

Jake swept his hand across his desk, violently slashing through a paper tray and a pen and paperclip holder. They all went crashing to the floor. Two pens hit the opposite wall. He put his hands on his hips and turned his back on Birdie and Boyd. Nostrils flaring, he walked to the other end of the room, trying to collect himself.

"Jake," Birdie said. "There's a reason I asked Boyd to come down here. Why we've been trying to get a hold of you for hours."

With his hands still on his hips, Jake froze. He didn't want to turn to face them. He wasn't sure he could handle any more bad news in one day.

"Jake," Birdie said. She came to him, putting a gentle hand on his shoulder. "Mark Ramirez was here. He waited as long as he could, but he had to head out to another case. Sit down. There's something we need to tell you."

Slowly, Jake walked over to the table where Boyd sat. He took a chair. His stomach growled. He realized he hadn't had anything today besides coffee.

Birdie grabbed a large gold envelope from the desk. She slipped a stack of papers out of it.

"Jeremy Lynch," she said. "You know we served the warrants for his blood and DNA. You have an email waiting for you, but Ramirez wanted to hand deliver this and explain it to you in person."

"The blood sample out at Ruby's," Jake said.

"It's not a match," Birdie said. "Jeremy Lynch's blood type is B positive. It's not the same as the second sample found in Ruby's kitchen. None of Lynch's blood was found at the scene."

The air left Jake's lungs. He felt ... nothing. He needed to replay Birdie's words inside his own head for a moment until he could fully comprehend what they meant. When he did, he dropped his chin to his chest.

"It wasn't Lynch."

"We don't know that for sure," she said. "We just know there's no physical evidence tying him to the scene. He might have been involved. Had an accomplice. We still have to run down his alibi."

"He wasn't there," Jake said. "So we're nowhere. Wesley Wayne Hall is innocent. He was telling the truth. The only other ghost of a lead I had was Lynch. Is Mark sure?"

He knew the answer to that. He understood the science. Of course, Ramirez was sure.

"Jake ..." Boyd started.

"I have to go," he said.

"I'm sorry," Birdie said. "I wanted it to be Lynch, too. I wanted it to be ..."

"Someone," Jake finished for her. He rose from the chair and grabbed his keys off the desk.

"Where are you going?" Birdie asked.

"I have to go to the Ingall farm. Boyd, can I trust that whatever you have to do, it can wait until morning? Sam Ingall and his aunt deserve to hear this from me. I need to prepare them for what to expect."

"What should they expect?" Birdie said. "I mean, how the hell do you do that?"

"I don't honestly know. I just can't have them hearing this on the internet or the local news. I owe them that much."

"Okay," Boyd said. "Please let them know I'm here to answer any questions they may have as well. And tell them ... God. I don't know what you tell them."

Jake clenched his jaw.

"Do you want me to go with you?" Birdie asked.

"No," Jake said. "This is something I have to do alone."

TWENTY-NINE

It seemed Jake would perpetually find himself interrupting dinner on the Ingall farm. He hadn't even thought to check the time. But as he walked up to the door, he could see Sam and Brittany's kids spooning mouthfuls of pumpkin pie into their faces. The youngest, Charlotte, had a dollop of whipped cream on her nose.

He wanted to leave them in peace. Perhaps wait on the porch until Loretta and Brittany cleared the table. Virgilene the chicken had other ideas. She marched right up to Jake and let out a strangled caw that heralded his presence better than any guard dog could have.

"Jake!" Dan said, spotting him first through the window. With a big smile on his face, he came to the front door and opened it, inviting him in.

Jake felt like a ghoul. Or some grim reaper. Always here to deliver bad news. And yet this family embraced him each time and welcomed him to their table.

Tonight, he didn't feel like he deserved it.

"I'm sorry," he said. "I don't mean to interrupt your meal."

"Nonsense," Dan said. "The kids are just finishing up their dessert. Brittany wanted us over to try out a new pie recipe she's been working on. Not that I couldn't afford to skip it." Dan patted his beer gut.

"Wash up then head upstairs," Brittany called out. "Sammy, you start the bath for Charlotte. I'll be up in a few minutes."

Loretta walked out to the living room to see who had arrived. Her smile seemed genuine when she saw Jake.

"Sam," she called out. "Jake's here."

Brittany paused, looking over her shoulder. She was the only member of the family who seemed wary of his continued presence. He tried not to hold it against her. She was Sam Ingall's staunchest ally and he couldn't fault her for it.

Sam walked out into the living room, chewing on a toothpick.

"Hey, Jake. What can we do for you?"

The kids tore through the living room on the way to the stairs. Little Sam, the oldest, nearly mowed Jake down. He raised his arms and scooted backward avoiding the collision.

"Sorry," Sam said. "They're on a sugar high. Good news is they'll crash hard in about twenty minutes. I think Brittany plotted it that way."

"She's crafty." Loretta laughed. "I was just about to put some coffee on. Would you like some, Jake?"

"No, thank you." He cleared his throat to cover the growling of his stomach. He still hadn't eaten a thing all day. He'd be damned if he'd break bread with these people tonight, in light of the news he had to deliver.

Brittany joined them in the living room, wiping her hands on a kitchen towel. She went to her husband and put an arm around his waist. "Is something wrong?" she asked.

"I suppose there is. It's good you're all here. Do you mind if we all sit down for a few minutes?"

Brittany looked toward the ceiling. The stomping feet of her children gave her pause.

"It won't take long," Jake said.

The family did as Jake asked. Sam and Brittany took the loveseat along one wall. Loretta and Dan took the couch. Jake sat on the ottoman in one corner of the room. He flat out didn't know where to start. So he ripped the bandage off as quickly as he could.

"Tomorrow morning, Boyd Ansel is going to file a petition to formally drop the charges against Wesley Wayne Hall and ask for his immediate release."

He kept his eyes on Sam. Of all of them, he knew Sam had suffered the most. Had seen the worst of what happened to his grandmother. Had lost his father over it as well. But Sam remained stoic. His wife rested her chin on his shoulder, squeezing her eyes shut.

"What's happened?" Dan asked.

"Boyd Ansel is going to give a press conference sometime tomorrow. But I didn't want you to hear it through that. Or somewhere else. I found Hall's alibi witness. He's credible. There was physical evidence found at the scene that wasn't properly processed at the time."

"DNA?" Loretta asked. "I thought they tested for that."

"No," Jake said. "Blood evidence. Not new DNA. But in addition to that, Hall's girlfriend has recanted her story. She never saw Hall washing blood off his hands or on his clothes the night Ruby died."

"Then why would she say that?" Sam asked.

"She was pressured into it. And Hall's alibi witness left town right after that night. He didn't know anything about what happened until much later. After that, it was too late."

"And he's just now coming forward?" Dan asked. "I don't understand."

"It's complicated," Jake said. He wasn't sure how much he could tell them about Zender's complicity. But they were going to find out soon enough, he figured.

"Ed Zender is to blame for all of this," he said. "I'm sorry. I probably shouldn't even say that much. But you deserve to know. It's going to become public anyway. I'm going to make damn sure of it. He made some ... mistakes. And he may face criminal charges because of it. That won't be up to me. But if it was ... I'd have him in cuffs right now."

"My God," Brittany said. "I don't ... what do we ..."

"Who did this?" Sam asked. "If Wesley Wayne Hall didn't do this ... is that what you're saying? It's not just some technicality."

"No," Jake said. "It's not some legal technicality. He's innocent. He was wrongfully convicted of killing your grandmother."

"You're sure," Dan said, his voice flat. "You're absolutely sure?"

"Yes," Jake said. "There's no doubt. He's innocent. He deserves his freedom."

"I can't ... I don't ..." Jake looked up. Sam had started to hyperventilate. His skin turned blotchy. Alarmed, Brittany reached for him, loosening his collar.

"Baby," she said. "Sam?"

Sam bolted off the couch. He tore his hands through his hair. "He has to be guilty. It has to be Hall."

"Sam, I'm sorry," Jake said. "But it isn't."

"Then who?" Sam shouted.

"I don't know. As of right now, I don't have any solid leads."

"But you will," Brittany said. She rose to join her husband. Sam was sweating profusely. He seemed in a full-on panic attack.

Jake knew at that moment, regardless of Sam's reaction, he had to be brutally honest with this family.

"I don't know," he said. "Right now, this case is cold. I'm sorry. I made you a promise that I'd keep you in the loop. I'm keeping that promise. Tonight, I'll make you another one. I won't give up on this case. As long as I have a job with the Sheriff's Department, I'll keep pursuing leads. But I can't promise you it will ever be solved."

Sam buried his face in his hands and doubled over. "Who did this? Who did this? They're out there!"

"Honey, breathe," Brittany said. "My God. Breathe!"

When Sam Ingall stood upright, Jake saw a change go through him. He no longer looked like a man. He looked like a kid. A teenager. A boy who had just seen the worst horror of his life. Jake knew with dead certainty that he was seeing what Sam looked like the moment he saw his grandmother's severed head in that field. And Sam was seeing it all again in his mind's eye.

"Come on," Brittany said. "Jake, I'm sorry. I need to take Sam out of here. We'll go for a walk."

Jake nodded.

"You go," Dan said. He was about to get up to go to his nephew, but beside him, his wife also slowly fell apart. Loretta buried her face in her hands and started to cry.

Brittany looked pained as she watched Loretta. But she had her husband to attend to. Sam more or less left with her willingly. They went out through the kitchen.

"I can't hear anymore," Loretta said. "I can't. My God. Not again. We have to go through this all over again?"

"I hope not," Jake said. Dan rubbed his wife's back. She got to her feet.

"I'm sorry," she said. "I need to go be with the kids. Charlotte needs help with her bath."

"It's okay," Dan said. "Do you want me to come with you?"

Jake started to rise, feeling his welcome more than worn out.

"No," Loretta said. "Hear what Jake has to say."

Loretta then bolted up the stairs and out of sight, leaving Jake and Dan alone.

"I'm sorry," Dan said. "They've been on edge for weeks with this. It's just ... such a shock. I thought ... we thought you were coming to tell us that you tied up whatever loose ends you had to with Hall. We thought you were going to tell us his new execution date."

"I know. And I am sorry. I just didn't know of a soft way to break this news."

"No. No. I know. You couldn't. And we really do appreciate your bringing it to us in person. You've been solid, Jake. It might not seem like it, but we trust you. All of us."

"But you trusted Ed Zender," Jake muttered.

Dan looked toward the stairs. He rose and motioned for Jake to join him in the kitchen. It would be less likely for them to be overheard there.

"You have your hands full," Jake said. "I can see they all depend on you."

Dan smiled. "Loretta? No. It's the other way around. She's my rock. Don't worry. She'll rally. She's stronger than she looks. She just got the wind knocked out of her tonight. But you watch. She's a lioness when she needs to be. She's just like her mother."

"Ruby," Jake said. Once again, he became keenly aware that he was standing just a few feet from where Ruby Ingall's life ended.

"Ruby," Dan repeated. "God, I still miss her. She'd know what to do. And she'd pull Loretta and Sam together. I can tell you that. She'd tell them to shake it off and do what needs to be done."

"I meant what I said," Jake said. "I'm not going to give up on Ruby. Or any of you."

Dan cocked his head to the side. "Are you worried we'll give up on you?"

Jake smiled. "I guess maybe I am. I wish I could give you something to hold on to. I wish I could tell Sam that the person who did that to his grandmother can't hurt him. And it's not that I think they will. They may be long gone by now. They're not coming back here to this farm."

"We'll tell him that," Dan said. "And we'll be there for him in whatever way he needs. That's *my* promise. Just like it was when he was a boy."

Jake walked over to the curio. Ruby Ingall's chicken collection didn't have a speck of dust anywhere.

"She was strong," Dan said. "And her blood runs through Sam and Loretta. They will be okay, Jake."

"Larry wasn't," Jake murmured. "Ingall men die at fifty-six. Isn't that what Loretta said? Sam's thirty."

"Sam's a lot like his father. That's true. And I worry about that. So did Ruby. So does Sam's mother. She thought taking him away from this farm was the answer. But like I told you, that boy's got enough of Ruby in him. I think he'll surprise everybody and outlive us all. He's a fighter, Jake. Ruby was too. God. She fought until her last breath, they said."

Dan came next to Jake. He picked up one of the glass chickens. "It's always made me feel weirdly better knowing that."

"Knowing what?"

"That she fought. Threw one of her damn chickens across the room."

Dan put the glass chicken back on the curio shelf. He went to the kitchen sink and looked out the window. Jake couldn't take his eyes off the glass chicken. It was an odd-looking thing with a body made of iridescent blue glass. Its tail feathers and crest were pink. It had a bulging white eye with a black pebble glued to it for an iris.

"Dan," he said. "How do you know she threw a glass chicken?"

Dan turned, leaning against the sink on one elbow. "Larry told us. He's the only one who sat in that courtroom every single day and listened to the testimony. I think that's what killed him more than losing Ruby. Just having to sit there and see those photos. Hear about her injuries and her last seconds. Larry always blamed himself for hiring Wesley Wayne Hall in the first place. That haunted him. God. I wish I could tell him. It wasn't his fault. I mean, of course it wasn't. But maybe if he'd known Hall wasn't guilty, that he wasn't the one. Maybe Larry could have borne it all a little better."

"Maybe," Jake said.

"You're all right, Jake. I believe in you. And so does the rest of my family. I won't lie. I'd like to take Ed Zender by the throat and squeeze the life out of him right now. I'm just going to have to trust the system. And you."

Jake felt a lump in his throat. He wanted to earn their trust. He would make good on his vow. He just didn't know how.

"Well, I should check on Loretta," Dan said. "Whatever you need, Jake. Always know that."

"Thank you," Jake said. Dan excused himself and headed upstairs. It left Jake alone in Ruby Ingall's kitchen for a moment. From the window, he could see straight to the barn where the unspeakable had happened. The corn husks swayed in the dusky breeze. They too had their own secrets to tell.

THIRTY

Hot water sluiced down Jake's back. He stood with his palms flat against the wall, his forehead pressed to the cool tile. He watched as suds swirled around the shower drain, matching the thoughts in his brain.

There had to be an answer. It was there. Somewhere. He could feel it. Almost taste it.

Wesley Wayne Hall didn't kill Ruby Ingall. Neither did Jeremy Lynch. She had no known enemies. She wasn't rich. The only thing of value she had was family. Family and the farm.

Jake squeezed his eyes shut, keeping the shampoo from running into them. He grabbed his razor from the shelf and ran it over his jaw.

He saw Ruby as she was. A happy grandma carving pumpkins with Sam when he was little. Teaching Loretta her secret chili recipe. Tending to her ever-growing flock of chickens, both real ones and her collectibles.

And Larry. Desperate for him to take over the farm.

Larry. Jake ran the razor up his neck.

They weren't angry. Loretta was sad. Sam was traumatized again. It left Dan to hold them all together as best he could. Larry Ingall hadn't been strong enough to hold on. What had Dan said?

He's the only one who sat in that courtroom every single day and listened to the testimony. I think that's what killed him more than losing Ruby.

Jake felt a stinging sharp pain as he brought the razor up. He'd sliced himself.

"Dammit!" He pressed his fingers to the cut. His hand came away red. A river of blood ran down.

Jake rinsed himself off and stepped out of the shower. His pulse raced. He felt it in the throbbing cut on his jawline. He looked in the mirror. It was a bad gash. One that would bleed forever. Jake dabbed it with the towel then stuck a piece of toilet paper on it, hoping to at least keep himself from bleeding all over his shirt.

Larry Ingall. He sat in the courtroom every single day of Wesley Wayne Hall's trial. Listened to every witness. Saw every piece of evidence the jury did.

Every piece of evidence. Jake felt as if his heart had just dropped out of his body.

Every. Piece. Of. Evidence.

He hastily threw on a suit, hair still wet, grabbed his gun, badge, and keys, and sprinted out the door.

J ake was still tucking his shirt in as he vaulted out of his truck and sprinted through the door. Lieutenant Beverly was still in the middle of roll call. Jake was late. He spotted Birdie standing in the back of the room. She turned, seeing Jake in the doorway. He motioned for her to follow him. Birdie gave him a curious frown and whispered something to Deputy Denning standing beside her.

She had to scootch past four other deputies to get to the doorway. When she got there, Jake grabbed her arm and led her toward the stairwell.

"What's the matter?" she asked.

"We have to hurry," he said.

She had her campaign hat in her hand. "Jake, Beverly wants me in Maudeville today."

"Forget that. This is more important. I need you."

The pair of them raced down the stairs. Jake fumbled with his keys and opened the storage room door. The Ruby Ingall evidence was still laid out on the tables as Birdie had arranged it. Jake went to the evidence table. His eyes flicked over every bag. Birdie had organized them into groups. Those pieces that had come from the courthouse. Those that had been part of the archives here in the bowels of the Sheriff's Department property room.

"Jake, what are you looking for?" Birdie asked.

Jake went from table to table, his eyes scanning every item.

"Jake!" She grabbed him by the arm and turned him to face her. "Geez, what happened to you? You look terrible." She picked off the bit of tissue paper still stuck to his face.

"Never mind that," Jake said. He turned back to the tables,

focusing on the items that had been introduced in Wesley Wayne Hall's trial.

"The machete, the blood samples from the barn," he began to rattle off. "Photos of the bloodstains on the floor. Ruby's body. What Sam found in the cornfield."

"Jake ... are you gonna explain what's going on in your brain?"

He could barely breathe and his heart beat so fast. He had to be sure. One by one, he ticked off every piece of evidence from Hall's trial. Forty-two exhibits. They were all accounted for there on the table.

Jake walked over to the other table. His hands shaking, he picked up a large plastic bag containing bits of iridescent blue glass.

"Something Dan Clawson said," Jake finally addressed Birdie. "I was there last night. Telling them that Wes Hall is going free. That he's innocent. Sam and Loretta couldn't handle it. They couldn't even be in the same room with me. But Dan. We sat in that kitchen. He told me about Ruby. How feisty she was. That Loretta was more like her. That she'd be okay. It was Sam he's worried about. That he's like his dad."

"Larry," she said. "Okay. But what's that got to do with that broken glass?"

Jake held it up into the light, letting the rainbow of colors shine.

"Her chickens," Jake said. He could see them in his mind's eye, sitting in Ruby Ingall's curio cabinet. There were two of them in particular. Blue, iridescent. Just like the shards of glass in the bag he held.

"Okay? Jake, you're cracking up."

"No," he said. "Dan said it made them all feel better knowing Ruby at least fought until the very end. That she'd used one of her chickens. Threw it at her attacker. Only, nobody ever said that. It's not in the report. This glass, it's from one of her chickens. You've seen them. The collectibles."

Birdie took the bag from him. "I guess so. Yes. I asked Loretta about a couple of them. They're blue like this. She told me Ruby got them at some shop in Saugatuck, Michigan when they took a trip there one year. She said they were made in Poland."

"It was a set of three," Jake said. "Now there's two."

"Because the third one was broken the night Ruby died," Birdie said. He could see her own wheels starting to spin.

"Only this was never entered into evidence at trial," Jake said. "Remember when we first started going through this stuff? You and I didn't even know what it was."

"How would anybody know Ruby tried to hit her attacker with one of her glass chickens?" Birdie said.

"They wouldn't. Not unless they saw it happen. Not unless they were the one she tried to hit with it."

"Jake ..."

"I asked Dan how he knew that. He said Larry told him. Larry was the only member of the family who attended every single day of that trial."

"Only that didn't come out at trial," Birdie said, her jaw going slack.

"We need to go over every single word Larry Ingall said to Ed. Pull his interview notes. I'll check the formal statements."

Birdie was already on it. She grabbed a thick black binder off the desk. Ed had at least been thorough enough to tab everything and use an index. Birdie pulled out his formal report. She grabbed a highlighter and started annotating it.

Jake quickly found Ed's interview notes. Together, they read as fast as they could. Ed had questioned Larry Ingall, his wife Julie, Sam's mother. Sam himself. Loretta. Dan.

"It makes no sense, Jake," Birdie said as she flipped through the pages. "Why would Larry kill his own mother? And if he did, it means he dropped his son off ... Sam was only fifteen. Larry would have known that Sam would be the one to find her like that. I just can't imagine ..."

It happened quickly, no more than fifteen minutes. Jake and Birdie combed through every page. Jake broke out into a cold sweat as his eyes darted over Larry Ingall's statement.

"Jake," Birdie said. She was sweating too. She had taken a seat at one table, but as she read through a different statement, she slowly rose to her feet.

"Jake," she said again, more sharply. "Julie Ingall said they were at an Ohio Farm Bureau fundraiser that night. The Ingalls and the MacDonalds went every single year. They were big donors. Loretta. Same thing. Julie, Loretta, and Larry. They were at the funder."

"Larry says the same thing," Jake said. "When I talked to Garth, he confirmed that. Said the whole family was there and he thought it was fitting that later it was the OFB that gave Sam a scholarship to study agriculture in college."

"Were they lying? If Larry Ingall was at the fundraiser, then he has an alibi for when Ruby was killed. The ME put her time of death between eight and ten p.m. the night before. Julie says the fundraiser went until after eleven. They got home just before midnight. She said she remembered specifically because Larry was stewing about an argument he got into with Sam before they left. Sam was supposed to go but Larry couldn't get him off his Xbox."

"Larry says the same thing," Jake said, leafing through Larry's statement. "It tortured him. He kept telling Ed he wished he hadn't been so hard on Sam the night before. And they were still arguing the following morning when he dropped him off at Ruby's. And then Sam found her."

Jake sat back hard, practically beating his head against the wall behind him. "It wasn't Larry." He felt equal parts relief and frustration.

"Larry wasn't there," Birdie said. "He was at the fundraiser with the rest of the family."

Jake pushed his head off the wall. That same cold panic started to go through him like it had in the shower. He reread Larry's statement. He grabbed Loretta's.

"Julie. Larry. Loretta," Jake said. "They were at the fundraiser."

Birdie was a half-step behind him. "Jake ... nobody said anything about Dan."

Jake grabbed Ed's notes about his interview with Dan Clawson. "Dammit, I wish he'd have recorded everything."

Birdie walked to Jake and read over his shoulder. "Jake, what if ... I don't think Ed ever asked him. Not point blank. He just assumed Dan was at the fundraiser with everybody else."

Jake curled a fist. Rage simmered through him. "He never asked him!"

"He assumed," Birdie said. "Ed was so focused on Wesley Wayne Hall ... he just figured the whole Ingall family was at that fundraiser together. My God. Dan wasn't with them. There's nothing in these notes that puts Dan Clawson at the same fundraiser as the rest of the family. Ed writes it here in his conclusion ... but it's just Ed's conclusion?"

"He never frigging asked!" Jake yelled. He wanted to punch the wall. "Dan Clawson knew Ruby used that damn chicken to hit her attacker because he was the one she tried to hit with it. He lied to me. When I called him on it. He blamed it on Larry, the one person he knew couldn't contradict him."

"Why?" Birdie said. "Why would Dan kill Ruby? That wasn't just some accident. Or something that got out of hand. Jake, that was sadistic. Brutal."

Jake sat down in the nearest chair. His head pounded. Why? Why? Why?

"We can't tip Loretta Clawson off," Birdie said. "How do we know she wasn't involved? And Sam? He was fifteen years old at the time. Do you think he'd have any clue about friction between Ruby and Dan?"

"No," Jake said. "But maybe there's somebody else who still does. We need to talk to Julie Ingall. How soon do you think you can track her down? I don't want to tip off any of the rest of the family. Not until after we've spoken to her."

"I'll find her," Birdie said. "Give me twenty minutes."

THIRTY-ONE

The ring tone echoed off the cement walls of Jake's office. She might not answer. Though the Sheriff's Department number would show up on her caller ID, that might be reason enough to avoid the call. Jake had no idea what Sam Ingall or the rest of the family had told her. Birdie sat across the table from Jake, her pen poised over a blank piece of paper.

"Hello?"

Jake gave Birdie a thumbs up. "Hello. My name is Detective Jake Cashen. I'm with the Worthington County Sheriff's Department. I am speaking with Julie Ingall?"

A pause. Jake heard some fumbling on the other end of the phone. He had a sense she might be putting him on speaker.

"I know who you are," she said. "I've heard of you."

"Mrs. Ingall?"

"It's Groves. I'm Julie Groves now."

"Of course. I'm sorry. I appreciate you taking my call. Do you have a few minutes to talk? Everything's all right, Mrs. Groves. If you know who I am, then I'm assuming you know I've been looking into your former mother-in-law's case."

"I talked to Sam. Yes. This has all been very upsetting for him. For all of us."

"I know," Jake said.

"What do you want from me?"

"Well, first of all, I made a promise to the rest of your family. Particularly to Sam. I told him that I'd keep him updated about any new developments in the case. I've done that. But it occurred to me you're probably owed that same promise. I'm aware of how much this has impacted your life as well."

Julie Ingall Groves let out an ironic laugh, signaling Jake had made the understatement of the year.

"What can I do for you, Detective Cashen?"

"Please, call me Jake. And I wish I could talk to you in person."

He heard something that sounded a lot like a chair being scraped across a tile floor. He envisioned Julie Groves had decided this was a conversation she should have sitting down. He couldn't fault her.

"You can call me Julie," she said. "I know you're on a first-name basis with the rest of the family."

"I am. Thank you. I've spent quite a bit of time out at the farm. I'm sure you know by now that we believe Wesley Wayne Hall is innocent of killing Ruby Ingall. By tomorrow, the prosecutor here is going to hold a press conference. He's dropping the charges against Hall."

Julie let out a breath. "Okay. Yes. Okay. You know? Brittany told me. I guess I didn't realize how much I needed to hear that from you directly until just now. It's ... it's a little hard to believe."

"I really am sorry, Julie. I know this reopens a lot of old wounds for all of you. I wish I could avoid that."

"What happened?"

"Well, if you're asking about the case itself, the investigation ... and I know this is going to sound like, well, an excuse. But it's still an ongoing investigation so I'm afraid I won't be able to tell you much about that ..."

"No," she said. "I'm asking you what happened to Ruby? Do you know what happened to Ruby? If Wesley Wayne Hall isn't guilty, then who is?"

"Julie ... I don't know. Right now, her case has gone cold. But that doesn't mean I'm giving up. To be honest, I had two purposes in wanting to talk to you. Of course, it matters to me that you know you can call me anytime. If you have questions or concerns. Before we hang up, I'll give you my personal cell phone number. It's the same thing I told Sam and your sister- and brother-in-law. I want you to know you can reach out. But the other reason ... for me, this is a new investigation. Now that we know Hall didn't commit this crime, I'm in the position of having to start from scratch."

Silence on the other end while Julie Groves undoubtedly tried to absorb what Jake had just said.

"Julie? If you have some time, I really would like to ask you some questions about Ruby. About that time. If you don't feel up to it right now ... I know this is a lot I'm throwing at you all at once. If you need time to prepare ..."

"No," she said. "I'd rather get it over with."

"Okay. I promise I won't keep you for very long."

"How did that other detective screw this up so badly?" she asked. "I know that's what they're saying."

Jake met Birdie's eyes. She lifted one palm up, gesturing she wasn't sure how he should answer.

"Yes. I'm going to be straight with you. Detective Zender screwed up. He may have done more than screw up. That'll all come out. There will be an investigation into his conduct. I know that's not much consolation after everything you've been put through. The only thing I can tell you ... I'm not giving up. I'm going to find out who did this. No matter where it leads. Okay?"

She made a noise. Maybe holding back tears. "Okay. What do you need from me?"

"Your memory."

She laughed. "It isn't what it used to be. I can barely walk into a room anymore without forgetting why I did."

"It's okay. Whatever you can remember is good enough."

"Okay. I'll tell you what I can."

"Thank you. Do you want to do this now?"

She paused. "Yes. It's just me here today. Carl, that's my husband. He's golfing today. He'll be home in a bit."

"That's good. So, maybe if I could just ask you about the night your mother-in-law died. Or that time frame. Can you think of anybody else who might have come to the house, or whom she might have hired to do work for her?"

"No. I just didn't have much to do with that end of things. That was Larry, my late husband. He'd go out there every week and try to get Mom to accept more help. She turned people away all the time. Getting Wesley Hall out there was a bit of a miracle. She didn't like him much, but he did good work. Until she caught him stealing her gas cans or whatever it was. Boy, she blew up. It got ugly. I just can't ... I can't get it through my mind that he didn't do this. Are you really sure?"

"I know. It's hard to reframe everything after you've spent so much time thinking things were one way. But ... if you can ... that's exactly what I need you to do."

"You're never going to solve this," she said. "If I'm having such a hard time remembering, how will anyone else?"

"We can only try," Jake said. "What about that night? Do you remember what you did? Where you were?"

"I did tell all of this to that other detective all those years ago. He questioned all of us, I think. The hardest was Sam. He's strong. But what he saw out there, it changed him forever. That place ... God. That farm. I'm sorry. I hate it there. Absolutely loathe it. I can't be there. And I hate that I feel that way. I know how important it is to Sam and Brittany. How happy my grandbabies are out there. But I just can't see anything other than death and misery when I'm there. It's why I left. Did Sam tell you that? After he graduated from high school. After we lost Larry, I just couldn't stay in Blackhand Hills. I begged Sam to come with me. So we could start over together. But he just had it in his mind he was going to make something of that farm. He's amazing, my Sam. What he's done out there? I'm so proud of him. So unbelievably proud. But it was a journey I couldn't take with him. You understand?"

"I do," Jake said.

"But that isn't what you asked me. You asked me about the night Ruby died. It wasn't a good time for us. I mean, before what happened. Larry and Sam ... they were at each other's throats all the time. Sam was your typical sullen teen. He wanted to be on his gaming system. Be with his friends. He and Larry were like oil and water back then. Now when I think about it, I smile. I would give anything just to hear those two go at it again."

"I can imagine."

"I bet you can. I know who you are, Jake. I don't just mean with the Sheriff's. I mean, I know who *you* are. You lost your father young, too."

"Yes," he said. "I lost both my parents. My sister wasn't much younger than Sam when she found them. They also died by violent means."

"I remember," she said. "I knew your mom a little."

Jake swallowed past a hard lump in his throat. But this is what he needed. It was good if Julie felt she could relate to him. Or if she felt maternal.

"Larry and Sam were arguing that night?" Jake asked.

"They were. They argued every night. We were getting ready to go to the Farm Bureau fundraiser in Logan. It's an important organization for our family. Honestly, Larry didn't want to go either. But he did it for Ruby. Her mobility was becoming an issue. She couldn't feel her feet. So we were going for her. Larry wanted Sam there too but Sam just threw a fit about it. I was always in the middle of them. And I just didn't want to deal with it. I wanted peace. So I told Sam to stay home. Larry was so angry. That whole night. We were just on edge. That's the thing I remember the most. If I could go back in time, I wish I could have just chilled out and enjoyed the moment. But how can you know everything's about to change?"

"You can't," Jake said.

"No. You can't."

"Do you remember how long you stayed at the fundraiser?"

"It was late. Maybe past ten. I know I wanted to go much earlier but Larry was schmoozing some of the other farmers. Again, he really wanted to represent his mother. I was getting restless. I was going to leave with Loretta, but Larry promised he was wrapping things up."

"Do you remember how Loretta was that night?" Jake asked.

"How she was? She was Loretta."

"Did she know you were restless?"

Julie laughed. "She wouldn't have cared."

"What do you mean?"

"Loretta was Larry's baby sister. He did everything for her. She worshiped him. Loretta wasn't really somebody I would have complained to about her brother."

"I see. Well, did you end up leaving with Dan and Loretta?" Jake asked.

"Dan wasn't with us," she said.

Birdie stabbed her pen into her pad of paper. She wrote down Julie's words then circled them in black.

"He came separate?" Jake asked.

"No. He didn't come to the fundraiser. It was just Larry and Loretta and me. I mentioned that to Larry. Made a joke. If I'd known Ingall spouses weren't required, I'd have stayed home, too. I was just so fed up with Larry. I thought he was being too hard on Sam. It was a constant source of friction between us in those days. Again, you just never know when something like that is going to change. It's so trivial now. It was just typical teenage stuff. But when Sam called us … when we found out what happened to Ruby. And we knew what Sam found. He was all by himself at that farm. That's the thing that haunted Larry. He blamed himself for dropping him off that next morning. He would say that over and over. He wished he'd have stayed. Walked the property with Sam. Been the one to find Ruby instead of Sam. He had more nightmares about that than Sam did."

"I see," Jake said. Birdie slipped him her note. In block, capital letters, she wrote:

DAN HAS NO ALIBI!!!!!! ZENDER JUST ASSUMED HE WAS AT THE FUNDRAISER!!!

Jake nodded. "I just want to make sure this part of your original statement is how you remembered it. You said you and Larry left the funder around ten thirty that night?"

"Yes. That's what I remember."

"And Dan and Loretta left at the same time?"

"Loretta did. Like I said, Dan didn't come. That was another thing. Loretta was on edge too. She was mad at Dan for ditching her. She was complaining to Larry about it. I just tried to stay out of it."

"That's probably another thing that seems trivial in light of what you all found out the next morning, huh?" Jake asked.

"It was. Loretta was such a wreck. Inconsolable. I remember … no … never mind."

"What?"

"I'm sorry. I'm just … it's just silly family stuff that doesn't matter."

"Julie," Jake said. "I think you never know what might matter. And it's okay. The more clear of a picture I can get about what was going on in that time frame, the easier my job gets."

"I was just so tired of Larry's family in those days. Tired of their drama. I loved Ruby. Don't get me wrong. But she didn't always make things easy for everybody. It was her way or no way. She had Larry jumping all the time. And he did. Loretta was the baby. So Larry jumped for her too. And I hate how that makes me sound. I know they've been a real source of comfort to Sam. I think that's the point I'm trying to make. All that stuff ... it's petty. It doesn't matter. And it all went away in an instant once we knew what happened to Ruby. I will forever be grateful to Dan and Loretta for being so good to Sam in the last years."

"He's lucky he has all of you," Jake said. "But Julie ... I get the real sense that maybe you didn't feel as close to them. To Dan and Loretta. How did Ruby feel about Dan?"

Jake wanted to tread very carefully. He couldn't let Julie think he had any suspicions about anyone in her family.

But Julie grew very silent. Jake could feel her unease through the phone. He wished he could see her face. Read her body language. For now, all he could rely on was her words.

"Ruby wasn't much of a Dan fan," Julie said. "He was ... in those days ... if I'm being honest, he was a bit of a screw-up."

"In what way?"

"Dan's just a perpetual bullshitter. One of those guys who's a jack of all trades but master of none. Always had some new get-rich-quick scheme. Thinking the rules don't apply to him. That kind of guy. Ruby saw right through that. I cannot even tell you how many times Larry and I bailed Dan out. Loaned him money when he lost his shirt on whatever crazy business venture he got roped into. Tens of thousands of dollars."

"Did he pay you back?" Jake asked.

"Sometimes," she said. "But I was suspicious that Larry was lending him money I didn't know about toward the end. I know it's different now. I hope it's different now. I've spoken to Brittany about it. You know, just as a bit of a heads-up. As far as I know, Dan's left those two alone. I told Brittany to be cagey with them about how much money she's making from social media. But if I ever hear that Dan's been sponging off of them, I won't be so nice the next time."

"I have to ask you something," Jake said. "Do you know what Dan was doing with the money you loaned him? Was it always for some business investment?"

It wasn't. Jake knew it wasn't. He'd heard this kind of story from families hundreds of times.

"I don't know," Julie said. "Larry always wanted to give Dan the benefit of the doubt. In his mind, every cent he gave Dan was really for Loretta. If it made Dan's life easier, it made Loretta's life easier. But I have to tell you, I think Dan was a user. I'm not a fool. You can't burn through the kind of money those two did without spending it on cards or drugs."

"You think he was on drugs?"

"I don't think. I know. He had that look about him in those days. I'm sorry. I really shouldn't say any of that. But you asked. He's okay now. Don't misunderstand me. After Ruby died, Dan turned himself around. I know my grandkids are very fond of him. In a lot of ways, he's stepped into a grandfather's role with them. I'm happy for them. I am. I won't lie that it makes me a little jealous. It should be Larry hanging out with those little precious babies. But as long as Dan is good to Sam and those babies, I'll never say another bad word about him."

WOW, Birdie wrote. Jake felt like he'd opened a valve somewhere on Julie Groves. Her truth and her grievances poured out.

"Well," Jake said. "I know it's a comfort to Dan and Loretta. They've told me as much. Especially since they couldn't have kids of their own. Loretta told me that never worked out for them."

"No. Loretta had three or four miscarriages. It was very hard on her. She was depressed for a long time about that. So yes. It does do my heart good to know my grandchildren bring them some joy in their lives."

Birdie wrote something else, her pen flying. She circled it again, then turned the pad so Jake could read it.

Dan = Money = Motive?????

Jake nodded.

"Mrs. Groves?" Birdie asked. "I'm sorry. My name is Erica Wayne. I'm working with Detective Cashen on this case. Can I ask you something? Do you know what caused Loretta's miscarriages?"

Jake frowned, confused by Birdie's question.

There was a pause on Julie's end. "Some kind of autoimmune thing. I'm not sure. Loretta didn't talk about it much. I offered to take her to this fertility doctor I knew. She helped some of our friends. Why are you asking?"

"Just curious," Birdie said.

"Well, you'd have to ask her," Julie said. "I just know it was pretty traumatic for her. As you can imagine."

"Of course," Jake said.

On the other end of the phone, Julie Groves started to peter out. She'd gotten what she wanted off her chest. Jake thanked her. He promised he'd keep her informed. She promised to call him if she thought of anything else he might be interested in.

Jake was sweating when he hung up the phone.

"Jake," Birdie said. "Crap."

"I know. Dammit. I know."

"Something she said. Something they've all said. I don't know why it just popped into my brain. It probably doesn't mean anything. Only ..."

"Birdie, what?"

"That blood sample. The one Zender never processed. And Julie just now ... she mentioned it again ..."

Birdie was on her feet, practically bouncing on the balls of them. "Brittany and Sam and Loretta. They all mentioned it, too."

"The blood?"

"No, not the blood. I mean, yes ... the blood. Not specifically, but ..."

"Birdie! What?"

"Loretta and Dan couldn't have kids, right? Julie mentioned it again today. It was a big deal. Like a defining moment in their lives. Loretta and Dan didn't have kids because Loretta had a couple of really awful miscarriages. So we don't know Loretta's blood type. But we know Ruby's was O positive. And we can find out, of course, but it seems pretty plausible that she'd share a blood type with her mom. And then you've got this mystery sample. The one Ed screwed up. And it's AB negative. And Loretta kept having miscarriages."

"Birdie, what are you talking about? Why did you ask her about that, of all things?"

"Her miscarriages. Jake, there's a thing. Rh incompatibility. If one parent is Rh positive and the other is Rh negative. If the fetus has a negative factor and the mother is positive. This happened to my brother and Abby ... before Travis was born. Abby had a miscarriage and they found out Ben and Abby had incompatible blood types. So the first time she got pregnant, it was like her body attacked the fetus. A whackadoo immune response. Maybe that happened to Loretta. Because Dan was Rh negative. A/B negative. If Loretta was O positive like her mom. And if the babies she was carrying had Dan's blood type, well, that could trigger an autoimmune response like I'm describing. It happens to a lot of women. And there's a treatment for that, obviously. Because Travis is here. And then ..."

"Birdie." Jake stood. She was spinning. Trying to process what they'd both just heard. My God. Could it be true?

"And Dan knew about the broken chicken," Birdie said, still rambling. "He *knew*. He couldn't have known. Not unless he was the one Ruby threw it at when she was fighting for her life."

"I know ..."

"Jake, you have to get Dan Clawson in here. Like yesterday."

Thirty-Two

He tried to imagine it. As Dan Clawson sat across the table from him, smiling, talking about the weather. Sipping from a cup of coffee Birdie brought over from Papa's Diner. He was easy. Relaxed. Eager to help Jake as he'd been since day one.

The boxes, Jake thought. The day he'd gone to Dan and Loretta's house, Dan had been affable. Concerned. He'd practically tripped over himself getting Ruby's ledgers and paperwork. Jake's veins turned to ice.

Dan Clawson knew nothing in those boxes would implicate him. They would only send Jake on a wild goose chase that would keep him from focusing on the killer right in front of him.

"Tessa makes the best coffee," Dan said. "I don't know what she puts in it."

"And she'll never tell any of us," Jake said. "Not even Spiros."

"I'm glad those two are still going. They've had some real

hardships in their life. Were you around when their daughter died?"

"No," Jake said. "I was in college at the time, I think."

"It was so horrible. Just heartbreaking."

"I imagine Tessa's always felt a kinship with your family," Jake said. "It's an exclusive club. Those of us who have lost someone we loved to violence."

Dan grimaced as he swallowed his coffee. "You know, I forget sometimes that you know exactly what that's like yourself. I didn't grow up around here. I met Loretta in my twenties. This church retreat we both went on. We were camp counselors. God. That was a million years ago now. We don't even go to church anymore. I don't know. After Ruby died, we kind of fell out of the habit. Loretta blamed God a lot."

"That's pretty common."

"Do you? Blame God? For what happened to your parents?"

Jake met Dan's eyes. He seemed to have genuine concern for Jake's answer. He got the sense that Dan Clawson may have been lying so long now, he didn't even recognize it as such.

Unless Jake was all wrong. Unless this was another wild goose chase. Wishful thinking. A desperate attempt to make sense of the nonsensical.

"No," Jake said. "I don't blame God. I blame pharmaceuticals and a disease process. My father? He wasn't himself in those last few minutes of his and my mother's life. I'd like to believe ... no ... I do believe that he didn't know what he was doing. You know? That maybe a person can be so sick ... or so traumatized that they can exist outside themselves for a moment. That they're not in control of their actions. Do you think that can happen?"

Dan sipped his coffee. "Maybe."

"I mean ... take your mother-in-law. The level of violence. I don't think anyone could consciously decide to do that to another person. And that's what I keep coming back to. Someone had to just be out of their minds. I mean, maybe it wasn't even motivated by rage. Maybe it was someone whacked out on coke or a hallucinogenic. See, that's what I think happened with my father."

"Wow. That's gotta be a really tough thing to live with, Jake. I'm so sorry."

A storm brewed inside Jake. As he looked at Dan, he swelled with hate. He knew what he had to do. He knew this was the way in. But his mother and father were tucked in a place deep inside of him. They belonged to no one else. And Jake had just given Dan Clawson a piece of himself. No matter what else happened in this room, he would never forgive him for that.

"I don't blame my dad," Jake said. "I'd like to hope whoever did that to Ruby was like him."

"Like him?"

"Not responsible. Not *mentally* responsible. Not that it makes what happened to her less awful. I just want to believe whoever could do that had something in them he couldn't control in that moment."

"Like your father couldn't," Dan asked.

"Like my father couldn't."

"Yeah. I suppose maybe it was like that for Ruby. Does it make it easier?"

"Easier?"

Dan leaned toward the edge of his chair. "Easier to absorb what happened, you know?"

"I think it does. Maybe she didn't meet evil that day. Maybe it was someone who didn't know what they were doing."

Dan took another sip of coffee. He looked wistful. "I suppose. Yeah. I suppose it could have been like that."

"I know you've been over this a thousand times. But you have to understand, I need to investigate this case as if nobody ever has before. I have to start from the very beginning. Reinterview everyone Ed Zender did. That means all of you. At some point, it means Sam. I will have to ask him to go back to that place in his mind. You understand?"

Dan's eyes dropped. "I hate this. I wish I could protect Sam."

"So do I. But he's a material witness. He found Ruby. He was the first one on that property after this awful thing happened. His recollections are crucial."

"It was bad, Jake. There was a time we didn't think Sam was going to pull out of it. He stopped eating. Started pulling his hair out. Larry and Julie were out of their minds with worry. We all were. There's a thing that happened. That we don't like to talk about. It was only once. And I believe it was more a cry for help than an actual plan ... but Sam made a suicide attempt a few months after he found his grandmother."

"I didn't know that," Jake said. "But it explains a lot. Brittany must know about it?"

"She does. They were friends back then."

"Well, Sam has a lot of support now. And he did then, too. Maybe he's stronger than everyone thinks."

"It's funny," Dan said. "We were all so worried about Sam, nobody realized how much Larry was suffering."

Jake had his portfolio sitting on the table. He opened it and took a couple of photographs out. The worst of them were at the bottom of the pile. But the ones on top were bad enough. It was Ruby's blood-soaked kitchen. He turned one photo so Dan could see it.

"Jesus," Dan said.

"I know it's hard to look at. But … it's what Sam saw that day. It's hard for me to imagine. A fifteen-year-old boy."

"What can I do for you, Jake? I'll tell you anything you want to know."

"Will you?"

Dan frowned. "Of course. I already have."

"Yes. You have. I can't tell you how much I appreciate you being my contact point with the family. I really have tried to insulate them as much as possible. It was never my intention to reopen old wounds. So … that's why I need to go over this with you. Maybe it'll help us both avoid subjecting the others to it."

Dan nodded. "Yeah. Okay. Yeah. I see that. What do you need, Jake?"

Jake pulled another photo off the pile. A close-up of one portion of Ruby's floor. Blood ran through the grout. A few broken pieces of blue glass could be seen.

"I just want to make sure I know what I'm looking at. You mentioned it the other day. Do you remember?"

"How would I know? It's the kitchen floor."

"But what is that, those broken pieces? Do they look familiar to you?"

"It's a mess. That whole kitchen was trashed."

"Did you help clean it? I always kind of wondered about that. After Ed's crew was finished processing the scene."

Dan squeezed his eyes shut. "Yes. I cleaned a lot of it. Julie and me. We thought it would be better if we did it. Keep Loretta and Larry away from it."

"That's really something, Dan. They really do owe you a lot, the Ingalls."

Dan shook his head. "It's just ... family."

"Sure. But I think you've gone over and above. I think the burden of this has fallen on your shoulders more than anyone else's. I see how you are with Sam. He's not your son but you've treated him like one. Loretta leans on you. You've been a rock for all of them. I didn't know Ruby, but I think she'd be proud of you. I think she'd be so grateful that you were there, taking care of the people she loved."

Dan let out a hard laugh. "Maybe."

"No, I mean it. Ruby was lucky to have you as a son-in-law. It's amazing to me."

There was a tightening to Dan Clawson's face. It was subtle. If Jake hadn't been watching him closely, he might not have seen it. But then, he knew.

"But I bet she wasn't very grateful to you when she was alive. I've ... heard things."

"What do you mean?"

"You know I've talked to everyone I possibly could. People who knew Ruby. How she was. Who she was interacting with in those last few months. The impression I got was that she was pretty hard on you. She was hard on Julie too, right? No one was good enough for her son and daughter. That kind of thing."

"Ruby was hard," Dan said.

"Yeah. I can see that. And it's really hard to do all the things you're doing and not feel appreciated."

Dan Clawson's lips turned white. He clenched his fists.

"Well, all I'm saying," Jake said, "is that I appreciate it. I see it. I mean, there was poor Sam. Just a kid. Dealing with all of that. And Larry? I mean, I can't fault him. But he fell apart too. Loretta. Then Julie just up and left. You've been it, Dan. For all these years. You've really stepped up. And look, this is none of my business. But I've seen the situation. Sam and Brittany are doing really well out there on the farm. Why didn't you and Loretta have a stake in that property?"

"That's the way Ruby wanted it," Dan said. "She wanted Larry to take it over."

"He didn't want anything to do with it though. That's what Julie said."

"You talked to her?"

"I did. Yesterday. I gotta be honest. She surprised me. She didn't have the greatest things to say about Ruby. Or ... I'm sorry, Dan. You. I had no idea there was family friction there. I didn't mean to step in it, but I kinda did."

"You should have told me you were going to call her. I would have warned you. Julie's ... she's pretty bitter. She hasn't wanted anything to do with us since after Larry died."

"Yeah, I caught that. She's another one. Has no idea what you've put up with. What you've done for everybody else."

"No," Dan said. "She most certainly does not."

"She told me something, though. And it's one of the things I wanted to clear up with you today. She said she remembered some drama the night Ruby died. At the Farm Bureau fundraiser you were all at. She said she remembers you and Loretta got into a big argument."

"What? Then she's misremembering. That didn't happen."

"Huh. Well, she was pretty specific about it. Said you stormed off and left Loretta there without a ride. Julie and Larry had to drive her home."

"I didn't ... I wasn't ... no ... that didn't happen. I don't know why she's saying that."

"Do you remember what time you left the fundraiser?"

"Not anymore, no."

"But you specifically remember leaving with your wife? You *did* take her home? Julie's wrong?"

"I don't ... yes. I would have taken Loretta home. Of course I did."

"You remember that?"

"No. I don't remember. I just know that's what would have happened."

"Huh. See, Dan, this is the problem. This is the thing that's been bugging me. I looked at your statement to Ed Zender. He never actually asked you about being at the fundraiser that night. He never asked any of the rest of the family to list off who was there. And you all talked to him separately. So nobody else would have known what you told him. Zender wrote down in his conclusion that you were at the fundraiser, but you never told him you were. He just assumed. Because ... you didn't go. Did you?"

"What?"

"You weren't there. You stayed home."

"Jake, what are you talking about? What is this?"

"Dan, where were you the night Ruby was killed?"

"Are you kidding me with this?"

Jake pulled another picture off the stack. This one showed Ruby's body in the barn. Her head was missing. He said nothing. He just laid it in front of Dan.

"She was leaving the farm to Larry. That farm was worth probably two million dollars, even back then. I've seen the ledgers. She was earning a pretty good income off the leases. But she didn't do anything with it. Wouldn't even pay for help in her home. And you were struggling. You just couldn't get things going. Right?"

"You don't know what you're talking about."

"I think I do, Dan. I think Larry was bailing you out. Thousands of dollars. What was it? Gambling? Or was it drugs? You wouldn't be the first. It happens. It doesn't make you a bad person. This, though ... this does make you a bad person, Dan." Jake slapped the final photo in front of Dan. The image of Ruby Ingall's head in the cornfield.

"You can go to hell."

"I found some things, Dan. You need to know that. Ed Zender messed up. He didn't process the crime scene thoroughly enough. We found blood samples in the house that didn't belong to Ruby. That didn't belong to Wesley Wayne Hall. But I think when I get a warrant for your blood and DNA, I'm going to find out they belong to you. She cut you. She fought. You said that. You said she threw that glass chicken at your head."

"I never said that."

"You did. And I called you on it. You lied, Dan. You told me Larry told you that. That he heard about it at the trial. Only ... that didn't come out at trial. The jury never heard a thing about some broken chicken. You know about it because you were there. And the proof of it is flowing through your veins, Dan."

Dan Clawson turned purple. Sweat beaded his brow.

"You wanna tell me what really happened, Dan?"

"Leave me alone."

"You were out of your mind. I meant what I said. A person would have to be out of their mind to do what you did to Ruby. You have a chance now, Dan. One chance. You tell me what really happened. I can't help you if you don't help yourself."

"No."

Jake took another piece of paper out of his portfolio. He put it in front of Dan. "Consider yourself served, Dan. You can read it if you want. But you're not leaving this building without providing a cheek swab and a blood sample. That's a search warrant. That's your blood in Ruby's kitchen. I know it. You know it. So do the one thing you can do. Help yourself by telling me the truth. Tell me how Ruby pushed you to the edge. Because it had to be that, right? You tried so hard. Did so much for everyone. And yet you were always the fuck-up in her eyes, isn't that right? And she was going to stick it to you. Make sure you never got a thing from her when she died. And Larry and Julie were going to get everything."

"She was a stone-cold bitch!" Dan shouted. "From day one. Coddled Larry. Thought he walked on water. Until she drove him half out of his mind, too. Needling him. Refusing help. I wanted to wash my hands of it. All of it. I just needed a break. Half a break. I am part of this family, dammit! I am not gonna be treated like some piece of crap she scraped off her shoe!"

"She must have said such awful things to you," Jake said.

"She called me a loser. A liar. She wanted to pay a lawyer to get Loretta to divorce me. Said I wasn't even man enough to give Loretta kids. Like that was my fault."

"It wasn't your fault," Jake said. "Loretta's miscarriages. You had incompatible blood types, right? Because she had the same as her mother. O positive. But you? You have a rare one. AB negative. Isn't that right?"

Dan Clawson's expression went stone cold. Jake recognized the truth in Dan's eyes. He had him. And Dan knew he had him. There was no going back.

"You didn't mean it, did you?" Jake asked, softening his tone.

Dan sobbed. "No. God. No. I don't remember. I just ... there was so much blood. She was screaming. She wouldn't stop. I just needed her to stop. To let me think. Just for one goddamn second."

"But she wouldn't."

"No. No. No."

"Tell me what you did, Dan."

"I didn't mean it. I swear I didn't mean it. I just wanted her to listen to me. Just for a minute. I didn't want to hurt her. I didn't go there to hurt her. But she just wouldn't stop. You have to understand. I was trying to get a handle on it. I was."

"What were you taking?"

"Oxy. Just a little. Just to take the edge off. I hurt my back. Someone rear-ended me at a stop light. It hurt so bad and the doctor gave me something. It didn't help though. It just hurt worse and worse. I didn't mean it. I swear to God. I blacked out. I just blacked out. And when I woke up, she was like that. Oh God. I didn't know. I didn't know. I didn't know!"

Jake rose. He took a breath to steady himself. Then he read Dan Clawson his Miranda rights.

Thirty-Three

How do you tell someone their loved one is dead by violence? How do you tell someone it was another loved one who committed the violence? How do you stand a foot away from someone on what you know may become the worst day of their life and be that messenger?

Jake had done it before. Countless times. Just like the legions of law enforcement officers, doctors, and first responders who did this every day. It was their job, their calling to be there on the worst day of a person's life. To be the deliverer of their trauma. To bear witness.

But this time was different. This time, he got to know a family. Had dinner at their table.

Sam Ingall sat at that table staring blankly at the wall. Loretta Clawson was in the living room, wailing. Birdie had gone to her. Two other uniformed deputies waited outside. Jake had no idea what he would encounter when he came here that day.

Brittany Ingall stood in front of him. Her father, Garth MacDonald, sat at the table beside Sam, his hand on his son-in-law's back. That had been Birdie's idea. She called Garth and asked him to meet them at the house.

"What happens now?" Brittany asked. She was poised. Decisive. She had been the one to make Loretta leave the room when she began to yell at Jake, calling him a liar.

"Dan's being booked. He'll be formally charged by morning. He should get a lawyer."

"Will you need statements from the rest of us?" she asked. "From Sam?"

"Not at the moment," Jake said. "Dan confessed. It doesn't mean my investigation is completely over. But I came here to tell you all in person what happened. I know what I owe you."

"You don't owe us anything," Brittany said. "You certainly don't think we blame you for any of this."

"I'd kill him myself if I could," Garth muttered. "Ed Zender has no business walking this earth, let alone running for sheriff. You've got the word out, Jake? People will know?"

"They'll know," Jake said. "There's a good chance Zender will face charges of his own. I'm sorry I can't get into the details of that. But he will be held accountable."

"Good," Brittany said.

"Sam," Jake said. He went to the table. "I can't imagine how you must be feeling."

"He wanted the farm?" Sam said, lifting his eyes to Jake. "Is that what he's telling you? Because Grandma wouldn't sell the farm?"

"It's still murky," Jake said. "But I believe there were money issues. Your mom said she and your father had given Dan and Loretta large sums of money over the years."

"She never told me," Sam said.

"She probably didn't think there was any reason for you to know," Brittany said. "She mentioned something to me. But she was careful. She knew how important Dan and Loretta are to you. Jake, I'm sorry. It never occurred to me that this was something that was relevant to Ruby's case."

"I knew there were issues," Garth said. "Nothing concrete. But I had the impression Ruby wasn't a huge fan of Dan's. God, I'm so sorry. I should have said something. I just didn't think any of that mattered after everything that happened."

"It didn't," Jake said. "Or it shouldn't have. You didn't do anything wrong. It wasn't your job to solve this case. It was ours. And we failed you."

"You didn't fail anybody," Brittany said.

"Will they kill him?" Sam asked. "My Uncle Dan. Wesley Wayne Hall was on death row for what we thought he did. Will they ask for the death penalty for him, too?"

"I don't know," Jake said. "That will be up to the prosecutor. But my guess is no. And if he gets a decent lawyer, they'll argue it wasn't premeditated."

"If that son of a bitch takes this thing to trial," Garth said, rising. "If he puts this family through that again ..."

"Daddy," Brittany said. "Let's not get ahead of ourselves."

"Brittany's right. None of that is for you to worry about now. Just ... be here for each other. And if there's anything I can do. Any questions I can answer. You all have my number."

"What about Hall?" Sam asked.

"He's being processed for release. He'll be a free man in a day or two."

"He must hate us," Sam said. "All these years."

"I don't think he's thinking about you guys much at all," Jake said. "He's been focused on proving his innocence. I'm sure he's grateful he can restart his life. If he hates anyone, it's Ed Zender. And it's going to be your Uncle Dan."

"No," Sam barked. "Not my uncle. I don't ever want anyone to call him that again. He's ... nothing."

Jake heard the front door open and close. From the side window, he saw a deputy put Loretta Clawson in a patrol car. She was in no condition to drive herself.

"Did she know?" Brittany said, tight-lipped. "Do you think Loretta was covering for Dan?"

Jake shook his head. "As I said, my investigation isn't over. She'll have to give a statement. But no, I don't have any reason to believe she was involved or knew anything about what Dan did. At least not now."

"Thank you," Brittany said. "But if you don't mind, Jake. Let me walk you out."

"Of course. Sam, I really am sorry for your loss. For everything you've had to go through."

"Sorry? Jake ... if it weren't for you ... God. He's tried to be like a father to me. A grandfather to my kids. All this time. And if you hadn't gotten involved, we never would have known. Wesley Wayne Hall would be dead already. And we would have just gone on thinking that was justice. So no, don't say you're sorry. Not to me. Not ever. I know what you did. I'll find a way to thank you someday."

Jake felt a hole in his chest. His throat ran dry. He said his goodbyes and walked outside with Brittany. The other deputies were gone. There was only Birdie, waiting by the side of Jake's car.

"Take care of him," Jake said to Brittany. "Just like you have been."

"I just hope we've done enough. With this place, I mean. It took a long time to wash the blood out of that cornfield. Figuratively. Literally too, I suppose. But if Sam doesn't want to stay here anymore, I'll understand."

"I think he will. I don't know why I say that. But somehow, I think he's exorcised those particular ghosts. And he wouldn't have been able to without you."

Brittany gave Jake a weak smile. "Get on out of here, Detective. Go home. Get a good night's sleep. You've earned it."

She did something that he wasn't expecting. Brittany Ingall leaned in and gave Jake a hug. Then she patted his back and walked back inside to be with her husband.

Jake climbed behind the wheel. Birdie slipped her seatbelt on. They drove past the barn where Dan Clawson had committed so many of his sins. The brown husks of corn swayed in the breeze as they drove away, almost as if Ruby Ingall herself was waving goodbye.

Thirty-Four

Tuesday morning, Jake parked along the curb in front of the Chillicothe Correctional Institution. It was nine a.m. Election Day in Worthington County. He had a long drive ahead of him. Just like he'd had a long night before.

A text came through from Boyd Ansel.

"You're not coming?"

Jake texted back. "Not a chance. It's your show now."

In fifteen minutes, Boyd would give a press conference announcing that Dan Clawson was being charged with the second degree murder of Ruby Ingall. For now, Clawson planned to plead guilty. He'd hired a big gun lawyer from Columbus. In exchange for his guilty plea, Boyd wouldn't pursue any other charges in connection with Dan's fifteen-year cover-up and the death penalty was off the table. Though his office's hands were tied, Ansel would tell the public state and federal charges would be sought against Ed Zender relating to his handling of the case. The county wouldn't be involved. The attorney general would handle everything for the state.

The gates opened. A lonely figure walked out. Boyd texted again.

"I'll make sure everyone knows this was your collar, Jake. None of this would have happened without you. Landry's not coming either. She thinks it's better for now."

Jake put his phone in the center console, leaned over and unlocked his passenger-side door. Wesley Wayne Hall wore a white tee shirt and blue jeans. He carried a small plastic bag containing what little personal effects he had left. He'd been given bus fare and an offer from the local deputies to get him to the station. But Jake was here instead.

"You didn't have to do this," Hall said as he climbed in beside Jake.

"I don't know. I kinda feel like I had to. You sure about where you want to go?"

"I'm not sure about anything anymore. I have a bed waiting for me at a halfway house in Yellow Springs. But I might just want to get as far away from this damn state as I can."

"I can understand that," Jake said, putting the car in gear. He pulled away from the curb. Hall was silent for a while. He'd had a long time to absorb his changed circumstances. Still, it had to be a strange thing, thinking you knew the date of your own death for so long.

"I know I should thank you," Hall said. "And I'm grateful. I just ... I don't know. It seems kind of weak."

"Wes, I'm sorry for what happened to you. That's all I can say."

"I don't know if I know how to do this, you know?"

"Be on the outside?"

"I've been institutionalized a long time, Detective Cashen."

"It's Jake now, Wes. Call me Jake."

Wes smiled. "Thanks, Jake."

"They gave you resources, didn't they? Maybe you should reconsider that halfway house. Just for now. Until you figure out your next step."

"I got lawyers calling me. A whole bunch of them. Famous ones. They're saying I might make millions when I sue."

Jake knew he shouldn't comment on anything. He still worked for the county that might be on the hook for Hall's lawsuits. Perhaps rightly so.

"You gotta do what you think is best," Jake said.

"I got a lot of reporters wanting to talk to me, too. Some of them are pretty famous too. One of the ladies on the nightly news. They all want a scoop. A couple offered to pay me for an exclusive interview. I just ... I don't know if I'm ready to talk."

"I get it."

"I'm sorry for that kid. Sam. Ruby's grandson."

"He's worried you hate him. When I told him about Dan Clawson, he asked about you first."

From the corner of his eye, he saw Hall get choked up. That surprised him.

"He was just a kid," Hall said. "How could he think I'd be mad at him?"

"He's a good man. He's had his life ruined in his own way, just as much as you did. His dad died because of Ruby's murder, too. Now ... well ... Dan's a murderer, but for a long time, he was part of Sam's support system."

"Well, you can tell him I'm not mad at him. But if I'm being honest. After today, I really don't want to think much about the Ingall family at all."

Jake smiled as he made the turn. The bus station was just up the road.

"I think that's understandable."

Jake pulled into a parking space. Hall clutched the small bag with his belongings to his chest.

"Do you want me to go in there with you? Wait for your bus to come?"

"No," Hall said. "I think I need to be alone. But thank you. Really. For everything. I want to … I know what you did. You didn't have to read my letter. I'm sure you get a million of them from guys like me. But you did. And you didn't give up. I just … I know there probably isn't. But if there was. If there was something I could do for you?"

Jake felt jolted by sadness. Wesley Wayne Hall might just be a good man. But the road ahead of him would be hard. He might not survive it. Odds are, he wouldn't.

"There is something," Jake said. "And you don't have to if you don't want to. But … somebody else got sideswiped during this investigation. I think maybe the two of you could help each other out."

Jake pulled out his wallet. He rummaged through it, looking for a business card he wasn't sure why he kept. He handed it to Hall. Hall frowned as he read it.

"She a friend of yours?"

"She's … hell. I don't know what she is. Not a friend, no. But like I said. She could use a break. Call her. Give her an interview. If you want. I can't promise she'll pay you. She probably can't."

Hall looked back at the card. "Yeah. I think I could do that. If she's somebody you think I could help."

"You could help each other, maybe," Jake said. "And it might be good to talk."

Hall nodded. He opened the car door and got out.

"See ya, Wes," Jake said. "Take care of yourself."

"You too, Jake."

Wesley Wayne Hall raised his hand and held it in a wave as Jake drove away from the curb.

Thirty-Five

Twelve hours later, Jake sat in his booth at Gemma's bar. It wasn't planned, but Cashen's Irish Pub turned into a victory party. As the day shift got off work, nearly the entire Worthington County Sheriff's Department filed in to watch the election returns. By ten o'clock, the local news anchor broke in.

"With ninety-eight percent of the precincts reporting, we can declare a winner in a couple of local elections. Probably the biggest one everyone's been watching ... Sheriff Meg Landry is gonna keep her job. She scored eighty percent of the vote over her opponent, the soon-to-be criminally indicted, Ed Zender. We've reached out to Mr. Zender's campaign manager, Tim Brouchard, for a comment and are awaiting a response. We'll have that for you just as soon as we get it. Also awaiting reaction from Sheriff Landry ..."

A cheer went up, drowning out the television. Meg was at the bar. She'd knocked back a couple shots of bourbon. She wasn't drunk yet, but she was on her way. Jake had a beer in front of him. Meg caught his eye. She raised her glass to him from across the room.

Gemma slipped into the seat opposite him. "Big night," she said. "How are you holding up?"

"I'm tired," he said. "I need a vacation."

"Yeah. You do. Only you never take them. I think I'm going to have to insist. You look like hell, little brother. You need a haircut. A proper shave." She leaned in close and wrinkled her nose. "And a shower."

"How about another beer?"

Gemma raised her hand. One of her waitresses gave her a thumbs up.

"I'm glad," Gemma said. "For Meg. And for you."

"Me too."

"Who would have thought it? For once, Dickie did something useful by giving you that letter."

Jake laughed. "Sure. Useful. How's that going, by the way?"

Gemma shrugged. "Dickie's Dickie. He hasn't royally screwed anything up yet. He's been decent with Aidan. But last night Dickie finked out on a ballgame he promised to take him to. I didn't make a big deal out of it. But Aidan was pretty disappointed. Maybe it'll be a one-off, but ..."

Jake sipped his beer. "Except we both know it won't be."

Gemma pursed her lips. "Yeah. I know."

"I'll pick Aidan up next week. I'll think of someplace fun to take him. It's going to be okay."

"Gemma!" one of the waitresses called out from the other side of the bar.

"Gotta go!" she said. "Thanks, Jake. Aidan will love that. I'll tell him tomorrow."

Jake raised his glass to her. The waitress she'd summoned earlier came to the table with a fresh beer. She wasn't alone. Meg slid into the seat Gemma had just vacated.

"Congrats, Sheriff," Jake said. Meg's eyes were just a touch glassy. She had her own beer and clinked it against Jake's.

"Thanks. You sure we can put up with each other for another four years?"

Jake clapped his hand over his heart, feigning chest pains.

"You wanna know the bitch of all this?" Meg said, pointing her beer mug at the television. "Zender still got over two thousand votes. Can you believe that?"

"He'll be a felon in a couple of months. And you'll still be sheriff."

"Still, it makes me wonder. Did I get this job because people didn't think they had any other alternative? Zender was gonna win, Jake. We both know it."

"I do not know it. Neither do you. And you know what? Who cares? He didn't win. He's going to jail, Meg. And you've got the badge. What difference does it make if there are a lot of people out there who don't want it that way? And now you can maybe start doing some of the things you've always wanted to do. Make this department yours. Not Greg O'Neal's. Not the county commissioners'. They have to get off your back for a while."

She nodded. "I have some plans, Jake. I haven't forgotten. First up, getting funding for another detective." Meg looked across the room. Birdie was at one of the pool tables. She just finished a great shot.

"She deserves it," Jake said. "Once again, I couldn't have cleared this case without her."

"Oh yes you could. But I take your point. I'll go to bat for Erica. I promise."

On the television screen, Wesley Wayne Hall's mugshot popped up. Then the camera cut to Bethany Roman standing outside Chillicothe Prison. Though Jake couldn't hear what she was saying over the crowd, he could read the crawl on the bottom of the screen.

TOMORROW NIGHT. EXCLUSIVE ONE-ON-ONE INTERVIEW WITH WESLEY WAYNE HALL BY OUR OWN BETHANY ROMAN.

"Was that you?" Meg asked.

"What do you mean?"

"You know what I mean. Exclusive. Did you ask Hall to sit down with Bethany Roman?"

"I might have," Jake said. "I figured she could use a win."

Meg smiled. "You're a good guy, Jake. You probably just saved her job."

"She didn't deserve Brouchard and Zender throwing her under the bus because of me. It was the least I could do."

"Oh, there was a lot less you could do. But this was smooth, Jake. Real smooth. You better be careful though. People are going to think you're a softie."

"I'll work on it," Jake said.

"Landry!" a group of command officers called to her from the other end of the bar.

"Better go," Jake said. "Because they're the first bunch you'll have to convince about Erica."

Landry downed the rest of her beer and slammed her mug on the table. "Drive safe," she said. "And don't come in tomorrow. You look terrible. Get some sleep."

Jake laughed. Landry sprinted over to the officers. It was as good a time as any for him to slip out unnoticed. He really was damn tired.

Jake made it as far as his truck door before Birdie shouted for him. Jake turned.

"Trying to make a clean getaway?" she asked.

"Failing, apparently."

"You okay to drive?"

"I only had two beers. I'm okay."

"Good. I've had four."

Jake laughed. "Hop in. I'll drop you off."

Birdie climbed into the cab. They rode in silence for a while. Jake decided not to tell her about his conversation with Landry just yet. She still had some hurdles to clear before she could offer Birdie the promotion they all knew she deserved. But for the first time in a long time, Jake had hope things might finally break her way.

As he pulled into Birdie's driveway, she slipped off her seatbelt and shifted in her seat to face him.

"That was some pretty impressive police work you did, Jake. I don't think anyone else could have solved Ruby's murder. If you hadn't gotten the Ingall family to trust you ... to let you in ... this would have gone cold."

"I wasn't trying to work them," he said. "This was luck as much as anything else."

"No, it wasn't. And if I've learned anything from you, it's that there is no such thing as luck. There's just good police work. Thanks for bringing me on."

"You're welcome," he said.

"Jake ... I just ... I want you to know. I know what this case cost you."

"What do you mean?" Jake asked, feeling immediately uncomfortable.

"You know I was on the other side of the glass when you interviewed Dan Clawson. The video of that thing should be required viewing at the police academy. It was a master class, Jake. Nobody but you could have done that. You have to know that."

"You sure you only had four beers?"

"Stop it. Take a compliment. Only ... what you said, Jake, about your parents. I know that cost you. I just wanted you to know that. And if you ever want to talk about it ..."

"I don't," he said, regretting how harsh he sounded. But it was a raw wound again. Another thing he could lay at Dan Clawson's feet.

"Okay. But it wasn't true. I know that. I just want to make sure you know it."

"What wasn't true?"

"Dan Clawson isn't like your dad. Ruby's case ... it's not the same. I know you said it ... er ... used it to get him to open up. And it worked. Brilliantly. But I just think you need to hear someone tell you that. Dan isn't like your dad. He isn't, Jake."

"No," Jake said. "Because my dad was worse."

"What?"

Jake stared off into space. "Dan Clawson hated Ruby Ingall. He can do all the legal tap dancing his lawyer tells him to about how it was a crime of passion. That he didn't plan it. Except he did. On some level, I think he always wanted Ruby dead. He hated her. He killed her. But my dad? He loved my mom. He loved her, and he killed her anyway. So I think that makes him even worse. Not because he loved her. But because she loved him. Ruby hated Dan. But my mom loved my dad."

"Jake ... no. Look at me. No. It is not the same. Even if Dan was crazed in those last moments. It's because he voluntarily chose to take drugs that altered his mind. Your dad? Jake, he was sick. He wasn't himself. And it wasn't his fault. I think even your mom would have understood that in the end. You did what you thought you had to do with Dan. It worked. But they are not the same. At all. I need you to hear that."

She moved toward him, closing the space between them. Before Jake could even take a breath, Birdie wrapped her arms around him and pulled him into a bone-crushing hug. He went rigid.

"I need you to hear that, Jake."

Then, something broke inside of him. He put his arms up, hugging her back. He took one ragged breath, then another. He let something go he hadn't realized he'd been holding in. But Birdie did. And somehow, he remembered how to breathe again.

They were not the same. He heard it. She was right that he needed to.

Birdie let him go. Her eyes glistened with unshed tears. She found a smile.

"Good night, Jake," she said. "I'll see you in the morning."

"Apparently not," he said. "Landry's forcing me to take a day off."

Birdie climbed out of the cab and leaned through the open window.

"Good for her. Sleep in, why don't you? And take a shower. You kinda stink."

Jake lifted an arm and smelled under it. "I do not," he said.

Birdie thumped the side of his truck with her hand. "A long, hot one. And use soap. Lots of soap!"

Laughing, she waved at him over her head as she made her way up her driveway. He waited until she was safely inside. She flicked the patio lights. Jake raised a hand and waved to her from the window. He pulled out. He could still hear Birdie shouting as he drove away.

"Soap, Jake. Soap!"

He flipped her the bird and honked his horn as he rounded the corner toward home.

Keep reading for an exclusive sneak preview of the next book in the Jake Cashen Crime Thriller Series.

How do you find a missing girl who doesn't exist?

Born to the secretive, prepper enclave on the other side of Red Sky Hill, Adah Lee has no birth certificate, no social security number, no school records. To the outside world, she simply doesn't exist. So when she's kidnapped on her 17th birthday, it might just be the perfect crime.

Only Adah means something to someone dangerous.

When an old adversary reaches out to Detective Jake Cashen for help in finding the girl, he knows the odds are stacked against him. Adah's community doesn't trust him. No one wants him there. But he is her only chance at justice...or revenge.

One-Click So You Don't Miss Out!

Turn the page and keep reading for a special preview...

Interested in getting a free exclusive extended prologue to the Jake Cashen Series?

Join Declan James's Roll Call Newsletter for a free download.

The Whisper Girl
by Declan James

She didn't think she was pretty. Nobody ever told her she was. If they had, she'd probably be punished for it anyway. Her mother didn't even keep mirrors in the house, saying vanity was a mortal sin. Adah didn't believe that.

She pulled her jacket tighter around her. It was too small on her. A hand-me-down from one of her older sisters. An awful pink puffy one with a horrible little purple flower pattern to the fleece lining. The sleeves only came down to Adah's forearms. It barely kept her warm. She should have thought to steal one of her brothers' larger, down-filled Carhart's. By the time they missed it, she'd be long gone.

Red Sky Hill loomed large. Behind her, Adah could hear the engine of one of the four-wheelers. It was moving fast but going in the opposite direction. The boys weren't looking for her. Not yet.

She pulled the little black cell phone out of her pocket. It felt strange to have it. That to, could be considered a sin.

Still no signal here. Her palms began to sweat. She was going to have to hike all the way around the base of the hill to get reception. Tiny fingers of panic snaked their way through her belly. It would be faster to hike one of the more well-worn trails up the hill. But then someone might see her. And it was the first place the boys would look once someone noticed she'd skipped out on her own birthday party.

Party. It really wasn't much of one. Miss Melva had baked a cake and invited everyone to the big house for a barbecue. But she did that every Sunday. Still, Adah's stomach growled. She would miss Melva's brisket. Since she'd made the decision to go, Adah felt the first pangs of doubt.

She looked at the phone screen. It wasn't a nice one. Not a smart phone. Just a burner. But that was the idea. She'd been promised no one would be able to find her with it.

Adah froze. She heard a shout. No. A wail. Had someone called her name? Or was it only the wind? God. If they weren't calling for her now, they would be soon enough. She was running out of time and out of light.

Adah's lungs burned as the ground sloped up. She was strong, used to hard work. But she knew she could stand to lose thirty pounds. Soon, she'd be able to. She would be able to eat what she wanted, when she wanted. Or more importantly, *not* eat when she didn't want to. No one would ever be able to tell her what she could or couldn't do again.

She was getting so close. Just another mile and she'd be on the other side of that damn hill.

"Adah!"

Her heart jumped into her throat. That wasn't just the wind this time. It was one of the boys. Probably Isaac. He'd be the one to notice she was gone before anyone else. There was a chance if he caught up to her she could convince him to cover for her. At least at first. Adah had no doubt Isaac would sell her out as soon as his father got a hold of him.

Adah started to run. Her legs burned. Her chest heaved. She

couldn't afford to fall. Couldn't afford to twist an ankle or lose any time at all.

She looked at the phone. One bar. Her heart soared. Adah dialed the one number she knew as she tried to keep running through the thick underbrush.

The call dropped. It was as if Red Sky Hill itself was trying to hold her back. She ran a few more yards then tried the call again.

"He—o?"

"Hello?" Adah shouted, panting. She came to a halt. "Can you hear me? It's Adah. I'm almost there...I..."

"Hello?" The call kept cutting out. The voice didn't sound familiar. Had she punched it in wrong?

"Hello? I said it's me. Adah. I'm on my way."

She couldn't make out any words on the other end of the phone. Just static chop. The call dropped again.

"Dammit!" Adah shouted. She wanted to throw the thing against the nearest tree. Instead, she started to run again.

A few minutes later, when her legs felt like rubber and she thought her chest might explode, Adah broke through into the clearing. The two-track road ahead of her made her want to sing. She knew to follow it. This had always been the plan.

She saw three bars on the cell phone and tried the number again. It rang twice. She heard a strong, clear hello. Before Adah could respond, her shoulder exploded in pain. The phone went flying out of her hand and bounced along the road, kicking up dust.

She didn't turn. Adah just lurched forward, trying to go after the phone. The next blow stuck her dead center in the back, knocking the wind out of her. Adah fell to her knees, gasping for air. A strong hand grabbed her shoulder, pulling her back. Another hand went around her mouth, blocking her from screaming.

A noxious smell filled her lungs. Her brain. Some chemical. Adah thrashed, but it was too late. It was as if a heavy blanket wrapped around her body, making her limbs stop working. Making her just want to go to sleep.

There was no time. No space. But there was pain. Adah's eyes snapped open. She tasted blood in her mouth, but she couldn't open it. Heavy tape sealed her lips shut and scratched the bottom of her nose.

Adah's arms were wrenched behind her. She was lying on her side. Her legs were pulled up, her feet touching her buttocks. She was hog-tied.

She jerked violently but rhythmically from side to side. She became aware of the sensation. Recognizing it. She was in a car moving very fast down a rough road.

She tried to kick back. Tried to loosen her bindings. Tried to scream.

Her head ached. Her limbs screamed from the pain. Her fingers and feet had already gone numb. But nothing felt broken. Just bruised. Scraped.

Still, she tried to kick backward. There was something. Some way she knew she was supposed to be able to free herself. A latch? A button? What had she read?

She had no sense of time. It had been nearly dusk when she reached the road at the base of Red Sky Hill. Was it night? Morning?

Then, as abruptly as the pain in her bound body awakened her, she stopped moving. She rocked forward as the car came to a sudden halt.

She didn't panic. She didn't feel anything at all. It was as if she existed outside herself. This couldn't be happening. This couldn't be her.

She felt the car door slam. Futile as she knew it was, Adah tried to make herself smaller. Tried to scoot backward, away from whatever was coming for her. If something was coming for her.

The trunk swung open. Adah was blinded by the glare of a halogen flashlight. She couldn't see a face, just a looming, dark shape. She moaned. It was the closest thing she could manage to a scream as rough hands grabbed her and dragged her out of that trunk by her hair.

A voice whispered in her ear. Hot. Hard. "You're so pretty."

Don't miss The Whisper Girl, Book #8 in the Jake Cashen Crime Thriller Series.

https://declanjamesbooks.com/twg

About the Author

Before putting pen to paper, Declan James's career in law enforcement spanned twenty-six years. Declan's work as a digital forensics detective has earned him the highest honors from the U.S. Secret Service and F.B.I. For the last sixteen years of his career, Declan served on a nationally recognized task force aimed at protecting children from online predators. Prior to that, Declan spent six years undercover working Vice-Narcotics.

An avid outdoorsman and conservationist, Declan enjoys hunting, fishing, grilling, smoking meats, and his quest for the perfect bottle of bourbon. He lives on a lake in Southern Michigan along with his wife and kids. Declan James is a pseudonym.

For more information follow Declan at one of the links below. If you'd like to receive new release alerts, author news, and a FREE digital bonus prologue to Murder in the Hollows, sign up for Declan's Roll Call Newsletter here: https://declanjamesbooks.com/rollcall/

ALSO BY DECLAN JAMES

Murder in the Hollows

Kill Season

Bones of Echo Lake

Red Sky Hill

Her Last Moment

Secrets of Blackhand Creek

Lethal Harvest

The Whisper Girl

With more to come...

Stay in Touch with Declan James

For more information, visit

https://declanjamesbooks.com

If you'd like to receive a free digital copy of the extended prologue to the Jake Cashen series plus access to the exclusive character image gallery where you can see what Jake Cashen and others look like in the author's mind, sign up for Declan James's Roll Call Newsletter here: https://declanjamesbooks.com/rollcall/